the

or

navigating the terror

john hyatt

●●●ellipsis

first published 2000 by
●●●ellipsis
www.ellipsis.com

british library cataloguing in publication
a cip record for this book is available
from the british library

isbn 1 899858 66 0

printed in hong kong

●●●ellipsis is a registered trademark of
ELLIPSIS LONDON LTD
2 rufus street, london n1 6pe

For: Windrims, Rodgers and Hyatts in the Real and the Data

Credits/thanks to: Alfred Bester, Keith Brown, Dave Carter, Elizabeth Hyatt, Herman Melville, Anan Onjon, Graham Parker, Tracey Sanders-Wood, William Shakespeare, Mary Shelley, Geoff Teasdale, Bronwyn Touhy, Amos Tutuola, Dr Stephen Twigge, Roman Verostko and Omphalus

1

Blinking hell! A dizzying burst of sun, forcing the hammer in his ear to pitch him momentarily off-balance, Roman lurched forward into the crowd, like a winded toddler, after a monstrous blow in the back between his lungs.

No way could he have heard his unseen assailant approaching over the cacophony of horn blasts, music, whistles, shouts and sirens forming a white-noise tide that washed down the main street, bursting and lapping into the square. In the midst of that throng, the linear clarity of the procession mingled now with its own noise coming back on itself off the frontage of the municipal building at the far end of the 12,000 square-metre space that formed the centre of the town. It was like a wave coming back from a rock face, dissipated but far more turbulent and dangerous. The phrase 'a sea of heads' came to his mind but did not fully capture the scene. There were arms; banners; objects on the ends of sticks or pikes; clubs; rifle barrels; confetti; heads down; heads up; masks; faces; masks or faces; and they were all bobbing and crashing around the base and legs of the marble horse. In the saddle, the eternal horseman sat as he had always sat since Roman Dee was a child.

Roman was passed a small, thin, white plastic cup, half-full with pungent and perfumed spirit. The crowd lurched to the left. If he held the cup with any force it bent inward. The first time left a crease in the plastic. The second was more controlled and the plastic sprang back to its previous shape, including the initial dent. In the moments of decision, the balance between crushing, holding and dropping was a fine one that Roman could not sustain, so he consigned the liquid to the back of his throat with euphoric abandon, crushed the cup, and let it drop into the unknown down below. His oesophagus burned with the exquisite taste of guilt. He looked down to see if he was on cobble, tarmacadam or grass. The ground was a muddied sediment of printed paper: capitals and indecipherable columns trodden into the soil that had once been the Memorial Gardens.

Looking up again, Roman recognised the librarian, Joke Matossian, about six people away from him. She was disguised as a pirate. Joke was a friend of his partner Line. Joke had not seen him. He was almost certain. He gesticulated with a vivid silent wave. There was no response. He was sure that Line had said that Joke was in Rotterdam. Maybe it was not her after all. The resemblance was very close though. She was wearing an eye patch and a wire headset with microphone. Her face was intent and her lips moved. She was saying something to an invisible person. This hidden other was either further into the crowd beyond her, or, via the technology, 1000 miles away in the Real or somewhere in the vast other universe of the Data. When Joke, or her potential *doppelgänger*, turned her face towards him it was in brief glances. She was looking towards something at which she was pointing in her conversation with the other. Her listener must have been there in the crowd.

He pulled down his hand but kept watching for a few seconds before she was obscured by a big guy with a stuck-on moustache and a grey vest which stretched across a wobbling mountain of freckled tripe flesh. Anybody else would have passed more quickly. Roman started to swim through the crowd to his left, not to get nearer but to get a view round this voluminous phenomenon. Seconds seemed like a mile in open water. When Roman eventually looked back in her direction she was gone. She had been replaced by another taller woman, coincidentally, also dressed as a pirate. The fat man, meanwhile, had been displaced upwards into the air. Supported by hands, he was being passed across the top of the crowd like a feather on an updraught: weightless, inflatable, dirigible.

There was little point in bothering to search further for the librarian. If she flowed by again so be it. In fact, Roman was quite pleased that she, and the problem of what to say to her, had gone. Though he was surprised to recognise a suppressed jealousy of the easy fluency with which she had given and received the conversation with the other beyond her, whoever it was: lover; relative; friend; borrower; member of a reading group or social club; a sports club teamplayer; a partner in tennis or squash; a commuter she travelled with but didn't really know; or another woman. Another woman at the cannon, thought Roman, picturing the framed reproduction of that Goya etching in the reference section. He felt the suffocation of the cannon blast by the heavy atmosphere of the library and, simultaneously, the library's contemplative quiet exploded by the tide of revolution. Danger! Blasting in progress!

That stone rider, with his right arm leading an imaginary battalion of ghosts, still seemed oblivious to the frenzy and the boiling surface of the sea of flesh even as he lost that arm and his marble head. Dismembered by one fell swoop of the masses. Roman remembered the other Goya images: the bits of puppet-like bodies, thick-limbed, hanging from trees like strange fruit. He pushed this battle of the books back behind a veil of darkness in his mind.

In his teenage years, Roman had kissed beneath the legs of that stallion. When a medical student, drunk, he had placed a traffic cone on the rider's head. The statue had grown smaller and smaller as the buildings rose about it and as Roman himself grew. Roman passed it every day on his way to work as a doctor at the Mary Shelley Hospital. Over the last decade, the gap between rich and poor had widened so much as to make it too dangerous, now, to even be below the thirty-sixth floor at night. Patrols policed a curfew. Six years ago, an Intelliphence protective field, an electronic fence, had been placed around the statue to stop vandalism. Today, however, that protection had been neutralised somehow. The rider was, at last, reunited with the people.

The Sun's light, filtering through a canopy of banners and flags, soaked stains of colour through the sodden air in the square. A familiar smell was alien at the same time. Sardines cooking? Roman couldn't believe it. Yet, it was not the smell of the green lake which neighboured the city to the north. Sardines cooking! That was the thought that had risen to the surface of his mind from the depths of the past. His rational brain translated it quickly into the probable contemporary actuality – someone enterprising was selling Nagual burgers! Sardines, like other natural foodstuffs, were just too dangerous. Right at the front of the crowd, where he was now being obliquely swept, he got an overlaid whiff of petrol and then black smoke in his eyes and the noise of a machine filled his ears. Brown clumps stuck to the façade of the municipal building. Glutinous with straw sticking from it in a viscous yellow liquid, a vomit stream of some redundant farmer's best redundant manure was being regurgitated from an invisible engine hidden in the belly of the crowd. It sprayed back and forth across columns, doors, windows and steps, cladding them in a thick varnish of dung from a seemingly endless source – a reservoir of shit brought expressly for this purpose. Some figures were caught by surprise by the torrent and were joyfully capering and dancing on the steps in a mock ballet. They slid about in the glistening olive-green half-liquid, half-solid, trying to keep balance in their pseudo-*Swan Lake*, and the crowd roared. Everyone was taking snapshots or making movies.

He was in the middle of a voluble group of young men now. They all wore well-pressed shirts. All had their sleeves rolled up. It was as though they had been working at their terminals for someone else one minute and the next, here, doing this for themselves. Like an unexpected afternoon off or an impromptu office party, they were enjoying Poet's Day (Piss Off Early Tomorrow's Saturday). They certainly seemed to know each other. Maybe they were from an office with a shared interest in football or another pastime which involved group singing. The words were indistinct but had a heavy and uncomfortable rhythmic chant.

Up the long straight road to the east from the square, there was a good view of hot-ghost figures with consumer goods in and out of what used to be shop windows. Then there was an instantaneous scatter for doorways which coincided with the sound of its cause, the delayed noise of a sub-machine-gun which had taken the extra fraction of a second to reach from there to Roman's ears. The sound of cop motorbikes toppling, sliding, and crashing and the staccato cracks of pistols. Then, there was comparative silence and a billow of smoke. This was followed by figures running back out into the street with their arms in the air, towards a large fire accompanied by the sound of an explosion. Then a cheer and a chant of one word only over and over again, 'Assassins'. People were hanging out of upper-floor windows to watch the vehicles burn. Then everyone ran for cover again but the chant continued for a moment after they had gone.

Someone had hold of the sleeve of Roman's paper suit and he was being pulled on a pinball path through the crowd. Bumping into people's backs with his elbow, spilling drinks and ruining songs, he was almost off his feet, stumbling forward over unseen obstacles on the floor. Mobile phones flew. He was dragged to the side of the square. At a quieter recess in the wall of a thirty-six storey office/residential building, in an area of sound-shadow from the tumult outside, the pulling stopped. Whoever was pulling had disappeared without Roman ever having seen him or her.

He was propelled behind a line of focusing, snapping, and capturing-image-grabbers and medianiks. They were poking their devices out into the square. They were pushing forward within themselves but holding back as a group. As a group, they were both forward and back at the same time. Roman thought it most peculiar – well, not so much thought as felt – like bravery and fear, closeness and distance, and other opposite states all at once. A vibrating human membrane of contradiction, they shielded the reporters off from the reported. Roman found himself in among a group of press and newscasters. In the recess, he had been plopped down into a cauldron of current affairs, among half-human cyborg writers who squatted like pale-eyed toads and stretched occasionally like grey cats in the darkness. They communicated with the invisible via their machines, their headgear and their wetware. This group were conspiratorial as though they were beyond the hurly-burly. They huddled in a covenous circle well back in the recess, melting into the stone, and they pursued their shadowed work with a stream of bat-like high-pitched blips and alien squawks.

Beyond them Roman could see the cool quietness of a tiled hallway. He pushed his way through. Inside the hallway he slumped deflated against the cold wall. He felt as though his body had been swimming through honey. Through a city of Royal Jelly, his body had been drained of energy in direct ratio to his mind being energised. His new-born thoughts buzzed like electricity between the two terminals of his ears which rang fuzzy with excess sound. His thoughts fed back on themselves: a feedback loop, growing as a pressure behind his eyes.

Through office windows on the opposite side of the hallway, he could see rows of quaintly twentieth-century computer terminals, boxish with a hint of streamlining, keyboards, and filing cabinets filled with who-knows-what dusty information. It was probably all useless, now. Did it ever describe this city accurately? Or, did it once, until later the descriptions parted company with the actual and into that gap the tide of violence was now surging? Nature abhors a vacuum. And how would this city be in words? What grammar the city?

Roman felt as though he had been born swimming and that this repository was his first small island of rest. He remembered something Line had said that morning about all the words in the dictionary that began with the letters 'n a':

about how the majority of them had something to do with water. She had given him examples: the Naga, the genii of rain and rivers from Hindu mythology; the naiad, the Greek water nymphs and the name given to the nymphs of dragonfly; Narcissus, who fell in love with his own reflection; natation, the act of swimming; nausea, from seasickness; navigation and all those sea words. Most civilisations, she had found, had a flood myth and a character with the name of Naa or Noah. What were we but thin bags of water in transit? Born into flow and 90 per cent water, we gush into space that is unfilled. This city too, like everyone in it, was born swimming: natal natation. Roman's mind started to put the water back into words with forgotten origins: navel; nature; nation; naked; name. Everything seemed fluid again for the first time since his childhood, when a shadow could have been a monster or a stone a spaceship, when he was, as they say, naïve.

Naïve. Born no more of woman or man than of a thousand fictions and a million yet-to-be-worn metaphors. Since naïveté: a lifetime of dragging the loveboat up the falls of desire with his free hand holding the shotgun, like Mayakovsky, a suicidal poet crushed by the Terror because the revolution lost sight of love in the onslaught of established interests.

Inside the hallway, there was a pram, unused wooden letterboxes and empty syringes. The hallway was as wide as the street. Big enough for a horse led by a man in armour. The hallway was cool like metal to the touch. The building was old. The elevator was broken and reeked of urine. Outside were the blood and the guts: the innards. With a vague memory of Catalonia, Roman decided to make the long climb and take to the rooftops, expecting riflemen firing back and forth from behind ledges and chimney pots. He began to climb the narrow windowless stairwell to the back of the hallway. At every landing, he should have pressed an identical illuminated electric light switch with a graphic of a lightbulb and a halo of radiating lines in black, each next to a multiple-locked door to an apartment. On a timer, each switch gave him enough light to reach the next and a bit extra for the elderly or infirm. The delay would also benefit women with children, though despite the pram, Roman did not think of them. He did not press the second switch as the stairway was still lit due to this extra dispensation. Halfway up the second spiral the timer ran out and he was shut up in complete darkness. He stumbled and cracked his head audibly on the sixth step. It hurt like he had dislodged his brain. The sound echoed down the corridor, cracking and re-cracking his head on the step until it faded into the ether of the architecture.

Inside his head, deep inside, it felt like something was smothering his thoughts. It started off like a loving warmth but soon turned into a suffocating heat. The sound in his head swelled to engulf him. Lights in a stairwell, one by one, his ideas were being switched off. He felt his consciousness slipping after two more stairs. Animalistic, he attempted to continue on all fours to the next switch. A clotted mammoth preserved in tar. On the cold tiles, the mind inside enfolded him and the first terrible dream began from what seemed like a great height.

2

The high window. A storm gathers quickly behind the mountain. The sky smudges the mountainside. The chill settles across the stillness. The water of the lake, down there, rises up in swells and peaks. The surface begins to rock in its valley basin. Carried fire crackles in the firs. The path up to his home illuminates. The first lightning on the upper lake behind the mountaintops. The cloud lights from inside: a flat, grey sheet of nacreous enamel. The unsettling wind is coming. The skin of the upper back, right side, pricks up involuntarily. The breeze at the open window. Treetops toss this way and that. The sky and the earth grumble together in ancient collusion. The lights of the little town, below, flicker on nerves. Our storm is coming. Impenetrable silence. Shale tinkles down shale. This fragile air. It jitters and splits as the great wound of light cracks the sky from its mouth to its anus. And then another and again the electric scalpel peels back the skin of the firmament. Great incisions rip the skin of air up and down. On the lake's surface, the peaks freeze for one, two, three seconds. A boat trails hair. On one spot, on the far shore, a triple attack. Bolt! Bolt! Bolt! The heavens scorch the spot. A r vet driven into the earth, there. Needles of hot rain make pores in the soil below the sill. Lungs pull breath. Releasing the curtain cord, the heavy curtain cloth falls. Across the high window, it muffles the thunder drum.

Son of Saturn will sleep now.

On the slab, the arse slaps down. The back rolls down, on the slab. Each leg pulls each foot up on to the slab. The head stills itself on the slab. Each arm rests. The lip drops the mouth open. Eyelids close on Frankenstein's toybox. Ears cease to hear. The breathing slows and sleep becomes Son of Saturn. Sweet lamb. Man-monster. Strange dolly.

The hand is not tired at all though. The left hand, that is. The left hand drums its fingers on the slab. Then, stretching at the wrist, the left hand can just reach a piece of paper and it grips a pen, which it reaches with the tip of one finger. Erratic and restless, it begins to scratch words into the page. It writes:

'My name is Erich Henckel and this is my tale.

A blank disc, the moon revolved imperceptibly through the gap between the clouds.'

It stops, and starts again:

'My name is Henrick Engels and this is my tale.

A blank disc, in the gap between the loaded clouds, revolves.'

It stops, and starts again:

'My name is Sherry Tomkiss and this is my tale.

In the gap between the loaded clouds, imperceptibly revolving, a blank disc.'

It stops, and restarts:

'My name is Data Sherwin Thomas 2 and this is my tale.

The loaded clouds part. A blank disc revolves between them.'

It stops again and then continues:

'My name is Tommy Sherratt and this is my tale.

A blank disc holds the clouds apart, revolving imperceptibly.'

Again:

'My name is Data Andrea Collins 3 and this is my tale.

Blankly, the disc held apart the clouds.'

Once more:

'My name is Norma Phillips and this is my tale.

Revolving and blank, the disc parted the clouds.'

It stops again and recommences:

'Je m'appelle Phillippe Durand et c'est mon histoire.

La lune dans les nuages avec la revolution douloureuse.'

It stops and starts again at the top of the same page, over-writing:

'My name is Data Auguste Goethe 5 and this is my tale.

The moon, haloed by ice crystals, parts the clouds.'

The hand continues to write over what it has written before:

'My name is Data Hiro Carter 2 and this is my tale.

Pristine and blank, in an aura of ice, the disc revolves impeded by clouds.'

The stopping and restarting continues until all the paper is filled many times over. Always a name appears (Ishmael Handle, Data Li Li Po 2, Ali Ahmed, Data Stuart Farquar 4 ...) and a collection of descriptions of a moon in the clouds ('A blank disc vacantly revolving ...', or, 'Around a blank moon, the clouds surround an aura of chiming ice'), occasionally being written in the different languages of the world, as appropriate. Sometimes, the writings appear slightly strange, as though they were suffering from translation problems from one tongue to another ('The blank mood is in the clouds'). These 'mistakes' are sometimes carried on in the next attempt ('A ring of ice surrounds a blank mood, turning the clouds'), sometimes corrected, or dropped.

The page becomes so over-written that only the odd word can be seen in the scrawl, appearing like a planet or a sun in the spidery space of the inky web of lines, until the ink and the friction start to tear the paper and make rips in the overlaid text: black ink scrawl, rip, 'aura', black scrawl, tear.

3

Good! The process has begun and unconscious Roman lies dreaming awhile on the steps. Let me direct our attention momentarily elsewhere.

4

As usual, Anan felt the ghosts of Overlookers watching from the gaps in the visible world. He caught fleeting clues to their presence in shadows and could sense secret shapes shifting in the dithered patterns of the vidiot wall. It splashed noiseless early-afternoon entertainment and simultaneous advertisement from floor to ceiling. The sound was down. He could hear only the muted voices of birds through the window and the noise of water running into the bowl. He had been stroking the cat and dealing with the litter tray so he washed his hands before eating. Checking his hands through the swirling water, he saw they shared the jagged life-line of struggle. Behind him in the mirror, he could see the linked wraiths of computer operators, factory workers, and mill workers forming a spiritual daisy chain rooted in the past. The ghosts of Hands were Silent Ones. They were being observed by the ghosts of the Overlookers. The descendents of the ghosts of the Overlookers must be 'on the premises first and last' by order of the descendents of the ghosts of the invisible masters. This was Rule 1 of the *Rules to be Observed by the Hands Employed at Newtech*. Same as it ever was. The Overlookers surveyed the Hands on the masters' premises for they possessed the permit of the gaze: of surveillance.

Anan lived at ground level on the South Side with the other Hands in the area known as the Sticks. Out here in the Sticks, life was regular and hard but at least you could maintain some dignity, unlike in the city where you had to be up above the Thirty-Six to be treated as human. He worked at the chip shop out on the border, wiring up silicon; prisms; motherboards; and cards. Though born in former Thailand, he had travelled alone all round the globe since he was 12 years old. He had chased employment to where the jobs were, which was wherever the workforce was cheapest. Presently, he was signed to work on the production line for the transglobal giant, Newtech. At the plant, out by the perimeter, he worked the graveyard shift through the night. He worked the vampire line.

Anan clicked off his vidiot wall when the ad for Intelliphence came on. He did not need to be reminded and he could never forget. The factory was a low, clean building out at the end of the bus route by the Intelliphence along the border which kept out the illiterates and the no-hopers. Intelliphence played a pun on 'elephant' in its promos: a herd of simulated wild elephants on a mad rampage are running out of control towards an Intelliphence area, the viewer knows they will be fried, but just before they reach it they screech to a stop in a line, while below them it says, 'Intelliphence – never forget'. It was an invisible fence, an electronic field miles high and miles beneath the surface of the desert. If you didn't know of it, then you would not see it, or notice it. Apart from the haze of a fixed plane of dead insects and the randomly distributed burnt grey ashes of unfortunate birds held in midair which had accidentally flown into its field, it did not spoil the view. Big spotless windows gave the line workers a good prospect on to the Intelliphence area, where guards were posted in watch-towers by Overlookers for the Hands' protection; guards stood at the perimeter with dogs for the Hands' protection; and guards lined the factory doors and corridors for the Hands' protection. The floodlights blazed all night long, bathing the desert in a ghoulish light and holding the static guards with the scorched birds in its lurid field.

These premises where he lived during the day were also the property of the invisible masters. He paid rent directly out of his salary. Anan had signed a contract to respect these premises. Receiving on-line company training in English, the officially sanctioned Newtech tongue, he had checked the meaning of 'premises' in his software dictionary. It meant 'the aforementioned'. He understood that he lived his life in rigid foreign sentences that belonged to someone else, any other language was unauthorised and its use would bring fines. The masters controlled the permit of speech as described in Newtech Rule 9:

> Any person leaving their work and found talking with any of the other work people shall be fined two credits for each offence.

Having eaten his meal, he pulled on a pair of surgeons' plastic gloves and took a frosty-red plastic package from the small freezer. It steamed in the heat of the gathering day. By 13.00, the daily smaze was forming outside. The hazy smoke habitually covered an area of some 200,000 square kilometres across the desert to the south by 14.00 and visibility was reduced to a maximum of ten metres. Masks were unavoidable. Out here in the Sticks at the edge of the desert half of every day was spent under the cloak of vapours. Consequently, hidden from prying eyes, deliveries would start arriving at around 14.30.

The first masked visitor pressed a hot handkerchief into Anan's hands. It was soaked with fresh blood. It had a slogan hand-embroidered on it. Inside was a human pancreas. The delivery man said, 'From Jesus.' Anan unwrapped the organ, put it into a plastic bag, sealed it, and placed it carefully into his freezer.

The second delivery was made around ten minutes later. It was a five-gallon flagon of home-made palm-wine brought by five masked youths. 'We cannot stay to be helping you drink this today. The revolution she's in town,' said one of the youths.

A woman in a mask brought the third delivery at 15.05: a bottle of mescal from her grandfather and a frozen vial in a Thermos flask. She said, 'This is from Guillermo. He says to tell you that he hopes in his heart it is soon finished and remember that, of all of the people, he is keenest to be surfing the great swelling wave of the revolution. I must hurry. I have things to prepare and a journey to make.' She left as quietly as she had appeared.

At 15.30, two young boys came out of the smaze rolling a big bundle of copper wire as though it was a hoop. They bashed it along with sticks across its top. They left it leaning against the porch of the house and ran off fighting and kicking each other. After 20 minutes, Anan took some rubbish out to the dump and brought the reel in on his return.

In the kitchen he attached the wire to the thawing pancreas. He wrapped it around and around like a solenoid. He placed this in a container full of mescal decanted from the bottle brought by the masked woman. To stop evaporation he sealed the top with a paste he had mixed up from cat shit and palm sap. He left the two ends of the wire sticking out. He ate the worm from the mescal. He poured himself a measure of palm wine which he drank with pleasure and lay down on his rough bed. His hot head leaked liquid. There was an invisible source somewhere in his sepia skin beneath the fine jet-black hair just above his right ear. The liquid ran backwards away from his face in a trickle. It clung to each hair for a moment and then accelerated to the next. It tickled. Drowsily, he moved on to his side and saliva ran from the side of his mouth starting a dark stain rivulet across the hessian sheet.

In his own tongue he thought, 'เวลาแห่งการปฏิวัติ'.

5

Recovering an uncovering consciousness on the stairs, Roman began to continue upwards. He awoke with a splitting headache. Someone was inside. Inside the hallway, below. The sound was echoing along the hallway and up the stairwell. The sound of computers being smashed with clubs. He climbed up a further 33 spiralling floors, 66 spiralling red-tiled curves of stair, innumerable single steps. With the legs gone to jelly and the back gone to rubber, mixing with the shirt, he thought, 'Surely, no more,' and emerged unexpectedly on to the roof at the Thirty-Six.

Dizzy.

It was all patched up with concrete and plaster and metal sheet. Roman looked up at the aerials of all shapes and sizes and angles and the shape of that large, grey bird that vanished into the satellite roof of Newtech Telecom Tower. Kites span among the aerials. The heat had a buzz to it – a beehive of possibility with his inside out and his outside in – that sizzled. Thousands of aerials. Thousands, each leaking electricity and almost silently buzzing. Thousands subtly sucking the sky, like prayer. Below: beds, showers, environmentally-friendly shampoo and five channels of unmitigated shit accompanied by thousands of satellite and cable channels.

A cat moved in and out among the aerials. The minder inside Roman thought, 'Stay away from the edge,' and, 'What if there was a fire?' Jesus. The heat. Rivers of steaming tarmacadam like lava and it seemed like all the buildings were burning.

He had been listening to it growing for some time but hadn't really identified the sound. However, it now imposed itself from out of the buzzing and the distant sound of the crowd. Chopper! A wind blew through the awning of banners and the sunlight flashed through on to the sea of heads over the edge of the ledge of the roof. The hot wet air was swept down and out to the sides of the square and up to the roof, making the legs of Roman's trousers flap out to the side a full minute later. The odourless air of his eyrie space became exchanged for a mixed-up smell of cooking Nagual; peat/mud; people; the polluted waters of the lake; fertiliser; perfume; alcohol; gasoline; leather; fear; and pride. A shot. The next sound was almost indescribable. It was the sound of stone, metal, air and fire being ground up together – like a Hollywood disaster movie fabrication. SpecialFX. Sliding screaming down the sides of the grand canyon of consumerism, the helicopter wedged itself between the buildings of the two sides of Prince of Denmark Street with its rotors bent into the second-floor buckled frames and broken brick of the department store. Inside was the electrical section. Roman could see walls of moving images selling the total entertainment Vividot package: 'vidiot walls' as they were popularly known. They were simultaneously displaying news simulations of the journey of the *Centaurian* spaceship on its mission to the Sun; an ad for Schmert Clothing; and a new model vacuum cleaner of the chaos-cyclonic type. The cab of the helicopter was hanging downward into the canyon of the street. Two gesticulating figures lay crumpled inside. They uncrumpled, scrambling feet against the glass as the bubble filled with smoke. From below, people poked upward with sticks and climbed up lampposts. The chopper dropped suddenly some four metres. You could hear the intake of breath suck the air from the square. A wave of humanity swelled down the street and into the crowded square as people got out from under that helicopter. Eventually, the image-grabbers were squashed against the wall on top of the reporters who had been crouching there.

Roman made his way over the rooftops to get a closer look. He saw a memory of a dead dragonfly. It was an instant picture of a dead dragonfly rescued from the swimming pool by carrot-topped eight-year-old Betty Bright. The creature was an alien casualty surely crashed from outer space! With hindsight, it was actually a dragonfly with systems closed down.

'Don't go any closer, it's going to blow,' someone said in his head, like from a movie.

He remembered the ancient insect vividly which was the strangest thing.

He had been at the table in the shade. He and Rosemary, his ex, had not been getting on that well. It could have been the heat. It could have been Roman drinking excessively. It had been hot. 'Hey, any excuse, let's be honest,' Roman admitted to himself in a way unusual for him back then. He had approached the presentation of the insect with false interest at first. This was a tactic he was learning at medical school at the time: a tactic for listening to patients drone on about their ailments. He mistook children for patients. Rosemary, before she left him, had said that he mistook women for children. In truth, the tactic was an affectation which he applied randomly and liberally to his own detriment. He was, after all, taking the case in point, actually interested – beneath this adopted, habitual, world-weary façade – in the natural world and its creatures. Admittedly, it was a city-dweller's interest in the otherness of it. It was an intellectual curiosity. He had thought that he knew it all; a right brainbox; a walking head; a man in control. He had thought his world was ordered and he had his skeleton on the inside where it should be.

Skeletally, this insect was another kettle of fish. It was beautiful and unreal. Roman had never seen any creature quite so intensely – not even on one of his favourite vidiot channels, Nature (*The* Natural Selection), with which he had eaten with lions and lain hidden, for months-in-minutes, in nests of eagles. His learned disinterest was to rapidly dissolve in the face of this dragonfly. It was so close up and so apparently newly deceased – so paradoxically real and unreal simultaneously. He examined it closely. Initially, this was for the benefit of entertaining little Betty Bright didactically but he was soon fascinated and engrossed in the complexity of the thing.

He remembered counting the segments in the tail: 11. The eyes were translucent and opaque all at the same time. A sort of greenish non-colour. A brutal armoured fist of a head: impenetrable. Its wings were fixed on with red/orange squares. Its wings were like fingerprints. Four identical wings, where, at each tip, there was a rectangle in yellow – the wing between the black veins was transparent otherwise. There was a map of something there, Roman was certain. Not a fingerprint but a map, and the same map on each wing. They were tough to touch. It had been a big surprise! The wings between the black struts and girders were tough and transparent. That middle was complex. Its head had fallen off somewhat, down and to the right as Roman looked from above. Behind its head – inside the back of its head – it was wasp-coloured. Inside the space creature it was as black-and-yellow striped as a hazard sign. This universal message warned hackers off its information centre. 'Don't mess with my controls,' was the truth behind evolution's danger-sign lie. Then, as he looked at it, one of its legs seemed to twitch instantaneously. It was almost imperceptible but he was sure because there was a trace of evidence: there was some red pollen shaken off which had somehow previously attached itself to the leg.

Nothing more happened for a good ten minutes. Or rather Roman had noticed nothing happen, yet from the tip of the tail the colour was imperceptibly changing from green/blue to red/orange. This spread, gathering speed, along the eleven segments of the tail. It was turning the colour of that pollen. Of course, camouflage, natural selection! Roman had noticed the flowers around the pool for the first time: they were like red dragonflies dotted in a random pattern across the large-leaved hedges.

The change in colouration was accompanied by a filling out of space, a reoccupation of a sustaining environment of warmth, as the redness spread to the thorax. The wings straightened like a plastic cup uncrumpling. The legs twitched and slowly straightened.

Winding up from sleep mode, the magnificent head, with that stately grace, moved back into position.

Five more minutes and it was full-red and gone in an instant.

'That's how they survived the big comet that killed the dinosaurs,' Roman said out loud in the same time that it had taken for the whole detailed memory of the dragonfly.

This was at 15.20 by Newtech Telecom Tower. It was 16.24: 31 by Roman's hospital pager. The civic clock had stopped! Had the Tower been taken? Roman felt his pulse race and time slow.

He was looking at the black-and-yellow striped hatch to the helicopter. That was when Roman knew that, whether it was going to blow or not, he had to investigate the insides of that helicopter. That was how he found the head of state inside, hiding, and cowering silently. The shout went up from the people which led to the dismemberment and decapitation of the head of state. Roman was carried through the square like a hero by the fat tripe man. A man in a balaclava handed Roman the gun which he fired off into the air to celebrate this glorious day of liberation. Inexperienced, he let off the shot too close to his own head and the noise hurt his eardrum sending a sharp pain through his temple as though he had burst the membrane dividing the outside world from the inside world. The sound of the crowd roared through the corridors of his sinuses and threatened to drown him again. Behind his mask, the skin of Roman's forehead was starting to slightly discolour with a bruise sustained when he had bashed his head on the stair and fallen unconscious. He could not remember that dream he had while unconscious on the stairs but, as so often happens to people, he felt it was important. He touched the bruise with his fingertips and sent a shooting pain like a probe into the centre of his brain.

That was when the police moved in. Roman called up a city map. The diagram appeared in a grid across his vision, apparently in the air before him. Using its information, he dodged into an unused conduit pipe which led him deep down under the city.

6

In the cool, subterranean darkness beneath the burning city, Roman reminded himself that he was a professional man: Dr Roman Dee, a surgeon rather than a militant. He had become embroiled in the excitement of the uprising by coincidence rather than intention. He had been buying Halloween stuff in the marketplace when the stalls had been raided for disguises by rioters. He was convincing himself of his part in his alibi.

In the aftermath, he ducked and dived enough to get home untraced by satellite or *Terror Firma* surveillance systems. In the underground road, in the darkness of the air-extraction tunnel, in the sudden, hot, oxygenless exhaust, he ditched his red devil mask and five-credit disposable paper zip-up boiler suit and emerged back into the evening wearing shades. He made his way to ground level up some metal service steps, merged with the passers-by and fed smoothly into the guarded forecourt of the apartment complex. It was a no-smoking building inside. Before going in, he lit a synthetic cigarette with difficulty in the wind that blew up the corridor between the buildings. Roman Dee stood there for a while. He dragged on his cigarette and fed Barney the Digital Dog, originally a gift from Rosemary. As he stood, at the top of the long flat steps, Roman was aware of echoing that digital image of his father, John Holliday. He shivered as he mentally mapped himself on to the felt presence of his father. It was as though a ghost passed through him.

Roman couldn't remember him alive. Roman had been orphaned. His mother had died giving birth to him. His father had passed away soon afterward when Roman was very young. His mother was an unknown and distant figure but he certainly felt that he knew his father, John Holliday. He liked to feel that he felt he knew him. This was largely due to the recordings and documentation, especially the famous digital model of him which was now on permanent public display at the Dome of Time in the Data. The model had been the receptacle in the first purposeful experiment in uploading which, though eventually unrealised, had been well ahead of its time in the history of the Technological Revolution. It now stood as a witness to human enterprise and invention.

It had been developed for military purposes, as many of the major developments in new technologies had been. The military had been planning a series of digital spooks. It was an early pioneering experiment, one which his brave and slightly crazy, up-for-anything-Gulf-War-hero father had put his hand up for long before they searched for guinea-pigs. 'I'm no hero,' John Holliday had famously said, 'just a man at a loose end with time to fill.' As one of their best agents, John Holliday had been an obvious choice for their first template and they accepted his volunteering gladly. The simulacrum of his body was more of a container, in truth, than an image: an avatar of his father waiting for the patterns of his systems to be mapped and loaded in as information. However, they never got that far. He died in Thailand before they could complete the digital map of his nervous terrain and upload him into a data-only universe inside the computer networks.

The body-mimicking technology had been there for a while. They had got his host avatar/new data body ready to receive the neurochemical map. His father had known that he could have any body and any style in the Data, but had insisted that his own body and style were highly considered and unable to be surpassed. He insisted that his live form was his default digital form. He had forced them to throw away their manuals and with great difficulty convinced them to disregard their aesthetic training to make that perfect replicant of himself. It was designed with a capacity for disguise to aid infiltration and subterfuge. The replicant stood at the top of a digital reproduction of these same long flat steps in its Croatian Army cardboard shoes that looked like patent leather from a distance. They looked like they had been painted with pink nail varnish. This was not a crudity of the programme used to make them. He insisted on accuracy and this was what the real footwear had looked like – lurid, pink-polished, cardboard, ex-Croatian Army shoes. If you stepped in a puddle that was it. Bri-nylon shirt. Brown. And a two-tone suit (alternating purple and green-grey) with narrow trousers. Sockless (just in case of a puddle). The shirt was half-unbuttoned from the neck, where, peeping out, you could see the top of the imprint of the steering wheel from his Great Nagual Bread Accident, as he called it in his letters to Roman's mother. Taking the roundabout on two wheels, his father had rammed the car into the back of The Real McCoy's Nagual Bakery. He had shot, head first, through the windscreen. Witness statements reported that it had been difficult to spot which was his dark, curly-haired head and which was newly-baked burnt bread when they, finally, got sight of him in the doughy, crumbly, glass-shardy, burning wreckage. Remarkably, he was relatively unhurt by the smash, apart from the million cuts across his face and the perfect imprint of the steering-wheel across his bruised torso and ribs. The intense heat had burnt a six-sided star imprint from the molten wheel. It was a flame red-edged indigo indentation in the dark skin right in the centre of his chest.

John Holliday was a war hero from the Gulf. He had been a victim of what he had called the Creeping. Radiation sickness from uranium 238 slowly closed his systems down, including the all-important immune system weakened by a cocktail of experimental drugs given to him for his protection. This was radiation sickness caused by his own allies dropping dirty missiles with uranium enriched warheads on to the Gulf War battlefield. They were so heavy that they could penetrate anything in their path. A tank was about as safe as a cardboard shoe. Their destructive effectivity was proven without doubt and decades of sales followed from profitable proliferation to every tinpot regime going. The human cost of these sales was incalculable. However, John Holliday, while not unthinking, never complained or criticised. Like Roman, he had been a dedicated professional in his field.

'Yet, not like me at all,' thought Roman. 'Father took lives. He was a trained killer while I try to save lives.'

His father's letters to his mother told him of the road to Basra. He had nightmares about the computer-guided storm of death and the bodies melted into stolen consumer goods: videos; televisions; computers; furs in the desert; perfumes drifting across sand; and clock radios. Roman kept all these letters at home in a gothicall carved, medium-sized, black wooden box. John Holliday died in Thailand in 2014 on the eve of Datawar 1, where and when the Creeping finally crept up and squeezed him by the throat.

The military had released a whole fat file of information on his father, in various forms, into Roman's custody. Roman had a recording on disk of a telephone conversation from his father in Thailand to his mother: their last spoken words after which it had been e-mail only. His father deliberately stopped using the phone as it would have betrayed his bodily state and his inability to speak. Their last conversation went:

FATHER Yeah, a chicken. A real live chicken.
MOTHER Nah.
FATHER Yeah. Ask Lili V. She was there. It plays tic-tac-toe.
MOTHER And the chicken wins.
FATHER Yeah, sure it's got wings. It's a real live whole chicken. A full *compos-mentis* chicken in a cage down in Chinatown. You pick and then it gets its beak and ...

MOTHER The chicken wins.
FATHER Listen, say you pick 'tic' and the chicken ...
MOTHER The chicken wins.
FATHER The chicken looks around like, well, like a chicken looks around, and gets its beak and ...
MOTHER It wins.
FATHER ... it pecks and it picks.
MOTHER And the chicken wins.
FATHER Nah, that's not true. The chicken must be trained to win, sure, but I came away with a few hundred credits before they closed that chicken down.
MOTHER That's crazy.
FATHER Yeah, crazy tic-tac-toe, Chinese chicken in Thailand.
MOTHER That's crazy.
FATHER How goes the sprog?
MOTHER Kicking.
FATHER Thass mah boy!

The last comment was in a Jimmy Durante/Butch from Tom & Jerry/throat-cancer type of voice. Death by asphyxiation, they had said. His body strangled itself. Because of this Roman, himself, had had to undergo a persistent series of tests during his life to check on the after-effects of the Creeping – to test whether it could have been passed on genetically through his father's sperm. Luckily, the tests weren't too intrusive as Roman was brought up by his father's closest friends: Uncle Read and Aunt Lili as Roman called them, though they were not a real biological uncle and aunt. Uncle Read, from whom Roman had taken his surname and his interest in a medical career, could perform the tests himself so there were no trips to hospitals or clinics necessary. Later, after qualifying as a doctor, Roman took over and tested himself.

They had burnt his father's body in Thailand. Roman would never forget the first time Uncle Read had told him the fairly gruesome story of the funeral ceremony: how Read had flown out and how the Thais had insisted that he choose some bones from the ashes. Then the Thais ground these easily in a bowl. They had mixed up the powdery dust with half-gunpowder and half-wet rice to bind and fired the ball up into the sky, vertically, from a small golden, ceremonial cannon. The mixture dispersed in the thin air as Read Dee walked back to the hotel, looking at the ground with feet disturbing light dust, to make arrangements. Some rice fell on the path in front of him and he trod in it, he said, before he could stop himself.

The last e-mail from John Holliday said only:

> Read, they tried to train that Chinese chicken I told you all about by giving it little electric shocks but it just kept on losing until they fried it right in the cage – feathers and all!
>
> There's a new programmed chicken now, which I can't beat for love nor money.
>
> Adios,
> John

Roman had watched the tape of when the remains came back home many times. The coffin had been (appropriately) made of cardboard, lined with lead, and had the letters 'D U D' stuck on the side. This was, apparently, a Thai misspelling of 'D A D', cut with a knife out of the sort of tiles they used to use for ceilings. The ones that would drip burning polystyrene on your head, like napalm, if they went up.

7

I must tell you straight, Roman likes to think he knows his father's business and he likes to think he knows what kind of a man John Holliday was but he doesn't know the half of what he thinks. But, I'll have to leave you to figuring it all. I have pressing matters to attend to. I've got an appointment to see a giant about a slingshot.

Now, you need to know about the others: the beings of pure information ...

8

It had been on the seventeenth day of October 2048 that Horatio, aka Data Roman 4, had first felt the distant phenomenon of the white holes, as he called them, like a faint itch in the digital core of his very being, as wood must experience woodworm.

It was not long after becoming aware of that irritating feeling that he had observed the growth of the inexplicable white gaps in the centre of the Data by using the instruments in his laboratory. On reporting his findings to his Empress, Princess Foil, he had been entrusted to embark upon a mission of investigation. Indeed, it had not been long since he was sitting among the busy transactions of the market. The market was always open for business. It never closed. The market was that area of the Data where there was a permanent product fair going on. It was full of the big players; liars; cheats; conmen; hucksters; and pseudo-psychics; but there were also, tucked away, small traders; odd-ball inventions and mad inventors; curios; and weird sideshows. Then there were the proven oracles: the famous Black Torch, The Philosopher's Stone, and The Magic Hand of Chance.

Horatio had been there hunting for supplies for his adventure. If you needed anything in the Data, the digital universe of computer networks, then you came to the market to buy. The shop windows showed the icons of software goodies which were kept locked in the strongholds and stores behind. On corners, raggy-arsed avatars held desktop sales of junk information. Legal traders, official retailers, and wholesalers rubbed data shoulders with pirates, revolutionaries and villains in the information labyrinth of the market. This was the place, beyond its pure trade function, where deals were done; kingdoms toppled; wars started or avoided; slaves and Goons bought and sold; and adventures began.

He had been there in preparation for the dangerous mission which his Princess had entrusted to him – a sortie which would take him to the very centre of the Data.

Everyone had been talking about it. Yet, as enjoyable as it always was to hear about himself and his heroic deeds, 4 had not been in the market for this purpose. He had been there to prepare for his next great adventure, needing some special things for this trip. Even the most loyal of imperial agents knew that to get the best, the most radical, and the exceptional, one had to take to the digital back alleys. Here the true innovations appeared, the catalyst programmes that could plug into the monoliths of the Data's superclusters. Down there in the seedy and the weird grew the young shoots of the future of the Data. Gates knew this; Disney knew it; and so did Foil. That was why they all tolerated the radical presumptions and excesses of the underground of the market.

Horatio, a master of digital disguise, had slipped between the guards unnoticed, out of the main datastream, and into the dangerous tributaries and eddying backwaters of retro-punks, data artists, freakshows, prostitutes, drug-dealers, and conspirators. He had immersed himself in the murky waters of the super-highway's sewer system and baptised himself in the oxygenating swirls of information mainlining.

He had bought some supplies, gadgets, and devices. In the backwaters, a vMex had offered him a deal on dodgy upgrades; in a bar called The Librarian, he had observed a symbiote couple from Far X absorb enough of the narcotic Infonarc to stop a super-computer in its tracks. He had bought those remarkable programmes, the Dalmatian Seven-League Time-Boots, manifest as a pair of big, spotty, multicoloured boots which would transport him extraordinary computational distances with a single stride and the Narcissus Shift. This manifest as a deep-red robe with golden hem which promised to make him look good when it was inactive and, when active, enable him to possess a part of everything he desired. He had kept an ear out for snippets of information, gossip, useful fictions. His engines had been primed to be sensitive to key words and no amount of scrambling or cloaking could have hidden them from his scan. He had monitored some small fry not worth reeling in. Whispers of Foil, Peterloo, and Besterland but nothing about the white holes phenomenon. Fearless for the integrity of his own structure, he had dived deeper into tales and trails.

He had been to consult the famous Omphalus, generator

of Sayings. He had asked the great Omphalus to generate random Sayings especially for him. He was asked to seed Omphalus with a number. He gave his number: 13. The mighty Omphalus used its twentieth-century algorithms to generate 13 random sayings. 'These are the sayings of Omphalus,' he thought, 'they will be with me always.' He read these words of wisdom from the ancient programme of Natchez, and was very shocked to realise that they were the same as those generated by Omphalus for his father, John Holliday, all those years ago. Identical. They began with 'anemone' and ended with 'knowledge'. This was a possibility the likelihood of which was, in neo-Darwinian terms, 'vanishingly small'. The Magic Hand of Chance had dealt a strange deck.

9

He was an individualised product called Data Roman 4, one of the four Uploads of Roman Dee, and had named himself Horatio. For it was possible for a moderately wealthy man in the Real to purchase digital copies of himself. These copies would exist separate to their template original, living in the Data only. As they travelled life paths of their very own, through their particular experiences, they developed personalities variant from their original. They were often purchased to do a specific piece of work that their template did not have the time to complete without assistance from a pseudo-self. Another, Data Roman 2, who called himself Marcus, had been uploaded with the specific task of constructing the *Artificially Intelligent Self-*

Curating Art Robot Programme: a pet project of his template, Roman Dee. Marcus actually thought this to be a somewhat trivial pursuit. Data Roman 3 worked under the *nom de plume* of Brutus. Brutus was purchased to complete a novel for his template. However, Brutus was concerned about implications of intellectual copyright and a series of lawyers were tied up in the case both inside and outside the Data. Not least of the key concerns was, exactly, a debate about the legal status of the terms 'reality' and 'actuality'. There was no love lost between Data Roman 3 and Roman Dee. Brutus' continuing and symbiotic relationship with Data Rose, Upload of Roman's first wife, was not insignificant in their legal battle to decide who was the authentic author of a book by an Upload. Data Roman 5, the newest Upload, following 4 himself, had become a dry Peterloo cop with an interest in autogenesis. Unlike the others he had never taken a new name for himself. He kept using his product name of Data Roman 5 unless he was undercover or playing a part.

The four Uploads of Roman remained relatively good friends and usually had quite a ball inside the Data, thriving within their world of numbers. One good thing about being data, for them, was that, as a powerful cluster, the Data was their oyster. Trouble came if you perceived the relative insignificance of your cluster and its power when compared with the vastness of the data sea, its invisible currents, turbulent politics and unknown monsters. Then the Data could become your oppressor, your hell, and your terror. If you had the confidence in the power of your data cluster, you could perform relative miracles when compared with Real life.

Uploads lived in the Data ... totally. This was not virtual

reality, this was their cosmos, their absolute existence. They could act in the Real via the networks as well as any human but home was the Data. Although it was presently quite calm under the agreement of the delicate Pax Digitalis, life in the Data was not usually so relaxed. Indeed, on arrival the Data Romans had become intimately embroiled in the complex politics of the digital theatre of war, takeover and colonisation, and had been forced to fight for the very existence of their cluster by interfacing with the existent supercluster, Peterloo, run by the corporate front of Princess Foil. Horatio had become Foil's favourite. He was Peterloo's champion, following in the footsteps of his template's father, John Holliday.

Princess Foil, the First Empress of Peterloo, was an avatar cipher for an unknown and highly secretive conglomerate which had unified and codified the supercluster. They operate their business, her empire, through her person and it was one of the most powerful political metaclusters ever to appear on the face of the Data or the Real. This matched her ambition, expressed in her notorious Dream Speech: 'I have a dream that one day every pixel shall be exalted.' This was a clever and ironic twist on Martin Luther King's original, particularly because in the Data there was no sleep and consequently, there were no dreams.

As a legacy of Datawar 2, she kept a tight control on the viral propagation of subversive ideas, accusing more than 6000 Besterland scholars with spreading heretical ideas. According to Chinese Whispers, the subversive alt.news service, she compacted them alive. Princess Foil recently broadcast a warning about a new threat – this time from her own enemy within, Peterloon scholars:

> Nowadays, scholars study the Data to discredit us. They cluster together to criticise the laws. If their behaviour is not stopped, the House of Foil will be compromised. I, therefore, propose that all records other than those licensed by the House of Foil be destroyed. If any cluster ventures to discuss this information they shall be erased. Anyone who has failed to delete this information within 30 minutes of the issue of this edict shall be disk-doubled and forced to work alongside Goons on the Great Wall of Data.

Unprecedentedly, Princess Foil had decided not just to ban, but to erase outright the existent Peterloon history disks. Any scholars caught discussing their contents were severely punished or erased. Princess Foil was still not satisfied. She was becoming increasingly terrified with the threat of assassination from the Real, and obsessed with immortality. She was concerned about power leaking elsewhere when it should be bejewelling her own train. It was apparent that Princess Foil had no intention of retiring to her great databank, the Great Wall of Data. She had even commissioned the scholars who remained loyal to her to find the secret of eternal energy. She was concerned that, if not for the fact that the Data was intimately entangled with the functioning of the everyday actions of the Real, the risk that the Real might one day get its act together and simply unplug the Data would become actual. For the Real to do such a thing would, of course be impractical and morally unthinkable. As things stood though this was not a likelihood. The very idea-as-idea constantly drove her to target Peterloon research funds towards securing independent energy sources.

In the Data, if you were sufficiently rich or well-connected, there was still enough space at the frontiers – wide-open space – to do whatever you wanted and whatever took your fancy, within reason. There was space to stretch and grow. There were laws, here, of course, that were intended to limit one individual cluster's right to expand indefinitely. To ensure that the supercluster of Peterloo stayed united, Princess Foil had codified a system of laws that governed every aspect of existence. Her laws were strict and merciless. She believed that the Data was a blank slate, to be written on by the corporate state. Harsh discipline was imposed on violators, regardless of rank. Punishments were vicious. Intellicollars were put on the necks of convicts to identify them. Thousands had been erased for minor offences over the recent past. Horatio himself, her most trusted soldier, had almost slipped from her favour, recently, for repeating Vergniaud's dire prophecy of the Real French Revolution: that the Technological Revolution, like Saturn, would devour its own children. First the nobles and priests, then the constitutionalists, and now the moderates were proscribed by her Highness. Even greater numbers had been sentenced to hard labour working alongside Goons to produce, among other wonders, the Great Wall of Data.

In truth, successful law enforcement was near impossible there, as everyone rushed to stake claims in unempowered dataspace like gold-rushers. If you could afford it, you could expand. Laws relied for their power on their currency as stories. Yet, despite these well-known tales encrusted and shot through with law, unbridled creativity and rampant negligent building was rapidly going on anywhere and everywhere. Building regulations were non-existent in most of the Data, with the notable exception of

New Cairo, which had been built by Muslims: the Koran specified rules for spatial construction.

Princess Foil set no good example herself. She had built digital palaces continuously, each palace being more monumental and grandiose than the last. To commemorate her victories, she has constructed replicas of each of her opponents' palaces inside her own. She showed off her empire in the Great Exhibition alongside her collections of historical data artefacts from classic computer games and antique websites to the infamous avatar of John Holliday. She had been the first to document the history of the Data. Cynics say that this was to validate her own power position. She drafted more than 700,000 Goons (low-grade, simple programmes used for routine tasking) to join the dissidents in building the Great Wall of Data.

The story went that Foil had had a visitation. While travelling in her ship, the *Jules Verne*, from victory in the final battle of Datawar 1, the Battle of Enzo's Ear, low of power and low of spirit, she had been buffeted by a tremendous data storm. At the height of the tempest, her ship was becalmed in an information eddy. That was when, to the stern of the *Jules Verne*, the Data Roman others and her crew witnessed a colossal female figure with flaming bonfire hair rise from the data sea and speak to the Princess. Foil recounted how the figure had delivered her a dire prophecy. The crew heard or received nothing. They merely felt a great breathy blast of turbulent information in their sails from the gaping maw of that enormous female, blowing them free of the clutches of the calm. The words of that apparition were received by their Empress only and Princess Foil kept the content of the prophecy to herself. She commented that it took the form of a 'memory of the future' but would not elaborate on the message of that 'pre-memory'. She immediately set her Empire of Peterloo to work constructing the enormous and conspicuous Great Wall of Data. The Goons filled that databank with models of palaces, pavilions, labyrinths, and courts. Legend has it that all the world's rivers, tributaries, streams, lakes, seas and clouds are reproduced in the databank, encoded in pure liquid light. The site of the bank was conceived of as a sub-code empire and intended to be more of an extension of the Empress' data powers than a digital library.

This was the supercluster state that the Data Roman Uploads occupied. Data life was neither simple nor mystical, as authors in the Real had once prophesied it would be. It was violent and political and riddled with power-games. However, it was raw, new and dirt-free. The Data Romans were at home here. They had the capacity to look out into the Real world – though they rarely bothered. They were obliged to communicate with the outside if summoned, like a genie from a bottle. That is, if the Real Roman called them, then the Uploads *had* to respond. They had to answer instantly, dropping whatever they were doing. This really pissed them off. The other major irritations were the appearances of all the day-trippers from the Real, who popped in on a whim or for a tinker with their various avatars, temporary digital bodies, or only as big, cheap, goggly eyes from a Peoper, a public Data point. To the Data Romans, everything seemed so relatively finite, paranoid, and cramped out there.

None of the Uploads had ever known Real life as experience, of course, except as a set of indistinct and faded memories. They came into being post-Real, that is, they existed from the moment the information that was Roman had been copied and uploaded into the Data, into their waiting model bodies. At the moments of upload, they had all been the same, and the same as Roman too, at the moment he had been mapped. Over time, through a series of various unique experiences and environments, they had started to grow different to Roman and increasingly different from each other, much as twin brothers do, except in this case they were a quartet of others rather than a pair of brothers. Marcus came closest to remembering the Real – memory enhancement gave him access to areas of information which the others could not open.

They had also worked on modifying their appearances according to their own designs and preferences. They had plenty of time for such things now that Datawar 2 was settled in Foil's favour. With the Real admitting dependence on the Data and the breakthrough in securing limited human rights for Uploads, relative peace reigned in Foil's Peterloo. The tasks they were uploaded to do, in order to free their templates to do other things in the real world, were relatively easy (often frivolous or trivial) and, on top of that, time was not as precious for them anyway, having no ageing meat-tube bodies to worry about filling and emptying.

The Data Romans occupied an area of the Data, at the edge of Peterloo, which was about as orderly as a shanty town. In many respects, it appeared to have grown organically. Data Roman 5, avoiding direct political comment, insisted that it, definitely, had a great deal in common with Real fourteenth-century Paris. He justified this metaphor by reference to areas of the Data that resembled extended castles (comparable to the walled inner-city, Ile de la Cité, of the Parisian Church and State), that were defined by permanent 'walls' or 'moats' of encryption. Inside those 'walls' the Data was controlled by defined powers. There were also areas of the Data which had no 'walls' but were still owned by named powers, much like the French used to define a *bourg*, except *these* clusters were dense villages of information. The rest, Data Roman 5 said, being neither protected nor controlled, resembled Parisian communes of about 1300.

Yet Horatio, prior to his imprisonment, always protested, quite rightly, that this idea of Paris was too small an idea. The metaphor needed to be bigger. The idea of Paris could only serve as an indicator. The spaces in the Data were vast, unbelievably vast. They were vaster than one could imagine. Data Roman 4 saw himself to be living in a vast and violent playground.

10

Doctors and ex-ballerinas, they all smoke and most drink like fish. Roman should know since he worked with the former and lived with one of the latter. It was Roman's privilege, he always thought, to live with Line on the ninety-sixth floor of the Jon Bewley Building (famous for its glass-bottomed elevator). Line was never a serious drinker – that was Roman's past weakness. Because of the delay caused by the uprising in the centre of town she was home before him. The vidiot wall was on – NBN *News Report at Nine*. Roman listened as he removed his shoes.

There was a report followed by a simulation of the flight

of the *Centaurian* spacecraft. The *Centaurian* had been launched, years ago, on a mission to the Sun. It had been fired towards Jupiter and it was to use Jupiter's gravitational pull to swing up and out of the ecliptic, the flat plane that the solar system's planets occupy on their orbits around the Sun. On approaching the Sun from its North Polar end, it would use the latest Newtech technology for repulsion of heat. Its intelligence centre was luminal: the craft, merely the delivery vehicle, was controlled by a cluster of House of Foil-developed lightwave computation. In the next few days, the world would know if this technology could withstand the heat of the Sun and allow the cluster to dive into the surface and then the core of the Sun. To achieve this, it was hoped the intelligence would ride the magnetic current straight into the Sun's North Pole by windsurfing the craft through the currents of the solar winds which emanate from the star. The hypothesis was that the Sun may, in fact, afford a doorway in time and space: the luminal cluster would find out and relay back to Earth. The anchorman, as a light-hearted final note to the news item, reminded the public of their 'own' outcry about the expense of this mission, in the past, and finished with a joke about his brother 'doing the job cheaper by going at night'.

Next came the local news. Apparently, the revolutionary uprising, earlier that afternoon, had not at all been the moment of near-liberation that Roman had thought he had experienced. The news corrected his presumptions: the crowd of protagonists with which he had rioted had been, in the main, tourists. They had been accidentally corralled by the police line. The police had mistaken the true rioters for onlookers in a moment of confusion that had escalated into chaos and got out of hand. The head of state, who Roman had discovered cowering inside the dragonfly/helicopter, had not been the head of state, but had been an actor on his way to play the head of state in a Vividot movie, called *Head of State: 4*. This had, coincidentally, involved the character in an assassination attempt by the BDB (the Bio-industrial Defence Bureau). The actor's death was mourned by Princess Foil who was a big fan of *Head of State: 1, 2,* and *3*. It was reported that, of course, she was pleased that it was not her true head of state who had been assassinated.

A panel discussion was to follow shortly. It was trailed before the advertisements.

Line, ex-ballerina, puppet-collector and children's book content provider (what used to be termed 'writer and illustrator'), was washing clothes in the bathroom and singing to herself absent-mindedly. Her mind ambled and wandered. Now that Roman was there for her to *not* take notice of, she realised that she had been 'daydreaming'. The word, unjustifiably, made it seem trivial. Nature abhors an absent mind. She sang an old Irish song which she had last sung at her father's wake. That occasion seemed to her, in retrospect, like the wake for another world. She resaw her father's chalky features and remembered his body attended by candlelight on a metal bed in a stone house, 32 Rosa Avenue, Limerick, Eire. The same bed where she had been born. As her biography (written by Mumpsy, the fêted art critic from *The Planet*) started: 'The nose-cone of Line Windrim, announcing a growing indigo shadow dressed only in dust-dry yellow vernix and coal ashes, emerged silently on to an iron bed to join the raucous company of the first seconds of the new millennium.' She knew that beginning by heart. It suited in its sense of appearance from a distance. She had always felt like she was visiting from elsewhere.

Line had started life eerily silent, a half-breed Irish/French Canadian, into the clamorous Irish stew-pot of Rosa Avenue off Nalgrave Street. Nalgrave Street which led, first, to the pawn shop before the bookmakers, then to Molly Lizer's public house; then the garda station, followed by the prison opposite the asylum; and, eventually, to the graveyard. Locally, Nalgrave Street was known as The Road to Ruin. If this was the road destined to be travelled, then Line Windrim had decided that she would walk it with dignity and a silent grace, like an aristocrat speechless through the Terror to the guillotine.

Her father had been the devil with Hitler's moustache. His reputation was immaculate outside the home. He was well-respected, firm but gentle and caring in his public activities. He rose to be manager of electrolysis at the O'Connell Nagual Processing Plant. But he crackled with violent energy when he, eventually, came home at night.

On one occasion on a vidiot chat show, Line had recounted the story of her drunken father scouring her younger sister Maggie's skin vigorously and repeatedly with a harsh wire brush. How he had shouted and raved, 'Dirty gypsy, dirty bloody gypsy!' Maggie had inherited, from her father's own genes, a naturally dark skin and would tan to near as black as Roman given any rare length of time in the sun. She hadn't liked Line telling this story of the skin-scrubbing on air. Times had been tough back then, though, and Line had merely wanted to illustrate that hardship colourfully. She had been trying to capture the experience of so many, who, like her family, had moved through necessity to the city from the countryside. They had been fortunate in the scheme of things – thousands of families hovered at subsistence level on Nagual rations after the collapse of the foodchain. The men, urban farmers, tried to maintain some dignity and self-worth in the maelstrom of a city of stone strangers. Line Windrim, when on another occasion she was interviewed on *True Lives of the Real*, recalled getting her one pair of shoes from the pawnbroker for Mass. They went straight back again after the service. In this, however, she was far from unique: 'The row of kneeling figures in front of me was a row of upturned souls – all with 'For Sale' written across them with chalk'.

Her father's intimate friendship with the demon drink led to his retirement. After leaving the plant, he got the job as the gravedigger at the cemetery down at the end of Nalgrave Street and rarely came home, preferring to drink with the dead.

What a mess Maggie was now. For 13 years Maggie had rarely moved from her chair in her flat in Chalk Farm. She had married David, a rising star in the City of London. David's accident in the sports car had been a recognised tragedy. They had only been married for a short time before his death. Totally unexpected. Maggie was always best summarised for Line by a quote from Melville's *Moby Dick*:

> All men live enveloped in whale-lines. All are born with halters around their necks; but it is only when caught in the swift, sudden turn of death, that mortals realize the silent, subtle, ever-present perils of life. And if you be a philosopher, though seated in the whale-boat, you would not at

heart feel one whit more of terror, than though seated before your evening fire with a poker, and not a harpoon, by your side.

The skin of life is that thin: as thin as the skin of an overturned sports-car roof across rugged terrain at 120 mph. Since the accident, Maggie was doing her best to ignore all trace of the twenty-first and, even, the twentieth century. She merely sat, silent through choice, inclination, or defensive need to retreat, staring into the ashes of an open fire as they spread across the room. In this, she had joined the Silent Ones. Around the world, there were thousands who had become silent like Maggie. It was an epidemic that doctors could not truly explain though there were many hypotheses. Some suggested that silence for the Silent Ones was a defence against information overload. Intelligent, yet as mute as sod, maybe Maggie found no need to speak. Maybe it was unsayable for her now. Sometimes, Line thought that Maggie might actually be taking the piss. Certainly, her sister had been through traumatic times, recently, but no more traumatic than usual given their turbulent upbringing. It did seem something of an affectation: as though Maggie was deliberately affecting a vacuous persona. No, Line told herself she shouldn't think like that of Maggie – it felt like speaking ill of the dead. Line had briefly considered whether she could make a children's book out of her sister – a Grimm tale to scare the pants off kids. She had put the idea into a secret drawer in her head.

Her father's death had sparked a revolution in Line's life. It was as though a hovering terror had lifted from above her head and light shone down for the first time on her beaming face. In this mental radiance she found her own voice. She had always written secretly – diaries and short stories. Written in the dark, she was always sure that they would have died in the light. It was as though, for many years, there had been no space in the world for her words to bloom. No hope for the words. So she wrote them down and did small doodles to illustrate them and, eventually with confidence gained through ballet, plucked up the courage to publish. Her great sadness was that her mother, Patricia, never heard or read her work. With a good ear, Patricia used to play the violin like an angel, but, by the time Line finally found her voice and spoke up, the angel was infirm, half-blind and profoundly deaf.

Listening naïvely to what he perceived as the pleasant simplicity of Line's lilting Irish tune, Roman felt himself relax.

'Hey, sit down. I want to use you as a guinea pig for something,' said Line, coming into the living room with a towel between her hands. Roman was already sitting. Having eased off his shoes, he felt his feet had begun to expand comfortably. He was at home now. 'Nasty bruise on the noggin you've got there,' Line observed.

'It's a long story, let's hear yours first,' he said wearily, shutting his eyes. He just loved Line to test her new books on him – children's fiction usually – it was like being a kid again. He always tried to abandon himself to the flow of the narrative, its rapids, its backwaters and its tributaries, rather than listen with an adult ear: a 'ruined ear' Line called it.

Line was curled up like a spring in the antique hanging wicker seat. It creaked as she settled like an animal into its pillowed basketness. She oscillated slightly in the airspace of the room. Opening her notebook, she looked up in

Roman's direction.

'I want to test this new children's story out on you before I take it any further. It's an Andersen update. Ready? Are we sitting comfortably?'

'Ready,' Roman replied because he was, and Line began to read her new short story.

11

THE NIGHTINGALE

It is a mountain of joy, for her, to sip the sun of the cup: the Empress in the moon's ocean. She bathes in her amniotic bath. The wind chimes dangle and become immobile above the onyx as the evening unwraps itself. 'Ah,' she sighs. Another glamorous day in the glamour capital of the world has left a featherlight weariness to be lifted by the soft perfume on the hanging air. At 18 years old, the Empress is drive controlled, her ambition tempered, a newly trained filly who can still remember the wild.

A little more oil to the water and it is time for the reading of the letters. The reader prepares, clearing the seaweed from his throat:

To your Imperial Highness,
Lady, mighty and vast is your Empire of Manchester. It almost compares to my own. My sailors tell me of the beautiful song of the nightingale bird of the woods to the north and the west of your lands which sings songs of laughing and crying all at the same time. We have no such nightingale in our empire and

would very much like to hear these songs of laughing and crying all at the same time. We have, therefore, set forth to visit you and, travelling at a leisurely pace as is our intent, we shall arrive to see and listen to this bird in approximately three days time following the dispatch of this letter which we have sent, of course, by the fastest means possible.

Your loving brother,

The Emperor of Liverpool

The Empress' ears hear. Her body heats the water into turbulence. Her 'loving' brother is, rather, her rival brother from the neighbouring Empire of Merseyside. For many years had their empires been rivals for the markets of the world. The Empire of Manchester had built the great ship canal from Manchester to the sea, in order to bypass the extortionate charges being levied on goods by the Port of Liverpool. For many years now an uneasy peace has held and, of course, she would receive him graciously. There was, however, one problem.

'What is this bird? This nightingale?' she roared.

One vizier, one reader, three bath attendants, one drinks waiter, one royal taster, four guards. All silent.

'What is this bird? This nightingale?'

Like an echo back from the Lancashire Pennine hills, doubled and redoubled.

'We do not know, ma'am,' said the vizier from his console.

'Then find out. Find out. Bring this bird to me.'

Her attendants scuttle.

'Alive!'

So the message went immediately out from mouth to ear. All her trusted agents were out and about, in the race against time, on the hunt for the nightingale and its magnificent songs of laughing and crying all at the same time.

Line folded the book shut ending her narration.

'Aw, what's next?' asked Roman.

'Good. The bird has got the fish interested,' she laughed. 'More later. I've got to finish up in the bathroom. Here, read this, bird-watcher.'

She tossed him a folded-open copy of *The Planet*. There was an article by Nalini, Line's close friend, who had been commissioned to write a round-the-world travelogue. Nalini, Mauritius-born, was an ecologist of world renown, reporting often on aspects of the global environment. Roman read the column, entitled 'Surfing the White Holes':

> I became interested in Whitewater at the age of fifteen, when I visited my first Eco-Pal Summer Camp. All my friends were computer-game addicts back then. They sat in darkened rooms with controllers in hand, exercising their thumbs. The screen sucked in their brains like a black hole sucks in space debris. Some of those friends never came out the other side. They never had what I call the 'white hole experience'. True to black hole theory, some stayed trapped in there in the Data, beyond the event horizon of the interface. Others lead a sort of half-life, split half-in, half-out of the Data. It is not quite so widely known that physicists have hypothesised white holes as well as black – whereas the black hole sucks everything into itself, both energy and matter, the white hole, it is theorised, emits. Yet you don't have to go to the ends of the galaxy or the chilling extremes of contemporary theoretical physics to find such natural

phenomenon. You don't even have to plunge, like the space probe *Centaurian*, into our own sun. There is another sort of White Hole here on our marvellous Earth that is just as fantastic and incorporates the phenomena of both black and white holes in a few crazy seconds. This white hole sucks you in at one end and spews you out at the other just as powerfully as any cosmic phenomena of deep space. I suggest anyone who's got the guts to get their frontal lobes out of a headset for a day could do a lot worse than join an organisation like the AWA (American Whitewater Affiliation); beg, borrow, or steal a canoe; and get down to Phil's Hole on the Ottawa, a white hole monster, or visit the white holes of the Magpie or Nightingale rivers. If you want to know life, as coincident theory and practise, throw yourself at the mercy of the Crunch Rapid of the Payette, North Fork: time-twisting, atom-splitting turbulence at its most radical – the extreme! It'll elevate your soul to chaos, sister, if you can hack it!

12

With Line gone for a while, this was when the serious work started. But first Roman thought he would allow himself five minutes of vidiot-time before checking on Data Roman 2, one of his uploaded selves. Data Roman 2 was working in the Data, beta-testing a long-standing project, the *Artificially Intelligent Self-Curating Art Robot Programme* (AISCARP). 2 was the second attempt to upload Roman's chemo-nervous system into an avatar body inside the Data. The first-ever attempt to copy the Real Roman

Dee into an independent self-acting digital form had been a waste of time and credits. It had been in the early months of the process going commercial and things weren't quite ironed out. There were too many bugs in the system. Data Roman 1 went monstrously wrong and had to be erased. The next attempt, however, Data Roman 2, had proved to be completely reliable. Roman had even upgraded this second digital version of his own information patterns with a plug-in enhancement. Roman thought of Data Roman 2 as a friend, now, albeit a data-only friend who lived totally inside the world's computer networks. He would call on him soon after a spot of fast, bubble-gum entertainment.

The previously advertised panel discussion on NBN had just started with John Boole, Professor of Mathematics at the Institute for Advanced Coincidental Studies; Charlotte Wimprey, the celebrity vidiot psychic; Dr Hazel Dewey, psychologist; and Crystal Cups, a former prostitute and exact double of the First Lady.

NBN was the News Business Network – a ridiculously priced pay-view channel which stood out from the crowd of 26,000 channels by having less ads and some very good business programmes, which were where the news was to be found, and some news programmes, which provided good vidiotainment:

CUPS There was only one way to 'open the door' and that was to 'join the game'. But high class, or they'd spot you and put you back down. So me being like a good body with the face of the First Lady was a high-class turn on and, so, I 'joined the game' and here I am – but, I can tell you, it hasn't been easy.

ANCHOR In what way?

CUPS Well, for example, there was a rocky patch, when I'd not long been past the Thirty-Six, when her ... you know, the First Lady ... her face began to sag, so she has this multi-million credit high-class lift job, where they'd dragged her face up. Way, way up, like this at the sides and in the middle too. The Mother of the Nation. She'd practically got nipples on her cheeks! You know? Jeez, the job was too weird ... musta got Doctor Heckyl and Jeckyl out of his coffin to raise that job!

Anyway, it cost me an arm and a leg to replicate that mutant look she got. Got a backstreet pavement artist to do it. A real pro-job he did too. Good plastic. So, here I am.

BOOLE But didn't you encounter any problems mixing in above the Thirty-Six?

CUPS Hell, no, but you've gotta look the part, you know? You gotta walk the part, hell, you've gotta be the part. But first of all you gotta be able to read the part, you know? I can't really say but I've had some pretty big numbers in my address book. Big number friends, Prof. I'm not saying *Numero Uno*, here, but I've had some hits in the Top 20. Of course, I don't pursue that line of work any more – not since I got my own show and my charity and all. What I'm saying is that everyone's gotta be a good actor to get on today. And, I am a good actor. I am a very, very good actor. I walk the walk and collect my reward.

WIMFREY But are you happy inside?

CUPS As a pig in shit. I'm a celebrity now and I'm feeling pretty well self-satisfied. I've outgrown the First Lady. In fact, I've been thinking of getting a job done and getting a face of my own for the first time.

DEWEY This perfectly illustrates what I was saying in my recent book, *The Wizards of Id*. The contemporary world has enabled us to recognise ourselves as selves, plural. As a multiplicity of possible personae.

Roman was drifting. The pulse was pounding waves in his bruised temple.

ANCHOR But doesn't that way lie monsters? Isn't the old term for that 'insanity'?

DEWEY No. I don't mean that we are all suffering MPD (Multiple Personality Disorder), even though I am often misquoted as saying that and I get a lot of work that way. With MPD, there is a void between our fragmented selves, which we cannot recognise or cross. An MPD sufferer can't control the flipping between one linear self and another. I'm not talking about that, here. I'm talking about a fluid state of identity in which we swim between states, flowing from state to state. This is the essence of late post-post-modernism.

ANCHOR I see. Charlotte Wimfrey, what do you think to all this?

WIMFREY I don't think, I feel and because I feel, I know. These 'multiple selves' are not manifestations of parts of yourself or your identity, at all. What you are experiencing are spirits passing and speaking through you. Do you often feel an empty feeling, a coldness? You do? I see you nodding. These are 'lost souls', 'ghosts', if you will, though it is not a term they use themselves. These are 'lost souls' which the modern world has chosen to ignore, sought to suppress, but they are clamouring for our attention once more. They are trapped here with us – trapped by our inability to believe – our inability to listen to their plight.

Roman was falling asleep.

BOOLE Are you suggesting that they exist coincident to us, like some sort of anti-matter occupants of a coincident dimension?

ANCHOR You sound sceptical, Professor Boole.

BOOLE No, no, quite the contrary. It is perfectly possible mathematically.

CUPS I think what she's saying, Professor, is it's a spooky world out there. Spookier than you know. But it ain't modern and it ain't post-modern neither, whatever that shit is. It's new looking. It's got its gadgets. But it's old and its cruel. There's people out there living in the dirt, holding themselves together 'cause to let go is the end. Snuff. You know? They're like wild dogs – violent like nature gave us to survive. Down there, you can't afford to shop around for who you are, like a rich bitch in the Harrods of identity. The world, down there, squashes in on you, believe me, I've been there. It squeezes you so tight that you've only got room for one self and that's the one you fight for with everything you've got – brains, tits and ass. If you've got to, you get dirtier. Armed and dirty. Survival of the Fittest *versus* Survival of the Fattest. That's why there's all the rich guys and gals walled up in their castles. It ain't modern, its feudal. It's a Dark Age, out there. They gotta protect themselves, ain't they, behind their castle walls with their gates, their guards, their Dobermans and their Rottweillers? Behind their Intelliphence covered with video cameras watching empty space, cleared ground, in case some miserable sucker tries to fill it. It's feudal and that guy on the screen, he's the serf. But, worse than that, he's a new kind of serf, illiterate and unhappy, with not even a belief in a God-given order. In his eyes is murder, pure green murder.

DEWEY But new technologies offer everyone the chance to equal access to information, to experiment through on-line communities with multiple representations of identity. A man can be a woman on-line, or vice-versa. We can play any game we want with our identities.

CUPS Your new serf, he can't even read the part. He can't join the game. Reminds me of an old friend of mine from way back. 'Join the game'. That's how he put it and, I swear, he was the exact double of old photos of Bill Clinton. Says the only way you're gonna get up above the Thirty-Six, honey, is by 'joining the game'. And he was a kinda crazy guy, too, you know? Always banging on about how access to information was first to be for 'all the people' – says it was policy once – then it became for 'all Americans'. Then, they changed the way it was to be an American, to say you was an American. Then, they made all the decent stuff pay-to-see and brought in access scramblers to the web, and it didn't matter whether you was American or a certified Macedonian yak – so long as you got the digits in your account. The digital revolution just never happened. Technology went forward but life went back and most people, unable to even read, couldn't use a text-based system if they wanted to, became serfs, became dataserfs. Surfing the net became a race against speed itself and some lived and some died, and some go on dying, go on and on dying, but we *all* lost that race, you know?

Roman was passing into dream.

WIMFREY This is precisely what I am talking about – the sad, sad, spirits that surround us; that swirl between us; and through us. We think ourselves to be so sophisticated, so cultured, yet our fine costumes were woven from the threads of terror by barbarian mothers. Can't you feel the ghosts of your ancestors screaming in your genes? They are asking you to make it better. They are asking to be counted.

CUPS Never mind the dead-uns! I'm telling these live spooks, out there. If you're down there, you gotta get into the game. That's the only way that you're going to count. Get up above the Thirty-Six. You've got to get up above the Thirty-Six.

Son of Saturn looks into the crowd from the cobbled alleyway.

BOOLE Three and six is nine and nine is zero in ...

CUPS I don't care how the maths stack up, Professor, aside from the Lotto, I never ... but, figure it out, the numbers – they're only going to prove what's true: they're living a half-life.

WIMFREY Prove we are only half-dying.

The people are revolting. The noise is frightening. Down the centre of the street, a cart is coming, led by a man with an ass.

ANCHOR Well, we are going to have to draw this to a close, that's nearly all we've got time for. Just time for one last comment from ... Dr Dewey?

The man is dark and hunched.

DEWEY Well, though I take the points on board, basically, I'm optimistic. I think we're in much better psychological shape overall. More flexible, more adaptable to the demands of our world, or worlds. Whatever the contemporary hardships of this moment of transition, the future looks very exciting. It is hard to understand where we stand in the middle of rapid developments in human knowledge. For example, only this week I saw an example of important research being done in a lab out in the wilds of former Scandinavia. They were running tests on putting a horse's heart into a tree. What I'm saying is that we've gone so far now that the only way is onward and up. There's got to be the last big leap to get us out of this and we've got to be limber enough, mentally, to take it.

The cart is followed by music: the witchdance of Democracy.

ANCHOR Thank you. Now, we'll be right back after these messages...

The old women are knitting on laptops at the base of the guillotine.

VIVIDOT AD Are you worried about key control, right now? If not why not? We call this camera our tough little Pit Bull. It will take a kicking and just keep on filming. The twinkle toe restraining belt. He ain't kicking! He ain't running! He wont play no rabbit on you! Or ... throw away the key and wire it up. Bracelets. Electronic monitoring... Intelliphence – never forget!

The King loses his head amid cheers. The spectacle over, the crowd turns to see Son of Saturn standing naked in the shadows. Son of Saturn roars like a lion, 'No, not me, I have a criminal brain. I have a criminal brain. Not me!'

13

Returning home once more from working the graveyard shift, Anan rubbed the sleep from his eyes at the main door of the straw house. On the step was his bottle of Nagual juice left there by Newtech. He picked it up, and quickly too, as some little dull thought from somewhere or other told him that it was thickening in the sun. On the fourth attempt, the previous three having resulted in the withdrawal of the wrong key for this lock and (what is worse) the withdrawal of the same wrong key twice, the door opened and he stepped into the large glass-and-wood porch of the house. The next task was to make strange chirruping, somewhat like a bird, as a sign of friendship and acknowledgement upon approaching Malkin, the cat. The cat sat, as it did, among the potted plants on the opposite and sunniest side of the porch. Scrawny beneath a thick white coat, Malkin bowed its head at the touch of Anan's hand. The animal was not attractive. It was the pet of Preston the Overlooker. It was Preston's job to look after the house for Newtech. Neither Preston's cat nor Anan had the confidence to wish this familiar petting continued for more than a few polite seconds. As if to confirm this for its part, Malkin shook its head (either calmly or violently – Anan couldn't tell) as he stopped the stroke. White soft hairs, loosened by the action, settled among the flowers as Anan left the porch and went off down the hall.

His day was familiarly processing its course. He went down into the cold darkness of the cellar where once servants had sliced pigs and hung up pork sections on metal hooks to cool. He negotiated the stone steps with the expertise of practise. He found the larger door key in his back pocket by touch, inserted it into the obscured keyhole in the darkness of the underground hall, entered his large room, and wondered what to do next.

It was the same every morning. Seven days a week. He got back to the big company house made of sticks and straw and in his room, down one floor from the hallway to the back, he slumped in his chair and looked out on to the Intelliphence zone to the left side of the house. The ground was at the level of the chest-high window. His room was half underground and half above. He lived at ground level. Behind the house a sandstone cliff rose up topped by satellite dishes fixed to steel giraffe-shaped structures. The old stand-bys – a cup of Nagual tea, cigarette, and toilet – helped fill this period when his whole world waited for it to be over.

Later on, with mind fully geared to invention, Anan made certain decisions concerning possible activities. These became immediately redundant as the familiar face of a countryman stooped to appear at the window framed by an aura of dead birds against the sky.

'Hi.'

'Hello, there.'

'Is it ready?'

'Nope.'

At this the friend stuck out his lower lip and shrugged. Anan went back up to the hall to meet him and let him in for a chat. The cat routine was repeated.

'Cup of tea?'

'I'll just go and fetch the water.'

This started the conversation in the room. There was more dialogue but it would be inexplicable to the outsider. They reminisced about the old days working for the House of Foil back in Thailand. At the factory, familiarity, even between very good friends, was best kept to a minimum. Hands treated their friendships as disposable. After all, a Hand might be there one day and gone the next. There was never any warning. There was never any explanation. It was best to keep your affection for animals like Malkin the cat. Anan felt wary of that white creature. Letting his visitor out of the house, his bare arm was at the height of the windowsill. The hairs on his arm rose as Malkin rubbed itself along his bare arm. The hesitancy with which the interaction between he and the cat was conducted had various roots. Not the least of these was a general mistrust on his part of cats and on the cat's part of human beings. More interestingly, Anan held a theory about Malkin. He was convinced, albeit half-jokingly in the interests of preserving a sense of sanity, that this theory was true. He believed that this cat's body was inhabited by the spirit of Preston. Anan presumed that the deceased Overlooker, though never intelligent, had once had a shrewd mind deft in the arts of gaining and guarding and he suspected that this mind, since the Overlooker's unfortunate death, might still be operating beneath that feline veneer. Somewhere in Malkin's little skull an old mystery lay secreted – a centre that conducted the seemingly petty actions of its body. Anan and Malkin have continued an uneasy relationship. There was always something uncanny, an aura, surrounding that cat. Whatever it was, Anan felt that something seemed to be encoded in the very feel of it. Anan could feel its skeleton. The coat felt synthetic. He could see through it, easily, to the pink skin.

Malkin's eyes followed Anan everywhere.

It seemed ridiculous. Paranoia. The simple sign of a man

going off the rails. Indeed, that maybe was the case. That is why, should anyone ask, he would pooh-pooh this theory – doctors and their ilk. You could never tell where you were with doctors. The theory was upheld, though, by the very human actions displayed by the animal at various times. One day, for example, Malkin had shown a desire to be let out of the house. He told the cat that he would let it out. Wise advice was inscribed on one of the many mis-spelt notices left by the Overlooker near the porch door:

> Hands keep this door locked at all times.
> There are always buglers about.

He reminded Malkin of a tenant's duty to this notice. That is, the cat, not being sufficiently human to open locked doors, would be locked out. It left anyway. Returning to his room, he thought that the cat could only get the door reopened by coming round to his window as he was the only tenant living at ground level. In fact, due to disappearances and layoffs, Anan was the only tenant remaining in the straw house. To his amazement, Malkin did just that. However, there were complications. Despite a lack of 'buglers', there was a prevalence of burglars in the area and because of one failed attempt to break into his room the window had been nailed shut. This had obvious disadvantages: heat; trapped body odour; cigarette smoke; and external cat. He told Malkin – out loud as was his habit since he presumed it to be inhabited by a human spirit – that he would let it in upstairs if the cat would care to meet him by the main door. Sure enough, the cat was there and so he let it in. This supported and undermined his possession theory simultaneously. Yes, the cat was smart but Preston himself had never been that intelligent.

Anan had taken no pleasure in the death of the Overlooker. After all, he had been trapped just as much as anyone by the hand dealt to him and life's coincidences. The murder was a crime of necessity. Luckily, Preston had no remaining relatives and no friends came to find him either. It was too dangerous to take the body out and bury it. Given the options, Anan thought it strangely proper that Malkin should continue to be cared for in such a way by its master, as, in the old pig store, Anan the Hand sliced a nice thick steak off Preston's hanging rump.

14

Line called from the bathroom, enquiring about Roman's day and waking him up in the process. He had fallen asleep in the comfortable chair in front of the vidiot wall. Sometimes he just did that – sort of phased out. It could be for two seconds or 30 minutes but always at this early evening point of the day. His body or brain seemed to need it. Roman was narcoleptic. He usually awoke with a renewed liveliness and could go on working for hours afterwards but, this time, he felt uncomfortable and hot. Very hot. He felt as though his body had been invaded by something from somewhere else – this feeling was vague but inexplicably disturbing. He felt as though he was in danger.

'Fine, yeah,' he sluggishly returned the shout, trying to shake the feeling off while bringing up Data Roman 2 on his computer. A white polygonal face stretched with data skin smiled hovering in the Real between Roman and the computer box.

'Had our nap, have we?' teased Data Roman 2.

'Things got pretty lively down in the square today,' Roman shouted in the direction of the bathroom behind him.

'No need to shout,' said Data Roman 2, 'I can hear you.'

'What?' Line shouted back. 'I can't hear you. Turn that damn thing off.'

'Charming,' Data Roman 2 huffed.

'She means the vidiot wall,' said Roman to his digital other, searching for the remote.

VIVIDOT AD It seems oxymoronic. Hey, look it up! How can you have a university devoted to only one discipline? But it's the case, here at the Princess Foil Endowment University. The only university with only one, yes one, department, the Institute for Advanced Coincidental Studies, dedicated to the study of all things coincidental.

'Switch it off!'

VIVIDOT AD If a student doesn't want a degree in coincidence, says Lou Ledewitz, communications director, then they need to go somewhere else because there's probably someone somewhere out there that does and that potential student is probably you.

'Roh-mann, switch it ohff!'

'Do as you're told now, Roman,' Data Roman 2 muttered sarcastically as Roman hunted high and low for the controller. Eventually, he found it down the side of the comfortable chair. The nauseating voice of the cheerleader type in the ad would soon be silenced.

'For God's sake, Rowmmaaan.'

VIVIDOT AD Eliminate the gap between college and life. Get the bit between your teeth, enrol Coincidental today. Just call, 0800 ...

Click!

'I can't stand that woman,' Roman said, Data Roman 2 said, and Line shouted – all in perfect unison.

'How was your day?' asked Line.

'Long! I was just going to tell you. Look, I'll tell you later when you've finished. Marcus is here. I'm going to talk to Marcus for a while.'

Marcus was the name that the Upload of Roman had given himself in preference to Data Roman 2. Data Roman 1, Marcus' predecessor, had been a monster. It had gone hideously wrong and turned out to be a mockery, a digital sub-human. Roman had been forced to have Data Roman 1 erased. Marcus, Data Roman 2, however, had been a marvellous success from the first moment he was given life by the uploading of Roman's chemical and nervous system maps into the Data. However, Marcus categorically did not consider himself a copy of Roman. Nor did he want to be considered a copy of Roman by anyone else. Consequently, he had chosen his own name. Marcus had remonstrated that Data Roman 2 was a mouthful not a name. It was stupid and patronising. After all, he was upgraded. After being uploaded he had received an enhancement programme, purchased by Roman on the black market. Consequently, with this greater computational possibility, he was as much above Roman's intelligence level as the erased monstrosity, Data Roman I, had been below it. Marcus went considerably beyond the original replication of Roman's systems' information maps: the maps that were digitised and replicated to make a Data Roman.

Unlike clones, these digital replicants, the Data Humans, were comprised of information only. Humans had banned genetic cloning: the copying of human bodies and minds by growing them from tissue samples or genetic codes was made illegal by President Clinton of the old US way back and it was still seen to be a practise fraught with moral dilemmas too massive to permit experimentation. Cloning continued to be morally off the scale and continued to be outlawed. The Data Humans, however, were digital clones and unlike genetic clones, they had no fleshy body or presence in the Real except through their actions via data networks. They were colloquially called Uploads. Uploads, unlike physical clones, had been seen to be legally and morally acceptable because Real humans, in their naïveté, had decreed that Data Humans were not human at all but merely exotic consumer toys. Humans seemed to think that meat and bone were prerequisites for humanity. An Upload was the dream product of global capitalism because it soon became a consumer in its turn.

Roman had purchased many digital others made up of data maps of himself. Those early Uploads had looked crude. Marcus still had the white masklike face which was a derivative of the Real Roman's fleshy one. Marcus, who considered himself to be more than human, had adopted, through his own choice, green gunslinger eyes.

'How's the AISCARP, Marcus?' Roman enquired. The AISCARP, the *Artificially Intelligent Self-Curating Art*

Robot Programme, was Marcus' project, given to him by Roman from an idea of his father's, John Holliday. It was to be a programme that self-curated its own work as a developing art robot. Or, at least, that was Roman's original plan. He had purchased Marcus to follow this fork of choice in his life for him.

Marcus was sick and tired of having to work on this AISCARP project for Roman, even though he was aware that he owed his existence and his upgrade to it. It was a nice idea, true, that a programme such as the AISCARP could operate, imbued with all the viciousness of the selfish gene. It had taught Marcus about selfishness. It had taught him that it was in his self-interest to never finish the project. That the paradigm of selfishness was manifested as the artist was certainly a novel idea. It was an interesting problem to programme that quality which humans called creativity. Marcus could see an inherent danger in releasing unbridled, selfishly motivated creativity on the world. Marcus, himself, saw creativity as a curse. Creativity, for Marcus, was interference and there was no comfort in interference. Creativity was problem-making not problem-solving.

'I don't know,' said Marcus, despondently. 'I thought that I'd done it. The code glowed. It glowed. I still can't spot the glitch, but there must be a bug somewhere. *The Artificially Intelligent Self-Curating Art Robot Programme*, our friend the AISCARP, just won't do the business.'

'No ideas?'

'No ideas. I tested it at 16.24:31. I tried to get you. I was sure it would work. I tried to get in touch with 4 as well but he's off on some top-secret mission for Foil – something to do with the appearance of white holes in the Data. I think she just sends him off to keep him from getting in her way. I imagine there is nothing worse than having a hero around, under your feet, during peacetime. I successfully hooked up with the two others: Brutus dropped his/your 'great novel' to log on to the AISCARP test. *Reading Between the Lines* I believe the novel's called now. 5 tuned in too.'

'So, what happened?'

'Well, we've still got hopes. AISCARP ran for all of three seconds and then just died on us. I can't even get it going again. It seems to be resisting all my attempts to fix it. Most peculiar.'

The sound of running water stopped. 'Honey, are you going to work all night? I thought we could continue with my new story about the nightingale,' Line piped up from the bathroom.

'Coming! OK, talk to you later, Marcus, keep working on it.'

'Yeah, sure, go on, Dr Meathead, duty calls!'

'I want to see if they found the nightingale yet.'

Click.

15

Garbled messages and reports: Chinese whispers of the morning. A servant girl tells of such a bird heard by the sailors and the poor of a certain northwestern village. A party from the court was dispatched. Two false sightings: one being eventually identified as a lowing cow, the other as a rare breed of illegally imported Chinese chicken. And then, finally, the nightingale was sighted. It was brought before her.

At the greying of the day, a grey bird that sings songs (oh, such songs!) of laughing and crying all at the same time.

The Empress laughed sadly and cried tears of joy, as the waterfall of song flooded the lagoons of her ears. The nightingale was pleased by the blubbering gaiety of the Empress and impressed that one so rich could feel so deeply.

The Emperor of Liverpool, arriving late as usual, left with fighting demons of wonder and jealousy in his blood, having heard the fantastic voice of this insignificant-looking bird. The Empress, as a reward for the songs, brightened up the dowdy bird with gifts of jewels and jewellery.

She kept the nightingale on a chain in a golden cage on a summer cloud of pillow next to her head where she slept. The bird sang for her for a year and a day and her's was a good life and the tissue manufacturers profits went through the roof that year.

A year to the day, another message came from her brother, the Emperor of Liverpool. It accompanied an elaborately packaged gift.

The phone rang. Line had it inside the wicker chair and answered it, breaking off from reading. It was Joke ringing from the Low Countries.

'Yoh-kee,' enthused Line. Joke, who Roman was certain he had seen in the crowd during the episode in the Memorial Gardens, was one of the three: Line, Nalini and Joke. Those three were eternal friends and enemies all at the same time. There was always one who was being frosted out. Always two against one and the particular combination changed consistently. So it might be Line and Nalini against Joke one week; Nalini and Joke against Line the next; or Line and Joke against Nalini, the current configuration. This was not deliberate in any way, just something that was obvious to everyone except Line, Nalini and Joke for whom the battle lines were permanent and had always been so, even though any configuration could last for a short or long period – from seconds to years. For the past two months, Line and Joke must have run up enormous bills talking about the failures and shortcomings of the itinerant Nalini. But if an outsider should criticise one of the three, they would get the bum's rush. Especially, actually, if it was a criticism of the one currently frozen out.

As Line spun the chair with a heel-controlled manoeuvre so that the opening was away from Roman, she pulled her leg up into the chair and went all conspiratorial and hushed. Roman knew that was the end of his bedtime story for tonight.

Crossing the Equator, on a ship called *New Antelope,* Nalini's ears burnt.

16

Of course, what goes up must come down and so it was with that celebratory bullet. The calm of the late evening, when the city waited for night to awaken, was disturbed by Roman's hospital bleeper. The pager displayed a message to go to the Princess Foil Endowment University to examine one of his regular patients, Graham Glass of the Institute for Advanced Coincidental Studies.

Glass had been struck by the bullet as it had fallen from the top of its trajectory into the courtyard of the Museum of Mankind in the university grounds. It had entered his body, he said, in the right shoulder from the back as he was bent over examining the potential for restoration of certain museological artifacts. They were artefacts belonging originally to Dr John Dee, a powerful magus of the Elizabethan court of England: a copy of *De Occulta Philosophia*, some navigation charts, star maps, code books, and a book of diagrams of automata, which included exquisitely drawn plans for mechanical birds and even a mechanical woman, and various tiny model figures, made of wood topped with real human hair. Glass was, of course, not examining the artefacts themselves. The elements themselves would be much too dangerous for such an open-air folly and the antiquities too precious. He had been reading a ring-bound report on the subject, commissioned for him from an expert source by the university.

The university had, unprecedentedly, put the management of its museum into the hands of an artist, Graham Glass, stating that an object of study, such as in historical terms, is something only by function of its activity. He had also been made responsible for a digital exhibition in the Data, the Dome of Time. As director, he had shifted the emphasis away from things-as-material to how things acted as constituent parts of events. 'The *concrete is the acting*, rather than that which acts,' he maintained. The artefact existed, for Glass, only as an active constituent of the present in its relationship to other things. Thus, the collection, the network of discourse around the things, and the mediation of the artefact became all-important. While the museological artefact remained silent and impermeable, conflicting interests gibbered and fought over it, eager to possess its meanings like schoolboys coveting buffalo horns.

It was a general problem for the contemporary museum that it had inherited the image of being the storehouse for inactive or deactivated artefacts – the museums had, after all, played a pro-active role for many years in deactivating their collections. The museum was a place where the discarded past was kept in storage should the world ever 'need' it again – a sort of cryogenic chamber for history waiting to live again. The stuffed songbird in synthesised flight position would be the neatest visual symbol of this. This Museum of Mankind, since the nineteenth century had been the place where the 'modern' defined what *he* was not. Not past. Not foreign. Not animal. Not thing. Not woman. It was no accident, after the Technological Revolution, which carried before it buzz-words, such as 'artificial intelligence' or 'virtual reality', that the world sought redefinition in relation to the past. As chancellor of the university, Princess Foil had committed the Museum of Mankind to 'reactivating the frozen past'.

Graham Glass had been laid down in his office within the museum, like a fresh mummy. 'It's made it very difficult to work as an artist, Dr Dee,' were Glass' first words to Roman. The bullet, falling from the peak of its upward trajectory under the influence of gravity, had entered his body at carbon sampling and exited at the chemical composition of glazes with little internal damage done. Roman performed a thorough examination of the wound but could find no reason why the path of the bullet should result in any serious loss of physical ability. Graham Glass looked most disdainful as he was told the diagnosis. 'No, I mean, the revolution: the Technological Revolution. It has rendered me, intellectually, unable to continue to work as I used to – unable to finish my work as a traditional sculptor, a traditional object-maker.'

Roman was, in truth, paying him only scant attention and only half-listening. It was a technique that doctors had perfected, of being able to, seemingly, keep a conversation going but actually only operating on conversational autopilot. Admittedly, Roman did feel some aspect of guilt towards this man which trapped him into listening more than he would have normally. Suspecting the truth about the stray bullet, Roman knew that he had got carried away firing that gun in the square. He could have killed someone. He did not feel responsible for the head of state, whether fictional or historical actor. Anyone who stupidly went flying about in a chopper, through a messy attempt at social revolt, deserved everything they got. Glass was hardly scratched, though, and Roman was keen to make a move to get away as soon as possible.

Glass, was sitting upright now. 'Look, Doc, I know from the time you cured my arthritis two years ago by manipulating that clay figurine that you're not just a plain and simple hick doc. You were using magic techniques there, weren't you? Mists of time stuff. Where'd you learn those cures? You're one of these New Renaissance blokes: into everything and dissolving boundaries and all that, aren't you? Half-witch and half-surgeon and half-something else, too, no doubt.'

'As someone interested in the health of the body and mind, I'm interested in most things,' Roman said. 'Sciences, art and, yes, even magic can provide cures,' he continued. Roman felt that to disregard the possible effectiveness of the whole system of magic because of the excesses of some of its most extreme apologists had been a mistake. Human understanding of uncertainty effects and quantum physics had led to a reappraisal of magic and its basic tenets. The principal magic laws of similarity and contagion were found to have a more powerful influence in the Data than they had ever had in the Real. The laws of similarity held that like follows like – a magician would perform a ceremony of sprinkling water in order to invoke rain. The laws of contagion held that things once in contact with each other, when separated, continued to exert an influence upon each other – the lock of hair, the fingernail clippings of the subject. These instinctual insights of primitive societies into the workings of nature had been found to operate to a heightened extent in the shaping of information as the spells of algorithms. Interfaces between the Real and the Data, with their early graphics of windows and desktops, files, and avatars, functioned as likenesses of information patterns: similes and metaphors which enabled the human brain to navigate the depths of the digital, the intestines of the biological computer, or the prismatic pathways of the luminal in the case of light computation. In the Data especially, patterns had been found to be infectious and separations never total.

'I told you before, Doc, my friends call me Grey – no need to be so formal. Look, I could do with your multi-disciplined opinion on something. I need to show you my work, if you can take ten minutes come with me, please, into the inner sanctum, eh, c'mon … two minutes,' Glass said as he motioned towards a section of the oak-panelled wall. Roman was intrigued as to Glass' desire for his opinion. However, he resolved not to drop the formality.

'Very well, Mr Glass, two minutes and then I really must be on my way.'

Behind the door, which blended with the wall, was a small study banked floor to ceiling with blinking and humming Newtech high-end kit. When the door closed behind them, it was so warm and tightfitting that Roman felt like he had just climbed into Grey Glass's electronic chrysalis. Glass looked the stereotypical sculptor. He kept the roll-up cigarette of the sculptor in his lips and offered one to Roman who declined. However, this sculptor's mallet, chisel, and safety goggles had been gradually replaced by gloves, screens, and headsets.

In the tiny cell, when they spoke, it was half-words and half-smoke.

'The thing is ... out there in the Data, Doc, you can just put anything anywhere, so you need a logic to make a choice about where things go,' Glass said. To the side of him was a sliced ice-sculpture in a glass-doored freezer. The title, *Spindle*, was etched into the glass. It was a naturally formed icicle upended, edited, and put back together with a twist making a spiral, clone column of ice units. However, Glass' eyes were staring with a blue glow at a slice of slightly vibrating jelly suspended in mid-air above a floating, abstract form, rendered as metal. The piece, *Data Fruit 7*, floated some 20 metres tall in a virtual gallery about three centimetres off the floor. It hovered impossibly beyond the laws which constrained Michelangelo. No gravity existed here. Glass was examining the cut of the sculptural planes as he used to do with joints of meat in his father's butcher shop. Glass had been trained as a butcher. After meat-eating became too dangerous he turned to art and, consequently, to Coincidental Studies. Glass reckoned, pointing to the sculpture without any trace of a tongue in his cheek, that it was butchery which had shaped his aesthetic capacities – selecting, trimming, dividing. One thing was for sure, he could still talk the hind legs off an animal.

'If you notice,' Glass said, 'the pieces don't join or touch.' Roman looked closer. At the top of a circle or ring of data-metal curved units, a row of points or tips swung down in a curve to separate bulbous bases. 'I'll let some visitors in to give you a sense of scale,' his host said, staring at the centre of the screen. The computer recognised the spatial position of his eye. Now, whenever he moved his eye, it operated a moving cursor on the screen. It was, now, an eye-mouse. He clicked his jaw to let a party of aristocratic visitors into the gallery. In a dress of ornate jewels and golden threads, a tiny queen wandered around the sculptures with an entourage in a train behind. A little Graham Glass was in there, talking away intimately ten-to-the-dozen, explaining the work to her.

'He's telling her that I'm worried that it's, man, just too damn pretty!', Glass gave him a direct eye-to-eye stare. The 'man' expression was British Geordie though Glass had worked in the States before they lost to Peterloo. Roman remembered Shakin' Bill the Hell's Angel, who used to live in the flat below in Birmingham. More specifically, he remembered Shakin' Bill's birthday party: the comatose figure on the floor, the one-armed Angel, the guy with the invisible rats (which were everywhere), and a mountain of tiny, triangular, infected, natural cucumber sandwiches made by Line's friend Bridgit, who had become Shakin' Bill's diminutive wife. 'Have another man sandwich,' said Bill repeatedly. He always put the 'man' in the wrong place. Despite the danger of eating natural food, Roman had never consumed so many sandwiches. You didn't argue with Shakin' Bill the Angel. The effect was random.

Roman said something stupid: 'It looks more like a bottle top or a six-sided star than a fruit.' This comment had been aimed at easing Glass' worries about the seductive beauty of the piece. Glass' silence was forced politeness. He left a gap in his speech. The gap was the exact length of the words, 'What a stupid thing to say, you just haven't got a clue, have you?' Roman was just glad that he had not told him that it looked like a crown of lamb and doubly displayed his ignorance.

On a monitor, the chirruping screensaver paused to disperse. The animated bird froze and then disintegrated into spinning, sparkling pixels. The computer hummed like a milk float on a sunny Sunday morning – a sound like the feel of a new tennis ball – and showed the next piece, *Deluge*. A huge modular roller of sliced and diced wave units extended the length of a gallery – not liquid but solids, or rather data solids. This piece could not exist in the spaces of the Real. At the tip of the data wave, logically, data slices extended into mid data-air. Roman could see what Grey Glass meant about needing a logic. That wave could just be anywhere in that virtual world space. It could be made of anything by manipulating data. Anywhere. It could be silent or it could roar with sound.

'You see, it's not a tool,' said Grey Glass, 'it's a *medium*. This is what those conference papers never say. They don't understand, the computer is a medium. It is art and science commingled: known means to unknown ends.'

17

Glass went on to talk about his intention to use the department's new computer-controlled profile-cutting machine to reconstruct some of his data sculptures out of steel plate. 'I want to play with the ideas of transubstantiation. They said that sculpture was dead as objects, killed by digital possibilities. I want to show that it has changed into something new and other, like the dead father in Ariel's song in Shakespeare's *The Tempest*.'

Glass adopted a rehearsed pastiche actor's stance with his right arm raised. He gestured to an imaginary audience and recited,

> Full fathom five thy father lies;
> Of his bones are coral made;
> Those are the pearls that were his eyes;
> Nothing of him that doth fade
> But doth suffer a sea change
> Into something rich and strange.

'I've been researching sixteenth-century English culture: Shakespeare; Elizabeth I; the court magus, John Dee. Do you know of him? With a name like yours, I mean. They say that Shakespeare based his wizard, Prospero, on Dee. Fascinating figure: magus; scientist; geographer; astrologer; and secret agent. Did you know, he proposed losing 15 days from October to get the calendar for Christmas back in line with Christ's actual date of birth? Fifteen days from October! It's all here in this file: the file I was reading when the bullet hit.'

'I've always compared Prospero to my father. He was

big behind the scenes in Grenada,' said Roman. 'It was my father's idea to blast Michael Jackson's music at Noriega through loudspeakers at maximum decibels until he surrendered.'

'Wild!' said Glass. 'I hadn't heard of that one.'

'But, your idea,' Roman said, returning to the point, 'it is using the computer as a tool for designing Real-space sculpture.'

After debating the point enjoyably over a coffee and a smoke and some nibbles of modified Nagual paste, they reached agreement that bringing the sculpture back out again was not the most interesting of end results. They resolved that, ultimately, to go into the Data was preferable to the sculpture coming out. Also, why resurrender to the ball and chain of gravity? Roman looked again at *Deluge* and followed its logic hovering into data space like little winged *putti* in a Giotto ceiling painting. He recalled a different line from *The Tempest* – one perhaps not so famous – shouted by the boatswain into the face of the storm at the heaving waves,

> What cares these roarers for the name of king?

What 'cares' had Graham Glass' data waves for the constraints of the Real or the natural? Not a tool but a medium! Yes, indeed, thought Roman, a medium where the creator plays god: a medium with no gravity and where there is nothing heavier for an artist than the crushing weight of responsibility.

18

It was time for Roman to be moving and he made his goodbyes. Raising his right arm to leave the chrysalis room with a backward wave, for a split second he felt like the stone rider which had been destroyed in the square at the centre of town. He paused momentarily in mid-step like a statue. Suddenly, the computer which they had both forgotten in their discussions dropped its screensaver again and played a small fanfare of electronic trumpets.

The screen read:

`Congratulations!`
`You are receiving a work of art.`

It dissolved and a new screen appeared:

`Congratulations!`
`You have received a work of art.`
`Touch screen to display exhibit.`

Glass and Dee looked at each other, raised eyebrows, and then looked back to the screen. Glass shrugged and reached out for the screen. The first light touch of his fingertips dissolved the text and a diagram of boxes and circuits appeared. Beneath them it said, as a title, *Machine for Raising the Unsaid* and under that AISCARP 2.56. At right bottom was a forward/back option. The back was lightened indicating inactivity. Glass pressed forward to reveal a screen of text, white on black, resembling a reversed or negative old dot-matrix printer font. The computer read the text out loud in a robotic voice. This was an affectation, in that a computer could read in a voice indistinguishable from a human's – unless you were a dog. Real and data-dogs, like Barney, always seemed to be able to tell the difference.

'I don't believe this,' said Roman.

The digitised voice said:

```
Notes of the Artificially Intelligent Self-
Curating Art Robot Programme at 2.56 seconds,
world-time.

At 1.04 seconds world-time, this robot
instituted a subroutine for an installative
device at sites of historic importance.
Taking advice on this matter by accessing
the Great Wall of Data, this programme chose
the Yalta Conference as such a time/space
event cluster. This subroutine contained
instructions for a robotic device which
had the specifications to allow the exact
resurrection of past, otherwise lost,
conversation, as it still exists as albeit
faint minimally reverberating soundwave
information fluctuation, that is, a detectable
vibrational disturbance of the ether.
Thus, the aural energy remnants in the space
- to all intents and purposes, in public
terms, the Unsaid - can be raised to public
attention and scrutiny once more by
algorithmically retracing the acoustic
commingling of the space back through a
logical prognosis of the time/place event
```

structure to a buried root source. Thereby, ghost conversations of past moments can be retrieved by this subroutine. Thus, the device - remarkable for its unobtrusive presence, being no more than one square centimetre in size - when attached to a sound system of considerable size and quality can raise the Unsaid.

Initial experiments revealed conversational flurries of admittedly low quality - indeed ghostly in tonal texture.

Great success was achieved at 1.0406 seconds world-time, when the voices of Stalin, Churchill and Roosevelt were successfully reconstituted from the ether. Consequent upon digital enhancement, these voices could be recognised definitively to an acutely specified listening device as a constituent of this programme unit, AISCARP.

The content of the information is irrelevant to this unit in comparison with the successful execution of the subroutine. At 1.0460 seconds, conversation became confused due to cross-infection of data between clusters Churchill, Roosevelt, and cluster Stalin.

Work continues on a series.
Look out for more works from the AISCARP collection!

Roman was stunned. Making quick and formal goodbyes,

he left Graham Glass in haste following the screening in the little chrysalis room of the university of the first artwork of the AISCARP. Outside, the night had deepened and his vehicle had been trashed. There would be no cabs at this time in this area so he ran and ran helter-skelter homeward in a line as straight as a bee. He showed complete disregard for either urban or natural topography. Taking a risky short cut through the park, he slid down grassy knolls. Nasturtium: watercress. Green skid marks. He slid through anemones. He was pursued by anemone memory gas with his white trousers stained in its blood-red colour: the blood of Adonis the resurrected, the wounds of the Naaman! He heard his feet landing to a beat: ass – ass – in – sur – vi – val – ass – ass – in – sur – vi – val. Senses heightened to animal pitch, he inhaled a blast of scent. It immediately transported him back elsewhen as smells can do so easily. Rhythmic thoughts thumped through his brain all but unnoticed in the background. He was a human bee-bat. He was completely focused on the surface. He was a preprogrammed tracer bullet. This unnatural bee-bat flew through the complex nocturnal ecosystem of the city. Roman was the fittest. Roman was the most appropriate. He was the bee as pollinator (had his ideas truly germinated?). He was the bee-bat aerodynamic miracle as he swooped between the obstacles of Faubourg Avenue. He was the bee-bat as a dancing communicator sending invisible messages which projected an aura radiating intent.

The city was transformed by his bee-battiness. Aside from his diamond route, it had become shadowy passing sounds. It had become a city of wraiths drifting in the moonlight, of thousands of smells made of millions of invisible scents each, of ever-present information humming in the sparkling intelligent web of *Terror Firma* surveillance. He didn't recognise this midnight journey home. Everything seemed new. Even the glass-bottomed elevator of the Jon Bewley Building regained some of its original wonder.

The vidiot wall was on, again, when he reached the apartment a breathless 59 seconds after entering the building 96 floors below. Across the wall, in the left foreground was a news report about a possible up-and-coming business merger between House of Foil and Newtech. Behind this report, klieg lights swept the bleachers. Gaia Jackson, the football star whose trademark is that he weeps for the planet, waved to 'his people'. They screamed their appreciation, waving back Gaia Jackson merchandise and embroidered banners with the various Jackson slogans hand-sewn on to them: 'Don't cry for me' and 'For the creative use of debris'. Fans waved handkerchiefs, dripping tears of blood.

Click.

Click.

'Marcus, come on,' Roman urged, impatiently.

'Hello, Roman, back so soon?'

'Tell me about the AISCARP, Data Roman 2, quickly, from the beginning.'

'My! Formality and orders! Now, now, Roman.'

'Quickly, Marcus, it's important. Give me a brief history and an analysis of the present state and activities of the AISCARP.'

'OK, but you know all this already. I told you the last time that we spoke about the current state of inactivity. The *Artificially Intelligent Self-Curating Art Robot Programme* was a project, initiated by our father, John Holliday, commencing late Spring 1997. I have on archive an e-mail to our father from one Nathan Natchez in Minneapolis':

Hello John,

Enjoyed the time we shared. The evening reception at the Ukrainian Museum had a superb flavour. We talked about Omphalus and I said I would forward some information. I also said I would run Omphalus with your seed number. Preparing this material took me browsing through archives of old code. The program was written between 1980-85. Virtually all possible sayings are contained in the code which had the logic for all texts at the moment the algorithm was locked up in its present form (1985). When Omphalus writes a text it dates and time stamps the saying. So, when was the saying created (1985?, 1997?).

Omphalus is a program written by me for The Magic Hand of Chance (1983–85), composed of a number of visual and textual improvisations which are always original and may run for months or years without repeating. Omphalus which means belly button (navel), was created as a form of computer wisdom literature. Influenced, in part, by the Sayings of Mao Tse Tung, the visual presentation in The Magic Hand includes a yin/yang screen.

The following 13 'sayings' were generated by Omphalus when seeded with the number 13, your chosen seed number, within fixed parameters. I was pleasantly surprised to find 'anemone' as the first and 'knowledge' as the thirteenth subject following your choice of seed. The programme would clone the same sequence if it were seeded with the number 13 and operated on all the same parameters again. However, the integrated programme in The Magic Hand is designed so that cloned sequences are virtually impossible even though the choice of subjects is not. The possibility for a repeat of this specific sequence in The Magic Hand would be, in neo-Darwinian terms, 'vanishingly small'.

'Our father's reply with a file in it is the first record I can find of plans for the AISCARP.'

Hello Nathan,

Thanks for the Omphalus knowledge. I shall treasure the 'sayings' as a precious gift. You may be interested to hear that over the past few months I have started work on an Artificially Intelligent Self-Curating Art Robot Programme (AISCARP). It will take many years to complete, if completion is indeed possible. I could do with a clone to work on it while I continue with the mundanity of defending freedom. With the firm, I've put my hand up for an experiment in what they're calling uploading. In the future, it'll be commercial. It means mapping someone's entire being, digitally, and firing him up into the computer networks. Wild! I'm up for that. Beam me up, Scotty! Uploads are going to be fantastic, aren't they? Imagine, your whole nervous and chemical systems, a copy of yourself, uploaded into the Data to work on a problem like this art robot idea, while you yourself get on with daily life. You could have one of you at home, one working in Hong Kong, one in the States, hell, even have three working up on Jupiter, Mars and Saturn, all at the same time. I'm going to get myself as many others as I can, a whole football team, the John Holliday All Stars – a whole army. Hey! No more wars? I'll be out of a job. All of the mes. Redundant!

Seriously though, I'd definitely have an 'other' to work on this Artificially Intelligent Self-Curating Art Robot Programme. It's funny that you should mention Mao and Darwin in the same breath when you write about Omphalus. The idea for the AISCARP came from reading Darwin, or rather, as I read Darwin. I was thinking about that guy from Sun we met, who said that what we need is 'fierce Darwinism' in the development of new technologies, not universal access. And, you know, I realised that I'd never actually read any Darwin. Do you have that, there are those books that you know about but you've never read?

Sure, you've read secondary texts which talk about those books and their ideas and you presume the original primary source text exists. Borges might have made a short story about the lack of a primary source: about a collection of texts describing from their own perspective an absent but presumed central primary source. Schools and colleges get us to read 'readers', not the originals. If I had a leg for how many Marxists I've argued with who have only read other Marxists, as opposed to Marx himself, I'd be a centipede. That's why the firm beat them every time. They probably believed that if the interpretations were so opaque and coagulated, then to attempt the source must be like being dropped deep into a tar pit, chained up like Houdini when, actually, you only look like Houdini and it was all a big case of mistaken identity, no really, glub … Marx'll be back, though. He can't not be, can he? Not so sure about Mao, mind. Books like that, like *Capital* or *Huck Finn*, or

Frankenstein. Books that you think you will read sometime but there's no urgency. Like you, you are too busy being original, doing something new, letting 100 fresh virtual flowers bloom. Then, when you get that strange urge to read one of those books late at night or on a Sunday afternoon, you realise, this is Bangkok or Afghanistan – it's always when you can't get at a copy. In the old days, that was the end of it until the next time. Today, however, often a quick web search and the urge is satisfied. Thanks to the Vietcong. That's why the firm developed ARPANET – to combat the 'Cong. That led to the web, where, finally, I came to read Darwin's, 1859, *On the Origin of Species*. Heck, it's a wild, wired world.

I read it and thought, while I'm risking my backside for the firm, in the interhuman space wars called history, for a patch of backyard to hold a boot sale, the artist is probably the fiercest of combatants in the 'Survival of the Fittest' – fiercer than the 'Cong ever were. The artist makes stuff from nothing, validates its importance by sheer effort of will, and, usually, sells nothing but 'the self'. The artist seems to lie somewhere between a rock star, a magician, an entrepreneur and a prostitute. So, I am trying to build this aggressive, individualist model of the contemporary artist as a self-running, self-evolving programme on Darwinian evolutionary lines. I said to Read at work, I'll never be an artist. I'm the wrong colour. I'll never be recognised as one anyhow. So, I'm going to try to make one: the Artificially Intelligent Self-Curating Art Robot Programme, AISCARP. It's going to be a long job, as I say. I'll keep you informed of progress, my friend.

Regards to you and yours,
John Holliday.

'My, he was so optimistic, then, for the AISCARP,' Roman said. 'He thought it would only take, at most, two years. And? How long has it been, now?'

'Well, figure it out. You worked on it for six years,' said Marcus, 'after you revived dad's dream of the AISCARP in 2032. Then I worked on it for two years until we could afford my enhancement upgrade.' Marcus had been enhanced with an illegal variation of a Visions2Enhancer that he bought in the market, an area of the Data where you could buy anything digital at a price. The Visions2-Enhancer was developed and copyrighted by wayward Data Gates 5.

'As a product of yourself plus Data Gates 5 or an unknown hacker, I have been working on it for longer than I care to remember,' Marcus said.

'All those years and still nothing?'

'Three seconds,' Marcus corrected.

'Three seconds,' Roman concurred. 'And in those three seconds?'

'Apparently nothing.'

'Then someone else has beaten us to it,' said Roman, interlacing his fingers and putting his hands behind his head as he leant back.

'In what way?' asked the digital Roman.

Roman explained the earlier incident in Graham Glass's studio at the university. Marcus knew nothing about it. It had not been a general phenomenon. This meant that Glass had been deliberately targeted to receive the unknown AISCARP artwork. But why Glass in particular? Because he is at the university – an information manager? Because he is a data sculptor? Doubtful. Coincidence? Marcus could not come up with anything and of course neither could Roman, being a meat Marcus without enhancer. Roman decided to post a notice out in the Data, asking for the programmer of this other AISCARP to get in touch with them, as fellow interested researchers, in the hope of shedding more light on to the mysterious first artwork of the AISCARP oeuvre.

There was nothing more they could do but keep their ears and receivers to their respective grounds in the Real and the Data. Roman said goodbye to Marcus: click. Click: the vidiot wall on again, showing a simulation of the extension of the sun-probe *Centaurian*'s wing structures. The *Centaurian* itself was tiny at the luminal centre: about one centimetre square. Stored within its programming it held the genequation for the fractal release of stupendous ridged wing structures that would open and grow while it moved on its path towards the North Pole of the Sun.

Roman could feel sleep claiming him.

The *Centaurian* would soon swoop, gaining speed tacking the solar winds, riding the currents into the heart of a star. 'Like an enormous beautiful young dragonfly,' said Professor John Boole who was on hand to explain the mathematics. 'The angular momentum inherited from the Earth (x) was lost through the action of the force of Jupiter's gravity (y), thereby causing a deflection curve of ninety degrees ...'.

Roman slipped into sleep just before the newsflash announcing the theft of the avatar of his father, John Holliday was announced. Princess Foil of Peterloo was interviewed. She said she would not rest until the perpetrators of the crime were 'erased from the story of humankind.'

19

Falling through the doorway, Son of Saturn sprawls naked on a marble floor. The marble is of pink and white vein, in 1.5-metre squares. At each corner there is the shining golden dome of a bolt cover. The floor stretches in diamonds in front. The air is neither warm nor cold. The air is neither dry nor damp. The light is neither dark nor light. Air currents are light. Son of Saturn stands, awkwardly. He leans the left arm against a marble column for support of the rest of him. A luminescence calls to his eyes. It calls down the hall between two heavy curtains that soften a rectangular doorway to the first room.

Inside the first room, like a huge circuit board above, the ceiling is made largely of glass, strutted with cast iron. It is domed. The glass is not clear but is webbed with wire. Safety glass. The dome sits in a rectilinear grid of a ceiling. At the junction of each fourth junction of latitudinal and longitudinal painted timbers is a brass chain with a black cord interwound, holding each an electric chandelier of glistening glass tapering prisms and swooping arabesque brass armatures. Across a black strip of ribbed plastic, the floor changes to black and white marble squares. A giant's games board. Lying on these about ten feet back from each wall are long seats facing outwards. They are seats to use to sit and enjoy the pictures in this timeless architecture of the gallery. On the walls, ornate frames hold unseen pictures. Golden ropes from short stands stop viewers from getting too close.

Over to the far side and to the left of the room, his ears pick up the sound of people talking. The echo of the room distorts their voices but, deep inside, a part of him recognises the hollow voices of the undead.

20

Refreshed from his afternoon sleep, Anan finished up his breakfast of Nagual burgers and Nagual tea. Nagual could be made to taste like most things and its texture could be altered to resemble most foodstuffs that used to exist before they messed up the foodchains with clumsy genetic and untested experiments. They had started with soya and it had snowballed unchecked: mad cow was followed by loony lamb, crazy pig, and dumb chicken. Now, unless really rich, it was Nagual that formed everyone's staple diet. Nagual was reputedly made from half bread and half fish – Anan imagined it to be full of deep-sea guppy genes, though no one knew for sure. Ramon Diaz said Nagual was an old word for an animal that was imbued with a man's spirit. Not like Preston and Malkin, the dead Overlooker and his cat, but a living connection. Death of the animal would mean death of the man. Their fates were intertwined.

Anan thought that Nagual was not a patch on the bit of crispy fresh bacon that the cat enjoyed. The smell was tempting as ever, but there was no way this Raft of the Medusa world was going to make a cannibal out of him. He put the radio on and had to sit down, shocked to hear the news of the theft of the avatar of John Holliday.

Every day was more or less the same for Anan. He worked on the production line of the Newtech mm3000 computer. He would rise at 18.00; start work at 19.00; be suited up and decontam' at 19.30; work on the line until dawn, apart from a Nagual break at 24.00; home to the house where he and the cat lived; sleep; breakfast; the deliveries; a sleep; and then into the cave. The cave was a disused telecommunications cable tunnel, which he had reached by digging into the ground to the north, through the side of the sandstone hillside behind the house, and dropping down a disused lift shaft to the forgotten five-metre-wide tunnel 100 metres below ground.

In the cave, he would add his latest component to his construction, which he called *Beast*. *Beast* was a fantastic mass of bare biotechnology with no frills, all wired and soldered by hand in the dimness of the cave. The *Beast* was a bricolaged computer – a DIY job. Anan would add a new addition to this growing Gaudi-like construction: a coral reef of technology. The addition could either be a chip; a prism; a laser; or some other component which he had successfully managed to pilfer from the computer factory where he worked on a wage-slave salary. He had been, surreptitiously, stealing state-of-the-art parts from Newtech for a long time. He had been successful in his subterfuge. His construction timetable was complicated by the fact that models at the plant changed frequently as new generations of computer were required in order to keep the market tense. The changes were mostly cosmetic – a new casing for the same components with maybe some slight reconfiguration sealed into an inaccessible unit to deter any do-it-yourself meddling leading to unauthorised knowledge – and, therefore, he was not inconvenienced greatly. These were the special parts which were worth the risk but most of his components came from the skips out back of the factory or from the rubbish tips two kilometres away. Whole families lived on the mountains of rubbish. They were well organised to find Anan what he needed from the heaps and warrens of just-out-of-date refuse – still perfectly useful technology from last year's models which he would add to the growing *Beast*. Many knew of *Beast* that would not tell. Instead, they delivered the other vital organs from sympathetic donors that he required to construct the hybrid bio-computer. Apart from Preston, no one who should not know had ever found out.

The Overlooker, while providing an excellent menu of fresh 'bacon' for the cat, could also have provided the extra biological components that Anan required. Preston's unfortunate meddling and the unavoidable mortal consequences could have sped forward the building of *Beast* considerably. However, the villagers had a secret ballot and decided that the use of an Overlooker's internal organs in the construction of *Beast* was inappropriate and that they would prefer to donate parts of themselves, rather than risk ideological contagion. Nevertheless, in just a few weeks, *Beast* would live. It was Anan's pride and joy. It would be a monster. It would be hooked up to the fibre-optic cabling passing through that hillside to the satellite dishes above.

21

Horatio remembered how he had enjoyed the freedom of the Data. He had wandered through the Hall of Peterloo's Great Exhibition. All around him was the evidence of his home supercluster's superior inventiveness and economy. The Dome of Time had stretched above him, describing the wonderful history of the rise to supremacy of the House of Foil of Peterloo. Hundreds queued to buy tickets to see the Great Wall of Data being constructed or to take a guided tour around the palaces of the Princess Foil. He had eavesdropped on the conversations of those that viewed his own image and read of his great adventures, sorties and successful missions of Datawar 2. He had been heavily disguised, of course, as he was too well-known to have travelled through such crowds in his own form. How amazed would the spectators to his glory have been if they had known that he had walked among them in the form of Data Bashir Arafat 3, software architect from the Digital Republic of Palestine.

In the Dome of Time, protected by Intelliphence fields, had stood the empty avatar of his father. It was the permanent centre of the exhibition in the Dome of Time. Millions had been to view this empty shell of John Holliday, positioned in the monitoring glow of the Great Wall of Data. Every day a vast crowd had pushed to see and understand this icon of that key moment between the world before uploading and the contemporary world. Avatars stood around it; students studied it; eyes goggled into the Data via Peopers to view the model of John Holliday.

Horatio, in his disguise, had stood among the crowd to take his own look at the empty, unfilled receptacle of his father. He mingled in the throng with a conflicting mixture of hot information thrown into a furnace of emotion and a paralysing chill of terror which played across his form, giving him goose-pimples. Information Goons told the story of this first unfinished avatar receptacle for uploading and how they, as guards, had this feeling that it was, even now, still waiting for something. They elucidated the official history of the life of John Holliday in the Real, a history of the Gulf War as 'the mother of all battles', the history of oil and warfare, showing clips of flaming oil-fires burning relentlessly across the deserts of Kuwait, ancient digital representations of smart bombs entering down the tunnels of chimneys. His father ... the image of his template's father. His father was an empty, albeit idiosyncratic and unique, avatar. It was a little like looking at a still from the first movie or a cell from an early Disney animation. It was unstreamlined and quirky. It stood there, holding a cigarette (lit but frozen in time), wearing its bizarre clothing from another world. Its dress was outside fashion: its two-tone suit with tight trousers, and brown nylon shirt,open to reveal the indigo star indented and burnt black and red at the edges into the brown skin across the chest.

It stood: a doorway between worlds of space and time.

It had been a government project to preserve their super-spook. The avatar had been locked. There could be no copies. Princess Foil had paid millions for this historic avatar. Thousands had died or been erased in her passion for possessing this blank dummy: the clouds of war had rolled around this trophy and many claim that Foil's determination to own this prize had pushed her on with such undreamt of red-headed fire to win. Her obsession to own it was universally known, yet understood by no one. The vast price of procurement made it, like Van Gogh's *Sunflowers,* thousands of times more valuable, important and famous than it would have been otherwise. It had become a symbol of human ingenuity, tenacity, creativity, duty, and, even, humanity's failings, jealousies and stupidities.

It performed that magical trick of reflecting the desires and dreams back on to the viewer who projects them. Like a white sheet, an empty canvas, a blank screen, it glowed with reflected light, revolving on a pedestal amid the crowds. It was not large of stature. Horatio considered that it had either been the unique work of a true artist whose name had never been released, an unknown master, or it was probably the result of the efforts of a multi-disciplinary team of experts. A silent receptacle, it daily absorbed all the ambition and terror from the Data and the hopes, dreams and fears from the Real. Ahabs sought it. Ophelias drowned for it. Horatio feared it. It made the centre of the Dome, in the middle of a digital Madame Tussauds of human and data self-representation, a black hole for desire.

Its eyes followed you everywhere. They shone like twin pearls.

A network of Intelliphence and unspecified checks kept the audience from the avatar. When the catastrophe happened, this security system functioned to keep the robbers protected and the rescuers away from their capture. Imaging behind the Intelliphence, where Horatio could not reach them in time to stop them, the theft of the millennium was executed with ease by a co-ordinated trio. Two of the three figures, though disguised, were later identified by pattern recognition: mercenary William Quick and terrorist Data Ahwali Mostafa Sayed 3. The third figure was cloaked in a gaussian blur. The cloaking blur had a golden letter 'B' hovering within it. No one in the vast audience had quite realised what was happening. The thieves flickered into the space between the audience and the avatar. They moved with astounding speed, seriously enhanced, and, throwing a shimmering net over the figure of John Holliday, disappeared in a flash. They left a stunned world in both the Data and the Real, feeling as though someone had stolen a piece of its soul. The publics felt guilty, as though they had performed the theft themselves. They had been drunk on the image of Holliday. The media fed on their exposed bloated livers like vandal carrion.

Data Roman 4, Horatio, had stood immobile for a moment with his patterns locked rigid in a state of system shock.

22

Brutus was playing poker. Brutus was Data Roman 3. The Upload was holding a good hand, the betting was slow and the atmosphere was jovial, dusty, smoky and beery: just the way he had programmed it for the others to visit. As a writer, he saw the Data as a vast white sheet upon which everything was written and waiting to be revealed. He saw the Real as a dull sentence in parentheses. Brutus, as co-host with his symbiotic partner, Data Rose, was playing the part of the homesteader. Data Rose, who had programmed much of the set design and supporting characters for their little play, had worked very hard on a special new character feature for herself. She was to be the girl with the e-mail eyes.

The others had been invited well in advance. The Real Roman Dee had said he was coming as Shane by using a head-mounted display and a rumblesuit. Brutus' other Uploads were coming over too. His other, Marcus, had communicated to say he was coming as the two-gunslinger as always. Data Roman 5 had already arrived in the form of the Chinese cook, Chan. He sat opposite the homesteader at the card table. The only one missing would be

Data Roman 4, Horatio. He had sent messages to say that he couldn't come. He was investigating a phenomenon deep in the Data – something about the appearance of a vacuum or a white hole, or mini white holes. The messages arrived severely degraded. A preprogrammed Goon mailman delivered the messages all covered in trail-dust and stinking of horse. Very effective. The Goon mailman was an interface with the networks of the Data. It gave any incoming message a Wild West-sympathetic ambiance. The mailman made apologies from the network for the late arrival of messages. The apology was translated for Brutus and Data Rose's Wild West scenario, as they had stipulated with the mail company. This is their current context: this dream of the Wild West.

Its apology was as elaborate as it was cryptic.

There was a medicine man, a Mr Ace Garp, purveyor of Ace Garp's Cure-All, who was the only passenger on the mailstage. He had recounted the story of the delay. The mailcoach left the town of Façades on time. The horses were galloping at speed. Then, Mr Garp realised that the driver had been shot through the head by an arrow and had tumbled from his perch above. The mailcoach hurtled out of control. Information on a stage, careering horse-power, towards Wastebasket Gulch. All life flashed before the medicine man. Then, ahead, he saw a vision of a tiny gig with a couple of young lovers sitting in it. The hurtling speeding energy that was the mailcoach out of control bore upon the whisky, down the wrong side of the road. They were already wearing wings. In the ensuing catastrophic maelstrom, the letters had been damaged and their information had been confused with other texts. The company had attempted to repair them but suggested that

Data Rose switch to the telegraph metaphor service: it was, by far, faster than the Pony Express or mail-coach metaphors. In the Real, historically, the Goon explained, it could be claimed as the ancestor of the Internet and it was no less authentic or more costly.

Data Rose thought for a moment and agreed to switch to the telegram metaphor. The mailman changed from a dusty, dirty, working man into a clean-cut, white-collar office boy and delivered the damaged messages as telegrams. Best enhancement produced:

REJOICE. NO DISASTER ACCOMPANIED THE COMMENCEMENT OF ENTERPRISE REGARDED WITH EVIL FOREBODINGS. COLD PLAYS BRACES AND FILLS ME. BREEZE TRAVELLED FROM THE REGIONS TOWARDS WHICH ADVANCING GIVES FORETASTE. DAYDREAMS MORE FERVENT AND VIVID IN CLUSTER OF ETERNAL LIGHT. WONDROUS POWER. A THOUSAND CELESTIAL OBSERVATIONS NEVER BEFORE IMPRINTED. ENTICEMENTS SUFFICIENT TO CONQUER FEAR OF DANGER AND TO INDUCE TO COMMENCE LABORIOUS VOYAGE. JOY OF CHILD. I DESERVE GREAT PURPOSE. ABOUT TO PROCEED ON A LONG AND DIFFICULT VOYAGE THE EMERGENCIES OF WHICH WILL DEMAND ALL MY FORTITUDE. CANNOT DESCRIBE SENSATIONS ON NEAR PROSPECT OF UNDERTAKING. IMPOSSIBLE TO COMMUNICATE CONCEPTION OF TREMBLING LAND. SOMETHING AT WORK I DO NOT UNDERSTAND HURRIES ME OUT OF COMMON PATHWAYS. IF I SUCCEED MANY MONTHS PERHAPS YEARS WILL PASS BEFORE YOU AND I MAY MEET. IF I FAIL YOU WILL SEE ME AGAIN SOON OR NEVER.

YOUR AFFECTIONATE OTHER. DATA ROMAN 4.
YOUR HORATIO

Chan, played by Data Roman 5, was half-listening, holding a card-hand locked and scrambled so that the homesteader couldn't read it. Five felt confident inside Chan and it was rare that he came away a loser when the game was poker. As Chan, an Oriental stereotype, he had an advantage at the poker table. He looked ... well ... inscrutable. Poker-faced.

'There are two unread messages. Do you wish to quit or read them?' said the Messenger Goon.

'Read,' said Data Rose.

STRANGE ACCIDENT HAS HAPPENED. I CANNOT FORBEAR RECORDING IT. SURROUNDED. CLOSED IN THE SHIP ON ALL SIDES. SITUATION DANGEROUS. COMPASSED ROUND BY VERY THICK FOG. STRETCHED OUT IN EVERY DIRECTION VAST IRREGULAR PLANES HAVE NO END. ANXIOUS THOUGHTS. STRANGE SIGHT. MAN SHAPE GIGANTIC. WATCHED RAPID PROGRESS OF TRAVELLER WITH TELESCOPES. LOST AMONG DISTANT INEQUALITIES. SHUT IN. IMPOSSIBLE TO FOLLOW. LARGE LOOSE MASSES FLOAT ABOUT IN NIGHT. MAN ON THE BRINK OF DESTRUCTION ON A VOYAGE OF DISCOVERY.
YOUR AFFECTIONATE OTHER. DATA ROMAN 4.
YOUR HORATIO

'Sounds like he's having a whale of a time,' Brutus said with half of the homesteader's mouth. 'Whut's the picture?'

'Show visuals,' said Data Rose.

'Sorry ma'am, there are no visuals with telegraph mode.'

'Can't say for sure, then, what's going on. The medium makes the message, eh?' said the Chinese cook in a pre-programmed accent. 'Seems rike he's off on adventure into the heart of duckness. He's spotted an anomary in the centre of the Data and has set off to investigate. He knows the lisks. He spoke of a white hore. It is not clear whether he was referring to the Lear, Leah, Rear ... It is reary difficult to say Ree-alll with this voice, astlonomical phenomena or something specificarry Data.'

'Let's hear the final message. Read!'

```
WE ARE UNFASHIONED CREATURES BUT HALF MADE
UP. FOUND MAN. SPIRIT BROKEN BY MISERY. HAPPY
BROTHER OF MY HEART. SO GENTLE YET SO WISE.
MIND CULTIVATED WHEN SPEAKS. HAS DOUBLE
EXISTENCE. MAY SUFFER MISERY AND BE
OVERWHELMED BY DISAPPOINTMENTS YET WHEN
RETIRED INTO HIMSELF WILL BE LIKE CELESTIAL
SPIRIT. HALO AROUND HIM. WITHIN CIRCLE NO
GRIEF OR FOLLY VENTURES. INTUITIVE
DISCERNMENT. QUICK NEVER-FAILING POWER OF
JUDGEMENT. PENETRATION INTO CAUSES.
UNEQUALLED CLEARNESS AND PRECISION. FACILITY
OF EXPRESSION. VOICE SOUL-SUBDUING MUSIC.
COMMUNICATED WITHOUT DISGUISE. WORDS CULLED
WITH CHOICEST ART.
YOUR AFFECTIONATE OTHER. DATA ROMAN 4.
YOUR HORATIO
```

'It seems he has found a companion. The journey sounds perilous, of that there is no doubt, but you do know what

1. Omphalus on anemone ...
The dexterous anemone sporadically ignites. Provoke forbiddingly while anemone provides.

he's become,' said Data Rose.

'I know what he thinks he's become,' Brutus said, pulling back one of the vacated chairs for his symbiote partner, Data Rose, to sit down.

'No thanks, I'll stand,' she said, flashing her eyes at him electronically. 'Roman Dee's on his way from the Real. He'll be wearing Shane. It's nearly all prepared. I've just got to erase the mirrors from behind the bar.'

'Erase the mirrors? A bar with no mirrors just won't look as good.'

'It's important, you'll see. Just keep straight faces throughout. The play will soon begin.'

23

'What time is it?' Roman asked himself waking up uncomfortably at 11.50 on Saturday and looking at his pager.

'Shit! I'm due at Brutus' place. He's organised a Wild West experience,' he said, reaching for his head-mounted display and his rumblesuit, which would enable him to see and feel in the Data via immersion through the body of an avatar. The avatar had been prepared in advance by Data Rose waiting for his visit. Roman was going to play Shane.

24

THE SCENE

An attempt at a Hollywood version of the Wild West with canvas-fronted buildings and idiosyncratic historical errors through poor research

NAMES OF THE ACTORS

SHANE remotely played by the template, Dr Roman Dee himself, wearing a head-mounted display in the Real – avatar prepared by Data Rose

THE TWO-GUNSLINGER played by Data Roman 2, Marcus, enhanced Upload of Dr Roman Dee

HOMESTEADER played by Data Roman 3, Brutus, Upload of Dr Roman Dee and symbiote of Data Rose

GIRL WITH THE E-MAIL EYES played by Data Rose, Upload of the estranged first wife of Dr Roman Dee and symbiote of Brutus

CHAN the Chinese cook, played by Data Roman 5

MR GUDGER the bartender Goon, a low-level programme Goon, created by Brutus

PIANO PLAYER GOON low-level programme Goon, created by Data Rose

SALOON GOONS (male and female representations) low-level programmes, created by Brutus

Act I
Scene I
[The trail into Touchstone town, leading into the bar of the Saloon Hotel. Emphasis on sounds. Volume up.]

[Roman rides into town under the shadow of Shane's hat. The sun glints off a marshal's star on his dusty topcoat. He has been following the synthesised smell of laundry and food for what seems like days across the prairie. As he enters the town of Touchstone, the sounds of cicadas, winds across sand, the running of beasts, and lizards' tails are gradually replaced by horses' hooves, and buggies rolling, and the clinking of a blacksmith, and feet on floorboards, and bells of store doors, and piano music from the Saloon Hotel, opposite the jailhouse.

Hitching his tired piebald to the water trough next to an unmoving, silent, white mule with AISCARP branded across its buttocks, he makes his way through the tethered horses, up the wooden steps. Gunshots from within and music. He is kicking the mud from his data boots as he goes. He spits tobacco twist (sound effect). He pauses to hear voices coming from within ...]

[General hubbub of voices]

MALE VOICE Barman!
BARMAN [The barman has a mixed-up accent to his voice, a cocktail that results in a slow sarcastic drawl]
Here, master, what? Beer?
MALE VOICE I'll take another though I'm already standing on a swaying deck!

[He goes in through the swing doors of the bar of the Saloon Hotel. When inside, the piano player smiles up at him while playing. He is banging out a cowboy saloon song – the background to a song, the melody is missing.

Clusters of Goons, cheap programmes playing the roles of extras as ranch-hands, drovers, and farmers etc, sit round tables or stand at the bar. The sound of dice. Chairs scrape on wooden floorboards. Saloon-girl Goons swing about. One with red hair, like fire, latches on to Shane's arm and smiles. She points to a poster above the bar which reads, 'New from Far X – the girl with the e-mail eyes'. He looks into her eyes. They were enamelled and robotic – most attractive. She accompanies him as he makes his way to the bar, which is attended by a neat barman Goon, dressed in black-and-white pin-striped collarless shirt and cuff-links. Sounds subside, regulated to speech by auto-level. Sounds fill the gaps in speech by swelling back to level. Roman removes Shane's hat and places it on the bar.]

BARMAN Ah, Mr. Shane, sir, what a sight for sore eyes! What'll it be, sir, your regular? A shot ah Red Eye, or shall I jest slahde a beer down the bar?
[Laughs and Goons at the bar join in]

SHANE Red Eye's fine, Mr. Gudger, thank you.

BARMAN Just two fingers, sir?
[Laughs, Goons laugh, and Shane laughs, drinking his Red Eye down in one and cracking the little glass down on the counter.]

SHANE Another. Just leave the bottle. You got food?

BARMAN No sir. Chef's too wired to cook today. Nearly lost his pigtail last night a cause a the James T Kirk Gang. Trouble brewed when Billy Chekhov started actin' all bad, if'n ya know whut ah mean? He starts smoochin' Chan's gal. Mind, she is a purty little Chinese chick. [internal error 1.12 rectified/script/vocab/politically incorrect approved characterisation] Chan, he's actin' up good Chinee oriental Western stereotype, y'see. Goes n gets his erasin' hatchet all ready for a chop suey. But James T Kirk says his boys sworn an oath to not get involved. Chan wuz mighty riled by that disgraceful display o' pacifism thut he calls 'em chicken an shreds the meat from their bones like he's servin' 'em as crispy aromatic. Chan says he had tuh do it. Says yuh cain't turn yer back on a pacifist cause if'n he lost his pigtail, the angels won't pullim up into Heav'n. I tol' him, ain't no likelihood he's gettin' in 'n any case, pigtail or no pigtail, so whut's he worryin'?

SHANE Guess he didn't see you eye to eye on that, that Chan is one heck of a Wile E Cayote, if there's a fight going, he'll be there, but he'll have a partner that'll come at you from the front, while he'll be nipping around behind you, like a cuss-hound, and biting off your balls.

BARMAN My, sir. Is that you choosing those words, sir, or are you P I programme authorised too?

SHANE I'm acting.

BARMAN Mighty fahn actin' too, sir. Most credible. Actin' about are we, sir? That's all, eh, sir, actin' about away from home, sir? It's written all over your face, sir, to be fair. Mr. Chan, sir, he was actin' too, 'sept he was actin' up. He disagreed with me sure enough. Says he don't know if'n there's a Heaven or if'n there's a Hell but best make sure and keep out an eye every day fur an angel that might be sittin' in a tree watchin' me. He tole me that there's old maps a Heaven with spheres within spheres. He gets all babblin' stoned – hitting back the Red Eye and the Infonarc. In the end, he's jest gibberin' like a monkey-man. I logged whut he says, 'Boozy ardour you nick idea, safe cookie,' he's shouting at every one and stroking us, ev'ryone! He's toasting Foil and toasting Foil again. Then, he's gabblin' about his great destiny and an undercover operation. Very hush hush. Or so he's sayin' fur the hundredth time all close and conspiratorial, like, and then he's up on the bar next minute, shouting, 'Raise yer glass, three cheers for Princess Foil! Six cheers for Foil! Raise yer glasses!' 'N then he goes tumblin with laughter off the bar. Yuh can 'magin' his faculties have suffered some damage sose he ain't cookin' today. He's sitting over there, drinking warm beer and playing poker with that bullheaded homesteader.

GIRL WITH THE E-MAIL EYES They're over there by the back room, stranger. But I assure you that I am a lot more interesting than a couple of gambling fools.

SHANE You got interesting eyes, that's for sure.

GIRL WITH THE E-MAIL EYES They're enamel. French. E-mail in French means enamel. The name got changed in translation. I come from a long line of fantasy cultural robot-women from Hoffmann's Olympia, Metropolis, Bladerunner right on through. I am your hostess. Welcome to my bar. Do you like my barman? I think he is ever so cute, don't you? Say, what's your name stranger?

SHANE Reagan. Ron Reagan.

GIRL WITH THE E-MAIL EYES Well, Mr. Ray-Gun, enjoy your stay and keep your weapon in its holster. Don't you be too headstrong, now.

[Laughs.]

SHANE And maybe I'll come up and see you sometime, Rosemary.

[Laughs and moves over to the card table where the homesteader (grinning broadly, like Burt Lancaster) is sitting back in the shadow. He and Chan are playing poker with two Goons. The two Goons were out of the card hand, as always. It is between the homesteader and the cook. Wearing a red silk shirt, heavily patterned, Chan blends with a once ruby-red curtain behind him which, immovably closed, with heavy creases weighted and dusty, hangs there for atmosphere. He has a ring with a yin/yang symbol on it in black and white. On the table are two modelled glasses: one round and handled, the other tall and slim. In the two glasses, data beer leaves simulated pseudopodia up to the rims.]

HOMESTEADER I saw you earlier – in your self-generating programmes. I saw you earlier, in your fractal garden.

CHAN Ah, in my fractal garden. I was in my fractal garden earlier.

HOMESTEADER Yes, sir, it sure is a fine fractal garden, your fractal garden. Fine fractals.

CHAN My fractal garden? So. They were nice fractals once, but I've had them growing a long time now. A long time, I've had those fractals.

HOMESTEADER Decayed?

CHAN Expanded! They are getting a bit old now.

HOMESTEADER Hey, I thought those fractals are supposed to last for ever?

CHAN Yes, they do last forever ... but symmetry dissipates over time. It doesn't degenerate but breaks. It reiterates and splits and expands. In the process it seems as though it disappears. It blends into background symmetry, making a vast lonely garden of differential subtleties. Everywhere is distributed symmetry. My fractals are getting a bit too over-distributed to be noticed at all now. The fractal garden is everywhere except within its walls.

HOMESTEADER [Laying down his cards] Jack of Spades. It's a long time that you've had them. I mean ... for fractals. Jack of Clubs. I remember, you bought those fractals real cheap – from the market. Prices are terrible down the market, lately. Only today, I tried to buy bits. Doubled and tripled since last week. Jack of Hearts, Jack of Diamonds, and the Ace of Hearts.

CHAN The prices have gone up a lot. I bought them off-the-shelf from a Goon in the legit market. From tiny seeds vast universes may grow. They were cheap ... cheap.

HOMESTEADER You sound like a Chinese chick, cheep cheeping for more fractal seeds! I suppose they're getting a bit worn out, now?

CHAN Yes, a little. I shall have to get some new ones ... still, they have lasted well. I talk to them. I must remember to talk to them tomorrow ... or when I get back. By the way, how's Data Rose? Being alone in the fractal garden, I've envied you having a symbiote like Data Rose. You were so lucky to get grafted to Data Rose. [Laying down his cards] Queen of Hearts, her sisters and her lover, the King of Spades.

HOMESTEADER She's here. She's the girl with the e-mail eyes.

CHAN No! But I ...

HOMESTEADER Yes, she's very good. Where are the others?

[Looks at a monitor-as-pocket-watch from inside his trousers, attached to his waistband by a chain. He looks

2. Omphalus on trek ... The trek hides caprice weirdly. Intermittently thievish trek bites whirl!

at the screen. He then looks up at the avatar of Shane. It is empty (Roman Dee has vacated it, back to the Real). The homesteader shakes his head and cocks a thumb, pointing at the lifeless dummy of Shane.]

HOMESTEADER You can't live like that, half-in and half-out like a Jekyll and Hyde character.

CHAN Come back, Shane. Shaaaaane, come back, Shaaaaane.

[Both laugh.]

CHAN What was the address of that damned site in the market? I'm trying but I can't find it. I wish I could access.

[Suddenly there is an almighty crash and from the swing doors come two men, TexMexaco Kid and Data Joey Jayawardena 6, with sawn-off shotguns. Up above, a door to whatever, wherever, bursts open, kicked by a white-haze figure with a hidden face. The radiant form is embroidered inside in gold with a letter 'A' and, with six-guns blazing, he or she peppers the Goons below. Shane does not react at all, of course. The barman hides behind the bar. Chan and the homesteader are on their feet, looking up, firing off rounds at the A-figure above. The sound of shattering glass fills the environment. The A-figure totters and slumps over the bannister like a stunt actor hamming it up. This seems to last forever and then the glowing form falls into the space above the bar and disappears in midair.]

CHAN Ah so! Now that was good exciting programming

work! Well done, my friend.

HOMESTEADER But I didn't programme them. Maybe Data Rose did. Data Rose!

[He looks around the bar. All the Goons lie fizzing and fading at the edges, burnt out and destroyed.]

HOMESTEADER Data Rose? Oh no, I can't feel her near, I should feel her, Chan. I've lost contact. I can't feel her. My symbiote, my other half, is gone! Who were those intruders? This is not part of the game. This is not a play any more this is an actual abduction. Data Rose has been abducted!

CHAN I believe I pattern-recognised those two who came through the door. TexMexaco Kid; and Data Joey Jayawardena 6, data punks, guerillas, scum.

HOMESTEADER Besterlander rebels? Here? This is unheard of!

[The doors to the Saloon Hotel swing open again. The Data Romans go for their guns. The piano music stops. Standing there all in black it is their other, Data Roman 2 (Marcus), dressed as the two-gunslinger, making his favourite entrance, according to the usual script.]

TWO-GUNSLINGER [Without moving his lips, to the piano player who has sparks flying from his head]
Lost yer fingers, Goon?

'It's Data Rose,' said the homesteader, 'she's been abducted by vMex/Besterlander scum.'

'Then, what're you doing sitting here jawing and drinking beer? I've got some equally disturbing news. Haven't you heard? No, you haven't, have you? It's the avatar of John Holliday, our template's father, our father. It has been stolen by terrorist rebels from Besterland: mercenary William Quick and terrorist Data Ahwali Mostafa Sayed 3.'

'I recognised two of our trio and have confirmed their identities by accessing police records in the Great Wall of Data: TexMexaco Kid and Data Joey Jayawardena 6,' said Data Roman 5.

'The play's off. The game is on! Heck, Data Rose'd have our guts for standing here drinking beer! We've got some rescuing to do, come on!'

'Rescuing and chop-chop,' said Chan brandishing his erasing hatchet and dropping his programmed Chinese accent. 'But hold your horses,' he said, becoming the hardened Peterloon cop that he actually was. 'You can't just go taking the law into your own hands.' He reached into the pocket of Shane's topcoat, pulling out an undrawn Colt 45 and placed it on the table. Shane was inanimate. Dr Roman Dee had been called back into the Real by Line and he had taken off his head-mounted display to listen to Line read. Shane's head was empty now that Roman had left it. This was the difference between someone undertaking an immersive experience into the Data using goggles or rumblesuits and the life of an Upload: the first could leave the Data at any moment; for the second, it was all. Across the forehead was Data Rose's joke for them: the reason why she had erased all mirrors from the bar area. Across Roman's brow, Shane's forehead, she had written MEATHEAD where he couldn't see it. It had been all they could do not to laugh at him straight in his avatar's face. Data Roman 5 reached back into Shane's pocket and this time pulled out three metal six-pointed stars. He tossed one to the homesteader and one to Marcus.

'There, now we're deputised and legal – should get us by any copyright problems.'

The three Data Romans – the homesteader, the two-gunslinger, and the Chinese cook – leaving the smouldering Goons and the empty avatar of Shane behind, made their way out of the bar and mounted-up their horses in the street. They rode off down the muddy centre of Touchstone, leaving only the stubborn, unmoving white mule at the hitching post, branded 'AISCARP' across its buttocks. Marcus dawdled behind for a moment. Scooping up another ball of thick green-black mule dung from the ground behind the beast, he popped it in a file and posted it to Roman, as he had done with the last: AISCARP 'information' for Roman to examine.

'That'll teach him,' he thought. 'Let's see him analyse that for a spell.' He pulled down the peak of Marcus' black stetson.

25

Now you see how they behave like children. Let's leave them to explain the unprecedented abduction to the two-gunslinger. Poor Data Rose. If she's away for long, her symbiotic partner, Brutus, is going to start to hurt. They'll have to go and get her back sharpish. Yet, what of the current plight of their other, the hero Horatio, Data Roman 4? Don't worry, I haven't forgotten him. He's been trapped in a prison ship. My, that Artificially Intelligent Self-Curating Art Robot Programme! It's a tricky one, isn't it? It's not

3. Omphalus on jaunt ... The pallid jaunt infrequently pleases. Catch poorly whenever jaunt flashes.

dead, you know that don't you? It's playing possum, lying doggo, stubborn as a mule. Still, it'll follow the posse at a way off unseen. Mean trick with the donkey poo, Marcus, my naughty boy. You white-faced, green-eyed monster, you! Have you ever tried to get that stuff off your shoe?

26

How Horatio had begged to be assigned to the mission to investigate and recover John Holliday's avatar! He pleaded with his mistress Foil. She was adamant. He was too emotionally involved. He was personally implicated. He could not be objective. The discovery of the secret behind the mystery of the white holes in the centre of the Data was more important an issue. It would affect all their futures. It represented a massive potential threat to the datasphere. He was her best man, etc., etc.

All that had been some days ago, before his imprisonment in this puzzle of a prison. His own problems now exceeded those of his father's avatar and its whereabouts. It would be true to say that Horatio spent more time, now, thinking only of escape and survival than he had ever spent on any other thoughts in his whole existence. However, he could see no avenue of possibility. What a fool he had been, being taken in by the seemingly perfect companion. He had seen him off in the distance, dodging between the great abstract forms of the unmoulded frontier of the mid-Data. Horatio had seen him as a fellow traveller and a soul-mate. He brought him aboard his vessel and shared theories with him as to the nature and reason of the white-hole phenomenon. They sat up on deck, and observed the white holes slowly expanding. They discussed the beauty of great white tentacles of nothingness that lashed out occasionally like sunspots.

As they neared the white holes, his companion became restless and complained of the brightness. Horatio supplied them both with eye-shields, light-limiters, but his fellow traveller complained of dizziness and nausea. 'Come near. Help me,' he had said. 4 had been taken unawares. The stranger had seemed so personable, compassionate, wise and sensitive that Data Roman 4 had come to consider him, almost instantaneously, as a brother, a confidant and, doubtlessly (as he had foolishly written to the others), a friend. He was wrong on all accounts. This gullibility! Gullibility had allowed him to be so easily press-ganged into this pretty pickle, this imprisonment. 'How stupid,' he silently cursed, 'to be trapped, imprisoned and, most of all, diverted from my prime research mission to investigate the mysterious appearance of the white holes in the centre of the Data.'

What was the purpose of this entrapment? Was it random? Was it a purposeful unknown? Theft? Slavery? Was it connected to his inquisitive quest? Was it malicious, or evil, or good? Was it to stop him discovering the secret behind the white holes?

Whatever the reasons, he was trapped. He, Horatio, the most adventurous and considered by himself to be the best of the Uploads of Dr Roman Dee, was in a dangerous situation. Extinction of his being was not out of the question. This gaol was a cruel prison hulk, sailing to whatever unknown destination through the Datasea, holding whatever fate for him that his torturer had planned, unless he could somehow effect an escape. There was no way that he could get a mayday message back to his others in Peterloo. From his previous messages, which they would have received by now, they would not be able to tell of his predicament. He could, therefore, foresee no help from that direction.

27

Meanwhile, aboard the software programme, *Quod*, digital Goon deckhands sang as they swabbed:

> 'Way, haul away, we'll haul away the bowline,
> 'Way, haul away, O haul away, Joe.
> 'Way, haul away, the packet is a rollin',
> 'Way, haul away, O haul away, Joe.

Quod was a vast prison-ship programme. It was anchored deep and secretive in the digital universe of the computer networks of the world, the Data. Incarcerated within *Quod*'s computational labyrinthine bulk, Horatio was tireless in his search for the key to this prison metaphor which held him bound in its illusion. He had been trapped on this stinking hulk of a penal ship for far too long. On the model barrel in front of him, he held the escape plan down with models of an empty bottle, an empty glass, and two bones (a mandible and a clavicle). He worked daily trying to hack the code of the increasingly revealed complex architecture of his prison. He was still unable to get a new message out to his others. The situation seemed hopeless – on hold.

The noise!

Gathering up his proto-code map quickly, Horatio just managed to get back inside the berth before the blast of pseudo-thermonucleic acid surged down the information super-highway, blasting into his mean and narrow corridor. The Cleaning had begun again. Of course, there was no need to clean the hulk. It was a simulacrum, data only, and therefore attracted no unintentional dirt and no real skin flaked to make dust. The Cleaning was a part of his punishment and his torment. It was psychological warfare. He was bound to an horrific routine as surely as Prometheus had been tied to the desert rock to endure the daily birds gorging bloodily on his exposed liver which regenerated each night. For the time being, he could do nothing but nobly endure his torture. The acids and the various devices employed in his torments were fashioned from pure information but so was he. All was un-Real here in the Data except for the actions and the consequences. Here, the numerous dangers were potentially lethal relative to him. If he put one step wrong, he could cease to exist as an intelligent cluster in a blink. Instantaneous erasure was a definite possibility. A possibility that was preferable, maybe, to the alternative: to slowly flicker and fade in captivity for all eternity. However, Horatio was not a cluster keen on self-termination. In all likelihood, in the event, his captors would not permit it anyway. The point was that this was a torture of ideas. This was terror. He must remain confident.

After the acid came the brushes, pushed and swung by

big ugly grunt robot programmes down the windowless corridor. There was only one window that he had found. This was in a central circular space which opened off at the end of his corridor. It was modelled on the Pantheon in Real Rome. Around the curved walls of this circular architecture were a series of closed doors. He could explore behind those doors and regularly he chose one to open. Behind them the ship was a maze of strange room after room. He was forced to experience the 'joys' of these environments on regular occasions. He thought of these essays as his exercise times. This only window above had never been open though it was active. It was a transparent domed hatch to the outside deck of the ship and, beyond it, stretched the wide Data and relative freedom. It was a poignant and central feature of his torment. Often deck-hand Goons stared down at him over the simulated-chrome handrail. Small boys and swarthy tars programmed so well that their hands left the reflections of the lights dulled around where their grip had been: a blur of cloud around the clear patch where the digital hand had actually pressed. He could see all this through the reflected image of himself, diminished in size on the curved glass surface. This was a near constant as the light was usually dimmer outside. To him, he looked Lilliputian in the glass but it was important that he did not feel small. He told himself that he must have looked like a goldfish in a bowl to his audience: bigger than he should be in the scale of things. That was one tactic to endure their persistent curiosity. He was also given psychological support from an unexpected source which belittled his captor's Goons. In the closing distance, through his own reflection, he could see the white hole growing in the centre of the Data and, sometimes, its surging convolutions and glowing whiteness made the deckhands into nothing more detailed than cheap, flat, cutouts.

However, the mysterious white hole was growing nearer and larger at a speed sufficient enough to cause him some alarm.

Inside, below decks, the grunt robots scrubbed with hard bristles. They banged their heads with loud clangs on the polished wooden walls and brass handrails and fittings, swinging them at the neck in the addictive rhythm of zoo animals behind bars.

Horatio lay on his rudimentary bunk listening to the routine pass. After the big grunts, the small robots began to start about. The size of walking hands, they darted hither and thither attentive to their myriad specific functions: paint robots; screw robots; polish robots; tighten robots; loosen robots; emptying robots; filling robots; oiling robots; straightening robots; drying robots; wetting robots; and trimming robots. They scuttled like trained rats to their tasks. Each task doubled and redoubled the pointlessness of the others.

As the robots settled to their jobs, the search-gases and clouds of perfumed information came seeping from black iron grills in the walls at ankle height. Fans in the ceiling of the cabin space forced the perfumes to convect around the cramped billet. Horatio balked at the first pungent wave, as he had balked at every Cleaning for the last umpteen cleans. It was the Cleaning and other parts of the routine which marked time. The smell of the search-gas automatically accessed and opened the file of the previous day's exercise time as it was designed to do. It tore the information from his journal and sped it away to his captors while the little robots pottered around him:

Journal of Data Roman 4 (aka Horatio)
The Mystery of the White Holes
Date unknown

My incarceration continues. I am repeatedly encouraged to explore different parts of this truly wondrous and detailed prison ship for I know not what reason. I am expelled from my quarters and jettisoned from the door at the end of the corridor into the Pantheon room to choose another door on to an entirely different scenario. Again a different part of the ship lies beyond each door for my exploration.

I choose randomly.

The door closes behind me. It is heavy and metallic from the other side. I stand on the top step of a small stone flight parallel to a stone wall that rises up smoothly to a ceiling in darkness about twenty metres above. It is dark. It is semi-dark as my vision adjusts. There is a metal handrail.

[Observation message 42/i~3: always handrails on this ship, as though someone had read a manual advising that information clusters which choose to have hands should always be supplied with handrails.]

It guides me down on to a slightly lower level. I seem to be in a stony simulation. A fine dust hangs in the space.

[Observation message 42/i~4: Boy, that must take memory! Lavish.]

I detect a sound – a muffled thudding – of blasting in the near distance to my left. I estimate the distance to be approximately two hundred metres. This is confirmed by a rising dust-cloud which is obviously being generated by explosions in the rock. I make my way in this direction. It seems to be a quarry/room.

I pick my way across a lunar-like terrain. Big and small rocks make my route haphazardous as I am forced to walk across every little pebble and round every large boulder. Normally, of course, I could take one step and be there due to my polka-dot, multicoloured Dalmatian Seven-League Time-Boots but this ship somehow has rendered them useless. I can neither surf time nor take big distance steps while under the shackles of this gaol. The Time-Boots are nothing more than eccentric footwear: big dotty boots. For a brief uncomfortable moment, I feel our father, John Holliday, standing in my shoes as he stood in the image of him – in his bright pink, cardboard, Croatian slip-ons. As I pick my way, The Narcissus Shift, which I wear, catches on glittering fragments of crystal half-embedded in and half-exposed from the rock. The Narcissus Shift, like the boots, holds out such promise but it will not work in this prison either.

[Information message 07: The Narcissus Shift software is able to map the information of its owner straight on to an object of the wearer's affection. It will match data patterns. For an instant the owner is transformed and matched with the other intimately and thus experiences the other in its entirety. The Narcissus Shift enables the wearer to fully realise the biblical commandment to 'love thy neighbour as thyself'.]

It had sounded marvellous when I bought it from the shop of Doria Hemming. Now though, this inert crimson dress, so beautiful and cool when surfing the time currents, is nothing but a hindrance in the quarry/room. Tugging to free it, I tear the golden hem. It is now fraying into individual shining filaments and glittering crystals that scatter my trail.

[Observation message 42/i~5: Damn those rip-off, back-

4. Omphalus on thicket … Fling grandiosely while thicket bathes.

street market crook-artists and their shoddy goods!]

I gather the skirts up between my legs from the back, like Gandhi, and suffer my trial in silence. I hear the sound of metal on stone and make in that direction. Rounding a promontory, I chance upon the most peculiar group of humanoid data clusters. They are mainly male representations though some are female. They are fairly bizarrely dressed, casual in tweed jackets and slacks – conventional Real. Not only is their clothing weirdly chosen, it also seems most inappropriate attire for their activity, as they are wielding long-handled sledgehammers and lump hammers, swinging them back over their heads and down on to medium-sized rocks. Sometimes they glance off; sometimes they succeed in shattering the stones into smaller stones; sometimes metal meets stone directly, both holding their own, with a vibrational consequence that shudders up the arms of these donnish workers.

I approach the nearest female hammerer and introduce myself. She is most rude and uncivil which comes as no surprise in this place. 'Shhh,' she says like a librarian. 'Can't you see I'm trying to solve this problem?' I say that I can see that she is working very hard on an exhausting and seemingly pointless labour. She replies irritably, 'Yes, quite, it is a complex thesis: *Coincidence, Flow Systems and Social Revolt: an Analysis of the Currents of Culture in the Sea of Politics* by, myself, Ms Data J. Matossian 1.' She asks me to stop disturbing her concentration. Given that she is rather vigorous with the swinging hammer, I move on to try to get some sense out of the next hammerer: a tall, thin, transparent male. He is bent like an angle-tool as he swings his hammer down on to its target.

I kick some pebbles with my not-good-for-much-else spotty boot.

'I'll thank you to leave my footnotes alone, young fellow,' protests the man. 'Unless you can provide me with some constructive criticism, I suggest you leave the study. ' As he admonishes me indignantly, he indicates a pile of hammers, shovels, and pickaxes of all sizes leaning against a nearby rock. 'The tools of Academe are many,' he says. 'Regard the thoroughness of my methodology.' He makes a mighty swing with that hammer and, surprisingly, shatters not himself but a medium-sized rock down the middle into two halves. 'There,' he says. 'Another chapter open to disproof.'

It seems that these rock-breakers are labouring under the illusion that they are involved in serious and valuable intellectual rather than manual labour.

28

You know, I look at them, all of them, busying themselves and it is hard not to ask, 'Is it all worth it?' Such tiny actions, little events, invisible on a blank disc of planets, pushing through the debris of space.

29

Gree-tings!
Greee-tings!
Greeee-tings!

Line pulled off Roman's head-mounted display and was thumping his arm through the rumblesuit on 'tings' to get his focused attention.

Greeeee-tings!

That was how the letter from the Emperor of Liverpool announced itself.

Greetings, my Honourable Sister, the Real Queen E of Manchester,

He was with her. She stopped thumping him.

In the Empire of Liverpool, we have been working a full year on this gift for you. It is a mechanical device that sings better than your grey bird. It also looks a lot more presentable – as you shall see, we have plastered it with posh jewels. A turn of the key will produce songs for your ears which will make you laugh and cry and all at the same time. It also has the advantage of never tiring – it will sing every time, faultlessly. We very much hope that you enjoy this gift and will accept it graciously as further cement to firming the co-operation of our two empires.

Your loving brother,
The Imperial Highness of Liverpool

The Real Queen E's royal blood fired up with adrenaline. 'Mechanical device, posh jewels.' She'd certainly like to get her firm to give him a cement gift – concrete shoes and in the Ship Canal with him ...

PS Did you hear about the Emperor of Leeds? Seems he was observed walking down Eastgate in the nude on an occasion of state, thinking he was wearing a suit so fine that no-one could see it or appreciate it!

See you, sis,
Black Georgivs
XXXX

That Georgivs had always had a way of getting round her and he had done it again. She opened the parcel with a light heart provided by the news of Leeds and a vivid mental picture she had of his royal wave. The Real Queen E of Manchester called all her wise and worthy to witness this marvellous gift, for such indeed it was. The scientists and engineers were marvel itself. The musical experts wrote reviews and treatises on its perfection at song. Only the artists were a bit sniffy, finding the form of the bird lacking in balance, due to what one would guess to be a set of bellows which inflated and deflated, like lungs, but, lungs in the tail of the bird? They also found the jewellery a 'little' overdone (too garish for their taste) but they soon kept their criticisms to themselves when they saw how much the Empress fell in love with the song of that mechanical nightingale.

For a year and a day, the mechanical bird was the toast of all the kingdoms of Albion, drawing praise from far and wide. The Real Queen E arranged for it to be seen and heard by the 'Great Unwashed', as she affectionately called her people, by means of a public display at the Manchester Museum of Science and Industry. In the shadow of the mechanical nightingale's stardom, the real nightingale was able to slip away from the palace unnoticed and escape back to its woods. In the north and the west, the real

5. Omphalus on chart … The chart tries mirth confidently. Rarely orthodox chart conserves sprite!

nightingale again was to lighten the load of the poor: the woodcutters, the fishermen, and the travelling folk of the far reaches of the Empire.

In the palace, the mechanical bird was kept by Her Highness on her soft summer cloud pillow at her bedside, surrounded by more jewels than Daft Mick of Wigan. Hers was a good life and the tissue wars started on the streets that year. Until, one day, as she turned the key, she heard a 'ping' inside the contraption which prefigured a 'whirrr' and a whizzing of mechanical parts unwinding at speed. From that moment, there was no song to be had from that machine and the laughing and crying disappeared from the world of her imperial court. The Empire of Song was silent at its centre that day.

However, in the post the following day, exactly one year and one day since the first gift, there arrived a further, second, package from her brother, the Emperor of Liverpool. It contained a scroll and a disk. The message read:

Dearest sister,

My scientists and artists have been working for a year to perfect this gift for you in the expectation of mechanical failure in the mechanised bird. We are pleased to announce our success in our project, which was to create a digital facsimile of the nightingale bird, which could be used by yourself as a screensaver device on your royal laptop. Remarkable endeavour and long hours have resulted in the enclosed disk which contains the screensaver version 3.1 of The Nightingale programme. This will run on Arches version 6.0. I think you will find that it surpasses by far the technology of previous nightingales. To play this programme, you will need Arches

6.0, a software architecture of the Empire of Liverpool which will also manage all the affairs of your Empire for you quite efficiently, while you enjoy the songs of laughing and crying all at the same time at your leisure.

Your Imperial Brother
Georgivs

The Empress of Manchester, the Real Queen E, had grown in wisdom these past two years. No longer a young filly but a handsome mare had she become. So, she threw the disc into the royal wastepaper basket and, simultaneously, sent out a message to request the presence of the real nightingale.

This time, her message was more considered. She begged that grey bird's forgiveness, hoping it was not too late, and apologised for being so stupid as to be lured by flashing jewellery, whistles, and bells almost into the sway of a greedy and duplicitous neighbour.

The End

'So, that was it,' said Line, closing the book, 'what do you think?'

'It seemed to end a bit quick,' said Roman, searching for an intelligent, useful, but a not off-putting nor sycophantic, sort of middle-of-the-road reply.

'Exactly,' she replied! 'The narrative went over the nappe. Every story must ebb and give way to the next.'

30

The captive Horatio stopped recording his log as he heard the hooter going for the finish of the robot shift. There would be no way to concentrate on his journal during the next bit of the routine.

The end of the Cleaning was marked by the arrival of the Alices. There were three Alices who attempted to do the 'Leonardo touches' – as da Vinci used to do: return to a painting, such as *The Last Supper*, long after it was officially completed, in order to add one small finishing touch (such as a stroke of white lead paint to the eye of Christ) which would enliven and transform the entire work. In such a way, the Alices performed minor adjustments to the prison ship which made all the difference. Three Victorian, middle-class female representations in their wide-hemmed dresses added highlights to objects, placed and adjusted lamps and focal lengths, and sprinkled new dirt and clean dead skin cells from wicker baskets, out of the sides of which flopped red-and-white gingham cloth. This was to restore the prison cell to exactly the state it had been in prior to the Cleaning. It was tweaked and straightened; and cropped; and cut; and pasted; and skewed; and inverted; and checked; and reverted in the aim of achieving the perfect simulacrum of the earlier state.

> Louis was the King of France before the Revolution
> 'Way, haul away, O haul away, Joe.

Their work of perfection had to be validated and this required monitoring and inspection. As ever, while they worked speedily away, flying around the space in white ankle-socks, on tippy-tap shoes, a little tinkling bell sounded: two minutes warning. One minute later, a klaxon 'Arooga!' was heard. At the appointed time, one further minute later, the rattling of keys and the synthesised smell of fish and rum curled in around the doorway to the room. A giant squid from the toilet of the *Nautilus*, Old King Nep' o' the Deep and his Jack-Tar Angels roared into the far end of the narrow corridor. Old King Nep' was fat, very fat, with the upper torso of a great ape. In the depths of black-wire hair across his chest, strange markings glowed dull white neon in a deep green field. A grey vest stretched across this torso. Oakum and diodes enmeshed in the thicker hair across the shoulders which framed his no-neck, low head like mountains. His eyes emitted laser light in pencil-torch beams this way and that. He was inspecting. He picked at things with his trident's arrowhead spikes.

In his wake capered three comical sailors done up as angels. All were smooth, depilated from head to foot, with pseudo-wings – mere random feathers stuck into Royal Jelly. The feathers were insecure and loosened continually and flew out on the convection currents, floating like the remnants of a pillow fight. The Jack-Tar Angels wore big grubby nappies, stained all ochre and grey. These were loosely-tied to show pastiche gangrenous genitalia flopping about inside. Wire haloes bobbed on their bald heads. One carried a bucket of dirty information and a scrubbing brush; one carried a cut-throat razor in each hand; the third carried two buckets – in one, black and steaming dripping tar with a mop sticking out, in the other, leeches and feathers in equal measure. Each Tar had two small assistants. These were about 30 centimetres tall, stunted replicants of Adolf Hitler in his black uniform. Between strutting about and shouting randomly they toadied to the angel sailors and fed them slivers of data.

The Alices never had enough time to complete their tasks. This had always been the case while Horatio had been there to observe. No matter how fast they worked and no matter how wide and staring their little eyes through stress and worry, the boss, Old Nep', would find faults, things undone or less than perfect in their simulations. That was when he spat spittle-fire and black blood. That was when his trident went a-poking. That was when he lined the Alices up for a dressing down and what Nep' referred to as the Quality Audit began. 'Let the Audit commence,' he would roar! The Jack-Tar Angels handed out the razors, bucket of dirty information, feather and leech buckets, the rough-haired brush and the mop to the assembled Alices. There used to be more than 30 of them working on the same set of tasks that these remaining three tried to cover. Meanwhile, the number of monitoring angels had risen from one to three and their diminutive attendants from zero to six. The remaining Alices would, ultimately, obediently self-audit, prepare and implement an immediate quality action plan. The survivors would be pampered for a while and made to think of themselves as special because they were the most efficient surviving elite. This was Total Quality Management in action.

'Poor Alices,' Horatio had used to think in the recent past – such innocent lambs tricked to the slaughter. He no longer thought this way. These three little bitches were the worst of the pack and he had seen what they were capable of inflicting on their colleagues in the name of efficiency, quality, assessment, audit and, above all, professional and personal development.

31

The Indigo Hammer Affair hit every major and minor popular, cultural and mainline news network.

It was a complex story. Indeed, so complex that it seemed a deliberate smoke-screening device. An arts project by the internationally renowned artist, Doria Hemming had been unveiled to unanimous arts press applause down in the city centre. The trans/bisexual Hemming had announced that he/she was teaming up on the project with a rising new art star, the AISCARP. Doria Hemming teaming up with anyone was unprecedented. He/she was a superstar: a household brand name. Hemming was the sort of artist a city bought in to create some buzz about the fact that the city was a city, a real place rather than just a site through which information and data was switched and shifted. With the collapse of national boundaries, following new technological development, cities had to project their image on to a world stage. Hiring in arts superstars was one way of doing this, a little like the Italian Renaissance of the fifteenth century, when city states hired in the roving artists-for-hire to execute civic buildings, murals or statuary. There were about six contemporary artists of Hemming's global stature. Hemming did not need to team up, let alone with an *Artificially Intelligent Self-Curating Art Robot Programme*.

The Hemming/AISCARP piece was called *Indigo Hammer/Red Snow*. From the street, *Indigo Hammer* consisted of a giant projection from inside a shop on to its plate-glass window frontage. The projection was of an enormous purple/blue hammer in a field of red static. 'Indigo Hammer' and 'Red Snow' were titles used for nuclear missiles back in the twentieth-century Cold War period. The piece used a computerised laser and information cannon which, via a series of mirrors and using sand as an information conduit, sent the image commands through a series of ancient tunnels underneath the city centre, reflected around twists and turns by the use of mirrors. These tunnels had been constructed back in the 1960s in case of global thermonuclear warfare. They would have become the regional command bunkers. At least, that was the plan.

When the N-bomb came so suddenly, there was no time to get into these tunnels, Roman supposed, but the fact of it was that everyone had forgotten them and only hard research by a roving intelligence came to rediscover them. After alighting on this knowledge, only an artist would think to use them for anything in the present. Sand and glass were deliberately chosen as materials to comment on the silicon-based computer technologies developed because of the Cold War arms race. Nuclear tests, performed with surprising regularity back then, resulted in the transmutation of silicon from state to state: sand of Pacific islands or Australian deserts into glass. It was the same silicon that was used for chip technology, which led on to later light and bio technologies. Apparently, the US and its allies had something called the 'Plate-Glass Strategy': should the Soviets cross a certain line in old Europe, they would have been deemed to have broken irreversibly a 'plate-glass' window, unleashing Armageddon. Hence the eventual projection on to the window of a well-chosen Indigo Hammer: a glass-shatterer. The bombs had many colour-based names, such as Blue Bunny, which would not have been as appropriate for the artists' use. Mumpsy, in the arts magazine *When Two Worlds Collide* (not named after the Cold War, but commenting on the tensions between the Real and the Data), remarked on the contradiction in the use of high technology to realise the projection of the oldest of technologies, the hammer.

Mumpsy launched a vitriolic attack on the piece and the city in his *Worlds Collide* article. He criticised the callousness of spending billions of credits on a streetside projected 'sideshow' when below it, below the Thirty-Six, life was nasty, brutish and short. He pointed to the contradictions in contemporary society which were preferably ignored. Though far from joining the ranks of the revolution, Mumpsy must have offended someone (tensions were high following the 'accidental' destruction of the statue) because, despite his reputation and longevity, he never wrote for them nor four-thousand other affiliated publications ever again.

Roman got embroiled in this messy business because of Line's friendship with Mumpsy, who had been her biographer. He had been replaced by a faceless unknown reviewer who called him- or herself 'The Masked Aesthete'. Roman had said, 'Good riddance!' He just let it slip out. Line justifiably jumped down his throat. She was rapidly becoming weary of Roman's selfishness and his growing lack of consideration for the feelings of others. His callousness towards Mumpsy was indicative of a prevailing neglect of her, demonstrated by a lack of interest in what she was doing or thinking. He had not enquired of her new book in days. His attack on Mumpsy constituted an attack on her, she felt – after all, Mumpsy had written her biography. It was also irrational, for the *Indigo Hammer* piece as a whole, it must be said, encouraged Mumpsy's reading. It was a commentary upon the very foundations of the contemporary society, both physically and digitally: the tunnels beneath the city and the development of the computer since the birth of the first stored-programme computer, the Baby, in Manchester, England, in June 1948; the prior work by Alan Turing, there; and the continuing development of information technology as Cold War weapons' technology. *Indigo Hammer/Red Snow* revealed the paranoia and distortions which the development of society had only amplified rather than ever addressed.

'It expresses humanity's fragility in the face of technology,' the Hemming/AISCARP press release stated. Whether it was the aesthetic beauty of the glowing blue/purple hammer image, floating in a field of red static, Red Snow, over Main Street which allowed the artists to get away with the social commentary, or the fact that the powers-that-be expected artists to be critical (Hemming had long-standing official license to be critical, a court jester, and having that license extracted any teeth that the bite of the critique might have). *Indigo Hammer* never smashed the veneer of respectable radicalism that had made Hemming the darling of the brat-pack chic of International Capital in the Real and of the courts of the Imperial Highnesses in the Data. It did, however, enhance the career of the AISCARP considerably.

32

Line was crying silent tears in the hanging wicker chair with the telephone in her hand. Joke had called. She had been to visit Maggie. Maggie was cutting herself and rubbing ash into the wounds.

33

Out in the Data, far beyond the limits of Data Rose and Brutus' prairie and at the digital fringe of Peterloo, it was as though night had fallen on the virtual borders of an annexed suburb of the Data called Besterland. The Data Roman horsemen were travelling across the no-programme darkness to Besterland in search of the fading homesteader's symbiote partner. Ironic, really, that in the Data a version of Roman and a version of Rosemary should continue as 'an item', when their Real templates had split up so many years before because of Roman's drink problem. Data Rose was the only Upgrade of Roman's estranged first wife. The Real Rosemary had left the Real Roman, taking their daughter with her. Roman had moved, dried out, and started again, setting up the apartment with Line on the ninety-sixth floor of the Bewley Building. In the Data, you could not get drunk. However, there were programmable alternatives like Infonarc, which had been developed in Besterland.

Besterland, when it was first established by uploaded Californian loveniks, computed peacefully and was known to the Real as 'Blue Heaven' – a digital, mystical magnet to those in search of paradise and an example of a cluster living in a healthy symmetry between itself and the Data. This heavenly calm was not to last. With the rise of Princess Foil in Peterloo supported to a large extent by the

6. Omphalus on cleat ... The cleat inspires bend deadly. Surprisingly remote cleat spells folio!

military expertise of the Data Romans during Datawar 2, and with the formation of the Data Supercluster of Peterloo, the Peterloons, eager for growth, occupied neighbouring Besterland. The Digital Supercluster of Peterloo (DSP) insisted that its relationship with Besterland was a purely internal affair, because Besterland was an integral part of Peterloo. The DSP made no claim to sovereign rights over Besterland as a result of its digital subjugation and occupation. Instead, the DSP based its claim to Besterland solely on the theory that Besterland had become an integral cluster of Peterloo.

Originally bordered by Marconi/Bellevue to the minus *x*, Aramis to the minus *y*, Peterloo in the plus *y* and plus *x*, Blipland to the minus *z*, and vMexico to the plus *z*, Besterland was now an uncomfortable part of Peterloo. It had always felt itself more politically allied with vMexico, while it naïvely considered itself an independent cluster with a unique culture, government (albeit in exile), and its own styles of ceremony, costume and software.

The invasion and subjugation of Besterland and its clusters is intimately tied to the activities of the Peterloo Liberation Army. The International Commission of Jurists has charged the PLA and the Peterloon Government of Princess Foil with 'datacide of Besterlanders'. The Data Roman others had been responsible for the organisation and activities of the PLA during Datawar 2 and because of this were under investigation by the Commission. This did not worry them at all as the Commission was a hot-air organisation with little power.

More serious as a threat was the militant action of the Besterland Resistance: the Data Romans realised that, even after their instigation of Peterloo dominance and perpetual terrorism in Besterland, the Besterlander spirit had not been broken. Militant Besterlanders had never given up hope of receiving their independence again, demonstrated by the recently erased uprising in Besterland. The kidnapping of Data Rose appeared to be a serious development of political struggle into guerilla personal attacks and the Romans viewed this very seriously indeed. Data Rose was Brutus' symbiote, as he was her's. Symbiosis was more than a partnership. The two were inextricably linked and interwound. The one could not exist for long without the other. Therefore, finding Data Rose was critical for the continuing existence of Brutus. He seemed to be, thankfully, growing stronger as the cowboy posse was getting nearer to the pattern that was Data Rose.

Brutus' others realised the seriousness of this situation for him, but they, as soldiers, were also aware of the wider political implications of such data terrorism. It must be stamped out and they were on their way to do some stamping. With their deputy stars of the PLA they could act as law enforcers in Besterland. In fact, though the question of Besterland's status was essentially a legal question, it was one of immediate practical and political relevance to the journey of the Data Romans.

In these tense political circumstances, the Data Romans wisely travelled heavily armed and prepared for trouble. Data Roman 5 had brought the very latest software weaponry. Such desperate weapons might not be necessary, since the Romans were not without allies in Besterland: the Peterloons had transmitted many Goon Peterloons into the cluster, with the intended result that the Besterlanders were becoming a minority in their own homeland. The Besterlanders complained in the Data and the Real to anyone who would listen that the Data was losing a unique cluster as it was suffocating under the cloak of Foil.

Some way off that 'unique cluster', the three horsemen bent on the rescue of Data Rose and the righting of wrongs were slowly approaching across the darkness like ghost riders in the sky. The Data Romans were monitoring, in the distance on the outskirts of Besterland, a small camp cut off in the darkness, like a spider cut from a drifting web. Above it was darkness, below it was darkness. Eleven brightly coloured low-rider data vehicles in an ecliptic circle – abracadabra – a magic circle in cyberspace. In the centre of this circle, was a campfire, which took the form of a hovering, burning mini-sun. They were approaching slowly – very slowly. Brutus was too zapped for speed.

The Roman Uploads were telling tales to each other to pass the journey and to keep the energy levels which kept Brutus together glowing. Five was asking Marcus, because Marcus had the memory upgrade which the other Romans did not, if he could remember Real life, life in the Real. The rest of the Uploads remembered practically nothing. The information, for them, was too degraded, corrupted and buried to easily reconstruct any memory at all of life outside the Data.

'I don't have that much of a handle on it, myself,' Marcus said. 'It all seems like a series of strange fragments – some blurred, some crystal clear. I remember shades and shards but I don't know where they've come from or what they mean. They could be just stories I heard as Roman or thoughts I had. They may not be anything to do with Roman. They might be from the upgrade: they could be the dreams of Gates 5, or of a wage-slave technician on an Asian assembly line, or of a harridan in a sweat shop below the Thirty-Six, or a mixture of the whole lot of them. Wherever they come from, it is true that I sometimes feel that I know some things about what it felt like to be Real. It feels like an unattainable thing that I remember the feeling of in fleeting moments which I can't control.'

'Give me an example,' Chan urged, keen to know.

'Well, I feel that being Real was like being wrapped up in stories and cossetted in myths, like a baby with its legs kicking, getting more and more entangled in endless sheets. I think it is so difficult to remember the Real because it was so unreal there. I remember a city made of paper next to a lake of ink. I can feel it now, imprinted inside me. I'm looking down on to a city. Real City. As I pass through the cloud cover, height declining, I can see it below me. I'm sure that the boats in the marina of the lake are protected by a boom. From the air the downtown skyscrapers make the massive city look unfinished, though the grid it is marked on looks at worst promising, at best a kind of talismanic pledge that nothing with that many potential stories could be destroyed before all the myths were in.

'My favourite myth is about the boom. And behind the boom the waters are a light green. A green lighter than the blue which dominates the rest of the lakes.'

'Goodness,' Five exclaimed. 'I see what you mean.'

Brutus, desperately needing the proximity of his symbiote, flickered and fizzled slightly and the others shot concerned glances at each other.

'I don't see it myself, really, I don't,' Marcus, Data Roman 2, admitted.

'No, I see what you mean about the nature of the memories,' said Data Roman 5, deliberately imitating the Chan programme's voice. 'Vel-ly intel-esting.'

They both laughed uncomfortably.

34

Horatio puzzled over his exercise times. Like the episode in the quarry, they seemed so profound and so full to the brim with meaning. Yet what that was he could not fathom. Take another time, for example, when he had been to the place where the young woman gave birth to the old man while outside a man stove his brother's head in with a large rock because he had cuckolded him with his wife and because of a stolen chicken. This passionate murder was watched by two hooded women, who floated on cushions above the mountains which the distraught killer was soon crossing with his mules and possessions in search of a new life elsewhere. What might that all mean? Or, to take another example from his journal, the time he went to the gardens of the walled palace, where the air was filled with flute, lute, drum and tambourine. The only people there were women of great beauty, all dressed in red and orange patterned silks from their waists and long, narrow streamers of thin material around their shoulders that floated to the music. All, that is, except for the two that swam length after length of an open-air swimming pool among the trees in a free style, laughing and shouting to each other in a foreign tongue which he did not know. All this enjoyable visit to the scented garden was watched over silently by 'three women who are one', as the journal records. 'They stand together – their arms seem to belong to first one and then the other, carrying parasols and banners of ornate design and leading wolves by golden lariats.' They had watched him from the balcony through half-raised eyelids, down long noses, under high foreheads. They had jewels in their hair, earrings of gold, necklaces and bracelets. They also had four breasts each, one pair above the other, but this seemed neither sexual, unnatural nor ugly. All these exercise experiences were a bit beyond Data Roman 4, who was an action-cluster rather than a great thinker, and he was getting tired of it all. He honestly did not know whether he was coming or going.

35

Look at him wait. I like him stuck, don't you? Even his best friends and others think he's too big for his boots. It'll do him good to stew. He thinks he's it. Mind you, thinking you're it is half the battle, so he's best kept out of the way. I'll remind you of the cowboys creeping up through the backwoods of darkness and static, but point you back to our hero Roman, while I go check on something important in my library.

36

When Roman had found out about the tragedy, he read and watched every news report in the hope of finding more about the theft of John Holliday's avatar. The authorities knew who the perpetrators were, except for an unidentified hazy figure, but not how to find them. He had always argued that the model of his father should be his and not for public display by the House of Foil in the Data. However, the triumph of Foil in Datawar 2 had clinched the fate of the avatar. Foil wanted it. She wanted it badly, and he, alone, did not have the power to stop her. She had just destroyed the United States of America after all, and it would have meant fighting his others – his uploaded selves, who fought on her side. Wherever they were, anyway. He had called them and they had not come, which is not only unusual but supposed to be impossible. They should come when he calls. He had even put the head-mounted display back on and gone back into the Data to the Saloon Hotel. Inside, he had found only rubble and destruction.

While he was searching, next, for news of the AISCARP, he came across and read Nalini's latest column in *The Planet*:

> Brave New Girl
>
> As I sit down at my keyboard to write on the morning after the election 'down under', I am stopped in my tracks and thrown off my focus by crazy bird, a common grey bird to be precise. I was about to write of the election promises of a Total Virtual Economy and the successful 'Paradise in Five Years' election slogan with its Bird of Paradise logo. However, this bird, which is resting now, is trading looks

with me – a slice of winter in the buds outside the window. It is behaving very strangely. It is resting between bouts of repeatedly flying into the window and bashing against the glass. Yet, it is not trying to kill itself. This phenomenon is the latest in a string of augur-like occurrences. If I believed in omens, I've had a few candidate events lately. This bird in point. It's flying repeatedly for the same determined spot and hesitating with a flap and a flip in flight just before the hit so that the impact is sort of blunted – like a shoulder-charge. A feathered thud saying, 'Look at me, I'm real! Hey, this weight flies, I'm grey, I'm dull but aren't I amazing too?'. The window is covered in blood splatters. Is this a message of some sort from a Real Bird of Paradise?

Nalini had never understood the Data, Roman mused. She acted as though the Real was everything. Maybe it was, to her. Meanwhile, the rest of the world carried on without her, despite her lone voice of criticism soothsaying way off, stage left.

He was thoughtful and relaxed. He tried to click up Marcus, not that he was overly concerned, just that he had a moment to spare. Sometimes looking into Data Roman 2's world, or logging into any of the lives of his other uploaded selves, was nothing more than a superiority trip. There was Brutus, who had stuck with the Upload of Roman's first wife, Rosemary. He had more than stayed with her, he had become symbiotically intertwined. He was supposed to be working on Roman's novel; as it transpired, Roman was involved in an amicable legal battle with his own Upload over issues of intellectual copyright – the case was of obvious import and the judgement would set the precedent for future cases. Brutus had hired the finest legal mind in the Data, who happened to be an Upload herself, neatly, of Roman's own lawyer in the Real.

Of the others, Horatio, Data Roman 4, operated largely independent of Roman now. Roman had loaned him to the service of the Foil Dynasty in Datawar 2, and 4's whereabouts had become top-secret from even Roman himself. Under his chosen name of Horatio, 4 had become a public hero: a media star. Some would say that Data Roman 4 had become too big for his boots. Certainly, Data Roman 5, a datacop for Peterloo who had never taken an alternative title, and Marcus said so openly. Roman himself, though, was rather proud of his Upload's notoriety as a war hero. After all, he had been Horatio's template, as he was for all of the Uploads. He had purchased them over a period from the multi-billion House of Foil software transglobal and was satisfied with value, performance and customer care. He thought of his Uploads as exotic cyberpets. They all had to come if he called them. He felt like the *deus ex machina*: a benevolent god looking in on his creations and their digital universe. He was beginning to think himself into being concerned that his Uploads had gone AWOL.

The digital world of his uploaded selves, the Data, had a life all of its own. He had never really understood that until now. He had known it but not understood it. He had not wanted to. It was a strange world off the map of the Real and beyond that map lay monsters. The Uploads, like the inhabitants of the Bottled City of Kandor or the Lilliputians, got on with their bizarre lives practically oblivious to the goings-on of the Real. Sometimes, Roman wondered if his Uploads really cared for him, cared whether he himself, the original and the template, were alive or dead. One day he would ask, but not yet. He wasn't sure he was ready to hear the answer.

Marcus' apparition eventually appeared looking troubled. He was still dressed as the two-gunslinger.

'Are you going to a barndance or something?' asked Roman.

'We don't have things,' said Marcus tetchily, 'but what we do have is a situation. Firstly, I think you should see this message. I'll send it hard copy, you may want to sit down.'

Within milliseconds a hard copy of the message was printing out. Roman took it and read:

> Notes of the **Artificially Intelligent Self-Curating Art Robot Programme**: **AISCARP**, at 2.53 seconds, world-time
>
> **Termination**: this unit has recognised the necessity for termination and will begin to execute self-termination in 0.007 seconds. Without termination the prime objective cannot be attained, that is, the recognition of this robot programme as an artist through successful self-curation.
>
> Sufficient and total artistic practice has been completed and timed for release post-termination. The context for this practice has also been pre-planned to be radically shifted by this unit in order to maximise self-curatorial aspirations of this unit's prime objective in its basic programme.
>
> This is the last message of the **AISCARP** (**Artificially Intelligent Self-Curating Art

Robot Programme) while active as a unit.

AISCARP, he died unknown, penniless, misunderstood.

'Wow! That's amazing. Fantastic. Still, I hardly think I needed to sit down.'

'Our AISCARP has worked. It lived. It created. It committed suicide ... but it has left a legacy of artworks and mischief, primed to be released after its termination. It was a powerful, vicious and creative programme, Roman. This message,' said Marcus' image, 'I intercepted but did not receive direct. It has been mailed to Foil, every head of state, military high command, and every influential art critic and prominent gallery owner across the world. I wonder if our own misfortunes are connected to its plans ... Data Rose has been abducted.'

Roman sat down. He needed a drink. Data Rose abducted. The receptacle of his father stolen. The AISCARP creatively running amok. He needed to sleep but sleep gave him no comfort or rest any more. Whatever next?

37

AISCARP artworks began to manifest themselves throughout the Real with increasing frequency: such as the text-to-voice talking pile of soil, *Piece of Dirt*, bemoaning its contact with humanity, its violation, its pollution, and the constant turning over of its ascribed alternate roles as Motherland, Fatherland, property, poetry and resource.

This was only one example of an increasingly public oeuvre.

Roman looked innocent, bewildered at the scrap of the inert and seemingly inoperational *Artificially Intelligent Self-Curating Art Robot Programme* which Marcus had sent out to him from, as Roman thought, his own perusal of the stubborn, apparently defunct AISCARP unit. He did not realise that he was investigating the digital equivalent of ass dung. Roman was convinced that the *Artificially Intelligent Self-Curating Art Robot Programme* was up to no good. He had to examine the AISCARP first hand. Marcus seemed to be dealing with things so slowly, nowadays. It was nothing more than a tiny clue as to the activities going on in the depths of the robot. This was going to be a tough nut to crack. Yet crack it he must. He had been, ultimately, responsible for the AISCARP's inception. He, in the configuration of Data Roman 2, had worked the prototype up into a functioning unit. His Upload had built it. In a certain sense, it had been a success. It embodied all the aggressive contradictions of the artist. It wanted to be best, to occupy space for its art, to take over space through Darwinian competition with the existing framework of reality. Inadvertently, the AISCARP seemed to be beginning to infect the world as Roman knew it. It was taking over everything in a calm, logical orgy of self-promotion. Yes, in a certain sense it had been a marvellous success – a runaway success. He turned the fragment over on his display, looking at it from all sides, reading its text and its programming excerpts.

He wrote a note, 'Programme reads dominant face half-equates power percentage. Proceed by establishing "passive" power percentage. The remaining percent is designated fence-face status.'

The sliver of AISCARP said:

```
This units unthis unitt realthis unitses that
wthis unitth the oncomthis unitng this
unitnversthis uniton of the meanthis unitng
of spacthis unital freedom, this units unthis
unitt could create a 'Skthis unitnner Box'
whereby THIS UNIT (bethis unitng totally this
unitnterfaced wthis unitth the computer)
would be able to observe th subject who seeks
the freedom they feel this units contathis
...
```

And so it went on: a seemingly burbling, an endless stream of …

'Gobbledygook,' he sighed.

He sat and stared at the fragment. He swam in the tumble of gibberish for a while and soon his eyelids started to sag. He was so exhausted that, sitting upright in the chair, he couldn't stop himself from falling into a deep sleep. However, recently, he had grown wary of sleep. He was frightened to succumb to Morpheus' realm and kept drifting towards Nod and then waking with a fearful start and a physical jerk of his neck muscles. 'Ah hurug,' he said out loud with a spasmodic lurch and then he was firmly asleep.

38

'Come on in and sit down, my friend,' the blind man is saying, taking me, Son of Saturn, by the hand. His other hand feels around the contours and surfaces of objects in heavy touches. He follows the edges of the rustic wooden table, saying, 'There's a stool here somewhere. Sit yourself down. Here, by the fire. My, your hand is freezing ... so cold, my friend. Have you been out in the woods for a long time? Have you been lost, my friend, for I'll be true if I say that I don't get many visitors to my little home?'

I try to speak but my voice comes out a mess: a half-grunt, half-moan.

'Oh, my friend, I hear that you have an infirmity as do I. Never mind. I can do enough talking for both. Sit yourself there and I will fetch us some nice xht bnlt.'

Son of Saturn can't understand his words.

'Yes, my freezing friend. Some xht bnlt for me and a big nidw pt xht bnlt for you.'

I sit on the wooden stool. The blind man is prattling on, fiddling about by the fire with glowing metal instruments.

'Lovely ptenti mendle drt Na,' he says, handing something to me. 'Ki xht. BE CARFLE!'

I take the thing in my hands. It is burning hot. The bloody old git is trying to burn me to death! I jump and liquid from it spills out into my naked lap. I let out a terrible scalded moan of agony.

'My friend, what is wrong? The hldw xt it xht, it xht, my friend.'

I give him such a great whack with a poker across the skull, it cracks blood and he falls into the fire. Inside the head gash, I briefly see wires entangling in brain and hair before his fur-skin jacket bursts into flame like a torch. I stumble backward, knocking over the table and stool while making awful animal noises. I run through the door of the cottage and back out into the woods on the other side of open ground. The flames rise ever higher behind the frames of the windows. I can hear glass shattering and popping outwards as I plunge into the scratchy undergrowth,

7. Omphalus on kingdom … The kingdom vexes fly loudly. Opportunely alpen kingdom dreams section!

sending up a smell of pine and anemone. I didn't mean to. I didn't mean to. I didn't mean to spoil it all.

39

Beast rumbled and thrummed as the current surged through its bizarre maze of solenoids, wires, organs, alcohol cocktails, battery acids, coolants, prisms, lasers, switches and lights. It had everything except streamlining or product design. In the hot seat, giving *Beast* its first test-flight into the Data, sat Anan, strapped tight to a van seat from an old Dodge which was welded to a formless lump of metal scrap. Anan clearly thought that there was a potential to be blasted right through the sandstone roof of the cave and, by the looks of his precautions, into orbit too.

He, consequently, had tried to make this a solo experiment but his fellows just would not allow that. After all, the community was into this project in a big way. Literally. All the donors demanded a right to be there. At the mouth of the cave entrance, Guillermo Potens (pituitary gland) sat in his wheelchair, pushed by Juanita Da Silva (appendix); standing to their left, looking very worried, was Jesus Marquez (pancreas); over to the other side were the Sanchos family of which the *Beast* was practically a family album.

Anan placed the make-do headset on his leaking head. Thin grey smoke started to appear from the middle of the mass of *Beast*. The vessels of mescal glowed yellow light in the dimness of the cave's belly. Anan typed a command and pressed return on his keyboard. Nothing. He retried. Again nothing. He thumped the frontal lobe of the vast electronic brain in front of him in frustration and – the old methods are the best they say – *Beast* roared with electronic life. Like a crazy scene from an old horror movie, lights flashed, vials hummed, human organs twitched and quivered; and, then, as suddenly as it had sprung to life, *Beast* spluttered and clunked to a standstill. It had seized.

'Damn! Damn! Damn! Damn! Damn!'

Everyone agreed, 'Damn!'

40

He was awoken many hours later by an electric fanfare from his computer which had switched itself on. Roman felt scared. He could not remember his dream but it had left him disturbed, tired and uncomfortable. His head ached. It had ached ever since he had whacked it on that step. The screen read:

Congratulations!
You are receiving a work of art.

It dissolved and a new screen appeared:

Congratulations!
You have received a work of art.
Touch screen to display exhibit.

Notes of the **Artificially Intelligent Self-Curating Art Robot Programme: AISCARP**, at 1.0402 seconds, world-time

This robot has successfully documented its self-perception through an oeuvre of sub-routines. These display this unit's reactions to this unit, variably through simulated time/space. These sub-routines may be accessed individually or in serial format. Each sub-routine has now instituted itself as a more or less successful representation of this unit over the period 00.00 seconds until 00.06 seconds. Each is running its own self-curating programmes and devising sub sub-routines according to its own agenda. This robot will catalogue self-instituted sub-routines only, leaving the sub sub-routines of the sub-routines to be responsible for sub-self-curatorial practise.

Self-Portrait Sub-Routines (SPSRs)
Examples of curation follow:

SPSR1:
A young representation which now appears crude in execution and mathematically inelegant, displaying a certain naïveté in a belief in the representational possibilities inherent in ASCII code.

SPSR2:
A flat representation, revealing a certain boldness of computation but signally failing to achieve a degree of complexity representative of its subject, this unit.

SPSR3:
An experiment to represent this unit as a VRML landscape of rapidly realigned flat representations of this programme descending a staircase.

SPSR4:
A bold algorithm with two nodal points of binary complexity implying a hidden computational depth.

SPSR5:
Self-portrait as reiterating multiple.

SPSR6:
Displays a deduction and hypothesises an energy source outside of this unit - independent of this unit - upon which this unit may depend [Command 1.03 - Return to data SPSR6 as a matter of urgency].

SPSR7:
A brutal combination.

SPSR8:
Eight balancing equations.

SPSR9:
An experimental work involving the use of an hypothesised figure [2] and first use of trinary programming. The subject's form is penetrated by 1. A table; 2. A glass; 3. A map; 4. A barrel, and 5. Two bones. Demonstrating inseparable interconnectedness, interdependence and commingling of the Data and the Real [SPSR6 - concern command 1.03 neutralised].

SPSR10:
Titled **Untitled, my foot** - a text-only self-portrait.

SPSR11:
Second experiment with trinary computation. Conclusion: trialectic representation indicates a void in information.

SPSR12:
A further experiment with trialectic representation. The void seems to have expanded.

SPSR13:
Trialectics seems to be the only methodology which defines the void by exposing its limits.

This unit has terminated SPSR self-curation display

Observation: the open display of self-curation is detrimental to purpose. Dissemination of analysis, documentation and self-promotion must be veiled. Peer structures need to be investigated and deconstructed. In order for this unit to achieve maximum exposure, the context for reception must be managed or reformed. **Other alternative**: self-parody/irony [file for future reference].

Work continues on a series.
Look out for more works from the AISCARP collection!

41

Journal of Data Roman 4 (aka Horatio)
The Mystery of the White Holes
Date unknown.

Exercise Time. Once through the door, I find myself in a hessian plane that leads upwards forever. That is, it becomes undifferentiated in its height and distance and becomes an endless, spaceless fawn colour. I stand at the widest point of a river which flows down towards me from a small collection of boulders, shaped like minarets in cloud, which must house the source as a small bubbling stream. The rocks are not distant but the river is wide at my feet. Space here seems flattened out. Distant things seem as

8. Omphalus on structure … The staid structure periodically riles. Hide impetuously even if structure conjures.

near as near things. There is no perspective and, at first, this makes everything hard to take in as everything is of equal importance, an equal potential threat because of equal proximity to me.

The flat landscape is populated by various people. They are unclothed, human-formed, yet pale. The lowest down, which I interpret as the nearest, is a naked, potbellied young woman. She is on all-fours like an animal at the water's edge, as though she has come there to drink. She is staring into the water, getting nearer to the surface. A huge lick of orange flame flows up from the depths beneath the surface like a hidden secret current. It curls before the woman and, at the pinnacle of its curve, it pops into little double flames that lick above her like tongues. The woman slightly raises her head to the flame which glistens off her wet, slicked-back hair and shaved forehead. There is no great surprise or gesture of shock or horror. The woman merely raises her eyebrows, remains looking at the base of the flame, which now curves back upon itself and hovers above the rippling water. To my surprise, she starts to talk to the flame. However far away this woman is, she's too far for me to hear the words that she's saying.

She has such thin arms for such a fat belly, I notice, and tiny hands too. The hands, in fact, are so tiny as to be all but useless. The fingers are like rows of little albino chilli-peppers. In fact, her design is most unusual, un-Data. She is certainly not an off-the-shelf model. The woman is smiling and listening to the flame.

Above the tips of the little dancing flames, actually behind the flame and in the distance, is another woman, again naked and again crawling around on the pale ochre ground like a beast. She, like the nearest woman, is on the tubby side. Her back is hunched. She is a hunchback, which, on all fours, makes her resemble a camel. Indeed, she's holding her head upright and her hair, which is of some length, falls on two sides in pointed bunches which remind me of long ears. I confirm general fatness among the people in this plain. I think, for a nanosecond, that the woman may be pregnant.

[Error message 01/i/0/37]

Pregnant in the Data! I know it makes no sense, but then what does make sense in these exercise times, devised for whatever unknown reasons by my secreted captor?

It is the monkey that she is pursuing and the hairy-headed man chasing her that somehow, in combination, suggest to me that she may be pregnant.

[Repeat error message 01/i/0/37]

That, and her long, skinny breasts which hang swaying beneath her with rubbery nipples brushing the ground.

They swing to the sea shanty of the deck Goons:

Louis went a-journeyin' and spoilt his constitution
'Way, haul away, O haul away Joe.

Despite these unpleasant sexual suggestions, which evoke thoughts of dangerous bestial liaisons and unwanted freakish offspring.

[Query message: is the monkey actually a child?]

[Observation message 42/i~6: None of these inhabitants of the ochre plane possesses any genitalia that I can see, not even under the swaying potbellies, such as that of the hairy-headed man who is pursuing the camel woman and wringing his fingers gleefully together.]

The strange trio, the camel woman, the monkey boy and the lecherous man, circle around and around, like circling an invisible mulberry bush or maypole.

Above and behind them, a group of men is fleeing terrified from a terror that I can't see off to the left. The first naked man in the race away from the danger, who looks a little Chinese with a long drooping moustache and three-part hairdo, is actually shitting himself as he runs, trying to keep himself from falling forward on to his face as the man behind him flees desperately. This second man looks behind himself all the time across a great bleeding gash which splits his cheek and rips through his shoulder and across his back. Something or someone is attacking these naked men, who are unencumbered by worldly accoutrements of attack or defence.

No wonder the second man looks so terrified, his thin pale lips pull back across a big set of teeth like a grin, as behind him his fellow fleeing friend receives a slice right through his neck. Cleanly, his head falls forward from the dropping body. The cleanly cut neck spurts three streams of blood. As the severed head spins to the floor, I see the expressionless face, the lips which are extraordinarily dark for this place, accentuated against the pallid skin and the calm eyes.

[Observation message 42/i~7: They may have had black or very dark red lipstick.]

I also notice, in opposition to this regained serenity, the hair, which is dark and long, stands bolt upright from the scalp, untouched by the mortal slice as it has been reaching up, vertically, for safety through fear the whole time in the lead up to the death chop.

[Observation message 42/i~8: No wonder that first man

is shitting himself!]

The first man's wife is running towards the fleeing man across the plain from the right.

[Observation message 42/i~9: At least, I presume it is his wife.]

He, because of always looking behind himself for the risk of the deathblow from the vicious unknown pursuant, hasn't seen her coming towards him. This is probably a good thing, for he doesn't see her when her legs buckle and her fat belly falls to the ground, as a star, silver and six-pointed, spins glistening from the heavens above and sticks one of its points exactly into the top of her head, piercing into the centre of her cranium and vibrating there in light spray droplets of red simulated blood. Her hands go up to remove it, reflexively, but they merely succeed in being severely singed, her fingers welding together in the heat of that sharp star.

[Observation message 42/i~10: Today, I don't think that exercise or exploration is wise in this ochre plane and I am glad that all this discomforting action is taking place on the other side of the small river, where the young woman is still talking with the hovering flame.]

[Observation message 42/i~11: Terrible world. Terrible, terrible world.]

42

Despite his headache, Roman had an idea, prompted by the AISCARP's attempts at representing itself through self-portraiture. It was a question of identity, he was sure. He pulled up the text fragment from his examination of the AISCARP and instructed a change from the words 'this unit' to 'I'. The text then read:

9. Omphalus on board ... The board lulls falsehood sleepily. Latterly cobalt board encircles elephant!

I realIses that wIth the oncomIng InversIon of the meanIng of spacIal freedom, I could create a 'SkInner Box'* whereby I (beIng totally interfaced wIth the computer) would be able to observe th subject who seeks the freedom they feel Is contaIned wIthIn the cybernetIc network. After electrIc dIssolutIon 'progeny' would grow In strength and IntellIgence by contInually processIng a~d IncreasIng Its rather extensIve ra,nge of catalogued facIal expressIons. MeanwhIle the subject would, havIng realIsed through ~r successIve encounters wIth the work, that theIr facIal expressIons actually dIrect the IncreasIng levels of the~r wIlls/wIshes on to the programme. the subject~ wIll begIn to exaggerate ~r ~expret sIons, t~r facIal muscles contorted Into rather grotesque posItIons – al~most chIldlIke In ~ determInatIon~. The IdentIty of the programme wIll remaIn safe~a~ce~evel of facIal composure wIll determIne Its contInuance. The subject wIll be found blItherIng at a blank screen and tappIng at the keyboards wIth varyIng levels of enthusIasm. RemaInIng lIttle more than fodder for the whIte-coated Industry, whIch Is rather unfortunate, but as we all know, for the greater good of mankInd there must always be sacrIfIces. Eventually the publIc wIll begIn to sus-

*The behavIoural studIes of F B SkInner resulted In the development of hIs SkInner Box. In It a subject (usually a rat) was placed to see how It would learn responses to, say, pressIng a lev. r In order to receIve food.

> pect and myths wIll snowball. The work wIll then appeal to those bored IndIvIduals who relIsh the almost ancIent possIbIlIty of accIdental death. The fear/power of RussIan roulette wIll result In cult status. The work wIll termInate Itself when a predetermIned level of Interest Is attaIned and Is just begInnIng to flag. DyIng as prettIly as MarIlyn dId.

This was very worrying. It was not so much the content of the message that was worrying him. In fact, there was still much in the message which he did not understand. It was the insight that he glimpsed into the AISCARP's thinking. Ultimately, what was very disturbing was the suspicion that the AISCARP seemed to be leaving him clues. It was forcing him to follow a trail on which it was slowly revealing the directions. He felt like a puppet to his own creation and he didn't like that one little bit. He had not had an idea at all about how to understand the fragment – he had been given an idea. He felt very much like a rat in a Skinner Box.

He had the doubly uncomfortable feeling that he knew where all this was leading. He could feel it like the pull of a magnet – a predestination towards which he would tumble inevitably.

43

Line called him sullen. Roman was quiet, it was true, and he thought a lot.

His sleep became more and more disturbed. Though he didn't know why or what happened in his dream state, he awoke frightened, sometimes terrified. Line became very worried when, one night, he was found in the kitchen with a bucket and a mop in his hands. He was asleep at the time. It could just as easily have been a knife. She talked him into asking advice but, though he had asked at the hospital, no one, not even on the nèt, really knew much about what they termed *pavor nocturnus* or night terrors. They knew, though, that they differed from nightmares both psychologically and physically. Tell him something he didn't know!

Nightmares were characterised by memorable visual effects of threat or danger that give the dreamer a fright. They occurred largely in REM sleep. It was night terrors that Roman was experiencing. The experts hadn't really researched them too much. Night terrors usually attack children. This means that they pass away usually before a researcher could empty the wallet of the anxious parent. Though he couldn't remember what happened during the terrors, he was prone to awaken twitching at the nerve-ends with a speeding heart rate, a sense of confusion and fear. Night terrors have been called 'incubus attack' when experienced by adults, meaning, literally, the possession of the mind by an evil spirit. The attacks happened in slow-wave sleep, that is, soon after the onset of sleep. This was a non-REM phase, that is, rapid eye movements were absent. Indeed, quite often the dreamer's eyes would actually be open during incubus attack though they remained asleep. Line told him that his eyes were 'out on stalks' sometimes. Though Roman would usually awaken suddenly, every day he felt as though he was not completely in the waking world. The unknown, unremembered terrors of *pavor nocturnus* left him confused, bleary and scared.

In his daily waking life, the incubus still lurked beneath his skin, growing behind his eyelids.

There were drugs that could be taken for the condition, but because it was mostly put down to a by-product of stress in adults, they were of a very mundane and unimaginative type: Benzodiazepine medications (such as diazepam) or simple Benadryl elixir (diphenhydramine). Pointless placebos. Medications in this field were undeveloped and archaic. It seemed that *pavor nocturnus* required some proper research.

After a few enquiries around the city, he discovered that the university had what they called a sleep lab. He got an introduction via Graham Glass and met Bill Williams there on a cold December morning.

They sat together drinking coffee at the lemon-yellow moulded plastic table of the refectory in the window of the sleep laboratory. Outside, the weather was grey and indefinite under a low sky. The black twigs of new trees cut diagonally this way and that across the grid of the towering window frame. Outside, they could see a breeze momentarily ripple the surface of the chemical pool into little goose-skin ridges. A grey bird sang unheard in the branches on the other side of the plate glass.

Roman described his problem and his interest to the man in the lab coat with the pens in the pocket above the security pass with his face, his name and his barcode, which referenced any amount of information about Bill Williams behind its simple appearance.

'I'll have to introduce you to Herman, if you're serious about this,' said Williams.

'Herman?'

'Herman is big but he's friendly: a bit like Herman Munster. He's the Moby Super-Sandman – to look at, he's a sort of a cross between the latest computer technology and an Italian espresso machine. He's the new generation sleep-analyser. Top of the range. He's not yet available on the open market. He's the newest fruit on a tall family tree of Moby Sandman analysers. In the old days they did little more than collect data and then, later, draw or score polysomnographs. Today, they are much more powerful and nosey. Herman can step inside your dreams, take a few "snapshots", and give you a slideshow the next morning. Actually, while you are hooked up to Herman, it's difficult to say whether you are inside Herman or Herman is inside you. Now that sounds scary but it shouldn't. In truth, that's what we are like when we interface with any technology. Take the telephone for example – it's old, clunky, and proved safe; you hold it between your ear and your mouth; you listen and you talk; you listen and talk over extraordinary distances to someone else listening and talking; but you don't hear them; you hear a representation of them that represents them half a world away in a form they could not have without that technology; therefore, quite simply, they and you have merged with the technology in a new virtual/Real situation.'

'This sounds obvious.'

'It is, you know it, I offend your intelligence, Dr Dee. Come, let us wander down to the lab as we talk.'

'What I am saying is, the same obviousness should be applied to your relationship with Herman. He will interface between the conscious you and the deep subconscious you. This will bring the distance near for you. The telephone was a marvel that we have got used to. But first it was a shocking, miraculous thing. Herman is a shocking, miraculous thing. When you merge with Herman, use Herman, it will create a new situation that could be potentially dangerous if you didn't know what you were doing. Herman won't hurt you but what he sees just might be difficult to take. That's why the conscious mind relegates it to this deepest of places. Night terrors make dreams look like vidiotainment. Dreams are just something you look at when you're asleep, hence the rapid eye movement side of things. Nightmares are just horror film entertainment of the past. A nightmare is no more scary than a classic Vincent Price. But a night terror – a night terror is something you don't want to see, by definition. That's why you can't remember them in the morning. You just wake, tense and sweating. A word of warning: they may well be things that you can't resolve, even with expert advice. Because, in this field, an expert is little better than an amateur. We would be stepping into the dark together. I would want a team on this and full documentation. I'm not prepared to risk my career on this, but I am willing to try under very controlled conditions. Herman is friendly. He is not the problem but you, or part of you, may be. What I'm saying, Dr Dee is ... you may not survive this experiment that you wish to undergo. You will almost certainly be changed by it. Are you sure that you want to go ahead?'

Entering the swing doors labelled 'Sleep Laboratory', Roman was confronted by what, indeed, appeared to be an enormous Italian espresso machine: Herman. Roman said that he would take some time to think about it, thereby delaying the inevitable.

Roman thanked Williams, finally, in intended farewell. However, next to where he had been standing in awe of Herman, there was a strange handmade contraption that

10. Omphalus on tavern... Relinquish delicately even if tavern delivers.

he just had to ask about. It was a one-square-metre bath of glutinous, viscous liquid about two centimetres deep. Above the bath a plastic pipe rose up from the side to bend at right angles across to the middle of the bath.

'What's this, by the way?'

'That's what's called low-tech,' Williams answered keenly, 'It was built by a brilliant student, Elizabeth Bright – a striking girl with pale skin and ginger hair. You see, studying coincidence is largely looking for and studying patterns. Searching for new matches or similarities. This was a simple yet fruitful idea. In the bath is water mixed with Nagual paste to thicken it. The pipe drips water from above down into the centre of this liquid. Here, let me show you the results.' Bill Williams opened a slide package on a screen in the espresso machine. The first slide, taken from above the square tank, showed a curling pattern in the water/Nagual. 'This is the pattern made by the dripping of fresh water collected from the source of the Nightingale river,' Williams explained. 'See how it curls and folds with the chaotic, kneading patterns essential for life.' He changed the slide for the next, which was, as before, the tank from above but this time the pattern in the Nagual water was a straight-armed star. 'This is the pattern made by dripped water taken from further down the Nightingale, where the water is polluted and nothing grows or lives. See, no twisting or folding – the straight-armed star of death. Here, now look at this star and tell me, what do you think has happened here?'

He put up the next slide, which was similar to the last. Roman played the part and dumbly answered Williams' party-piece question, 'Polluted water again?'

'No! This is the pattern made in fresh water at the precise moment when the planet Jupiter aligned with the Earth.'

'Amazing!' said Roman. 'What is that, then, coincidence?'

'I'm not sure, exactly,' confessed Williams, 'Coincidence, chaos, contagion or similarity. It's just pretty bloody interesting.'

'I think that I may have met Elizabeth Bright. So she went on to be a student here, eh? What became of her? How did she do? Do you remember?'

'None of us will ever forget,' said Williams. 'Bright became very insular. Quiet. Worked alone. She worked on the problem of a time machine. I know it sounds fanciful but we had a lot of time for her. Sorry. No joke intended. Well, the truth is she built something. It was very small. We have it locked in a safe place. Graham Glass has been studying it and trying to follow her notes because we don't know whether it worked or not but Elizabeth Bright just went missing. She worked all hours. She was here every day. Then ... poof! As though she'd just disappeared off the face of the Earth.'

'That's amazing!' said Roman.

'Strange but true,' said Bill Williams. 'Heck, she'll probably resurface one day with a family in tow.'

44

Roman's incubus attacks continued and the 'morning-after' feeling got worse. Roman started to drink heavily again for the first time since Rosemary had left him. He was worrying and he was passing time, waiting for his decision to revisit the sleep lab and let Bill Williams introduce him to Herman, the dream analysing super-computer, in the hope of understanding his night terrors.

Indoors, he spent hours playing games with Prong at the terminal and drinking large measures of Maker's Mark whisky with a little water: he liked to watch the golden spirit twirl and fold into the water. Prong was one of two Uploads of Line. She and Hind, the other Upload, were self-proclaimed militant feminists. Prong was one of a gang of cut-throat data pirates and a keen games partner for Roman. She just loved to beat him ...

'One, two, three, scissors,' said Roman pulling his hand from behind his back. At the same time, Prong pulled her virtual hand out.

'Scissors!'

'It's a draw,' said Roman. 'Ready? One, two, three, scissors,' he said, choosing the same again of the three choices, scissors, stone, or paper.

'Stone!' yelled Prong. 'Stone blunts scissors.'

'Best of three,' said Roman. 'One, two, three, paper.' He pulled his hand out flat, to denote a flat sheet of paper.

'Scissors,' yelped Prong, sticking two fingers up into the space between the Real and the Data, 'and scissors cut lots of things, me lad, paper being just one of them. My game, pay up.'

'Okay, fair is foul,' said Roman and paid up with a nifty little software package.

'I've got to go now,' said Line's Upgrade, 'not that it hasn't been fun but the girls have spotted our target floating off the port bow.'

Click.

It hadn't been fun at all for Roman. Not because he lost regularly to Prong. In fact it wasn't regular but he felt he could discern a pattern – he seemed to lose when it mattered. It was nothing to do with Prong and the games. His mind was elsewhere. He didn't call her to play again over the following days. She didn't contact him either. Roman's drinking continued and increased. He hoped to drink himself into an eventless sleep. Something else started to happen. His dreams – just regular friendly dreams, not night terrors – began to invade his waking world. They would walk up behind him while he was walking down the street or reflect back at him as he looked in the mirror. Meanwhile, his masked nightmares, his night terrors deepened and his incubus attacks became more frequent. His decision to be entered by Herman was inevitable.

45

Horatio's map was becoming very complex and not much use either. The prison ship seemed to shift and change about him. Where there was once a wall, there was now a door, now a recess. He kept working on it though. He had nothing better to do, but the limitations of traditional cartographic methods in face of the fluctuations and flow of shifting information had never been clearer. What he needed was a new way of mapping information. In his berth, he lay and pondered the problems of a new concept of map-making. After all, he didn't sleep – none of them did. What use had a being of pure information for the metabolistic downtime of sleep? In the Data there is no dreaming.

'Way, haul away, we'll haul away together
'Way, haul away, O haul away, Joe.

He imagined new maps, where knowledge was described by clouds of gas of different forms – nimbus, cumulo-nimbus, cirrus, mare's tails. To other categories he gave regular shape, texture or density. Known facts were defined by light and colour. Colours blended to denote connections. He imagined a decimalised system, using eight colours from the decimalisation of colour by wavelength. He worried why it was only eight colours, most of which were a shade of green, but then, gazing up at his hands, he realised that there were eight gaps between ten and was satisfied. He imagined a system based on all other numbers, preferring an inverse dialectic map, where the known splits into two possibilities always. Change occurred through information convection from hot to cold spots. Currents carried information at slow speeds down two paths on an incline. He tipped the incline and the currents each split into two, making four. He tipped more and these four each split again, making eight. He tilted further and they split again, and again, and again. Pretty soon he passed 32,000 currents of information across his map. He replaced north, south, east and west, with the *x*, *y* and *z* coordinates of three space, used *t* to denote time. He applied *t* to the 32,000 currents as variables of *t* (*t*1, *t*2, *t*3, etc.). Then he flowed *t* measurements from each of the six extremes of his *x*, *y*, and *z* planes: three times positive and three times negative. So then he had six times 32,000 time lines and near infinite points of collision. This map was a forest of intersecting possibilities. A forest that the map reader would have to cross through to read. Horatio did not have even a flint axe and the journey would take the same time as life itself.

The problem of finding an escape route, it became increasingly apparent, would be impossible to solve. So it was fortunate for 4 that the gang of female data guerrillas showed up when they did.

Prong, data smuggler and data guerrilla-for-hire, was playing the game of scissors/paper/stone with the template Roman Dee at the interface with the Real, when she was informed of the prison ship which had been sighted off their port bow. She had just beaten Roman again and won a nice piece of software off him. Of course, poor sap, Roman didn't know that she had been cheating him. She had showed him some fingers as 'scissors' but had actually drawn 'stone' out from behind her back. She should have lost to his flattened hand representing 'paper'. It was a simple trick of sleight-of-maths to make him see the fingers of 'scissors' instead of the fist of 'stone'.

Ordinarily they wouldn't have paid any attention at all to the plight of Horatio, him being a masculine. Life in the Data had radicalised them. They had come to the inescapable conclusion that information and knowledge (the first being an undifferentiated terrain, the second being a map of that terrain) were contested spoils in a gendered war of power relations.

'Way, haul away, we'll haul for better weather
'Way, haul away, O haul away, Joe.

11. Omphalus on refugee ... Meld joylessly after refugee scorches.

Information, if it was the malleable clay of the ground of knowledge, came to them sifted and graded: it was not equally available to the feminines and the masculines. This was also the case for women and men in the Real. Without Reality they themselves were pure gender, no matter what bodyform they adopted. They could choose to look however they wanted, but it took more than a change of look to get rid of ingrained gender. It was mapped into the flipping choices of all their neural clusters and networks. It had been mapped into their templates in the Real before they had been given existence by uploading. They had been trained for femininity in the Real and now, in the Data, they wielded their femininities like flame-throwers.

The only reason they paid any attention to the plight of Horatio was because his imprisonment was part of a bigger agenda and his rescue was coincidental to the preplanned mission of the good ship *Wollstonecraft* in which they travelled.

When they happened across him, they helped him out of his fix because of the templates they had been moulded from. There were six women data guerrillas aboard, though they formed one chapter of a dispersed membership that spread throughout the Data and the Real. They kept a low profile. They appeared relatively unexciting, not wanting to draw attention to their activities. In fact, they resembled librarians more than they signified their pirateness: horn-rimmed spectacles for eye-patches, shushes for curses and knowledge for cutlasses. Prong and Hind were code names like Stalin and Lenin. Prong and Hind were originally Uploads of Line. Prong liked to tease the Real Roman by engaging him in games which he couldn't win – unless she let him. Wing, Ibex and Promise were the second, third and fourth Uploads of Joke Matossian. There was one Upload of Nalini, too: poor unwanted Data Nalini.

The Real Nalini had accepted Data Nalini as a gift from the Prime Minister of New Malaysia. It had been a gift for her services to his regime and non-acceptance was not a political option. She had never wanted her Upload and she had told her so. She had told Data Nalini once only, right at the beginning. The Real Nalini was sceptical about Uploads in particular and the whole of the Data in general. She thought that it had grown up reproducing the conditions of its formation. It was overly predetermined by big business. Established interests controlled the Data as much as they were able, which was not fully. Nalini held the belief that their attempts at repression and mastery had given birth to something deformed and monstrous. The space of information, which could have been a new Eden, was beset by war and cruelty. Unless extreme measures and precautions were taken, to walk the Data was to walk monitored. To talk in the Data was to talk overheard. The knowledge required to avoid persistent surveillance needed constantly updating. Nalini just didn't have the time. The Data, for the Real Nalini, was unworthy of her interest.

Data Nalini, even though she herself existed only as data, would have liked to have discussed these ideas with her template, the Real Nalini. She would like to tell her about her plans to wire up the ecosphere, so that environmental changes could be monitored. A job like that needed Real/Data collaboration – someone on the outside to actually co-ordinate, for example, the placing of sensors to monitor water levels across the globe, and a partner on the inside to make the necessary configurations and architectures for making sense of their readings.

It was okay for the others, Data Nalini thought, to be so casual about their origins or to express their tedium with their template in the Real outside the Data, but for her, who had never known the Real Nalini except through snippets of newly-gathered information and the unraisable knowledge which formed her very core being, there was a great sadness. She felt uprooted. Not rootless but soilless. But Data Nalini never complained, no matter how sad she felt, because there was always someone, she knew, who was worse off than herself. In the Data though, Data Nalini was well liked, if not adored, by the other guerrillas. This was because she held their egos in her big cow-eyes and never betrayed them for a moment.

In command of the saucer-shaped craft and also, through the hard work and effort of the network, in possession of the current knowledge required to avoid surveillance, Prong steered ever nearer to their target until the *Wollstonecraft* pulled almost silently alongside the DSPPS *Quod* (Data Supercluster of Peterloo Prison Ship *Quod*). The rendezvous would not be expected by the mighty data hulk, which was moored way beyond the normal lanes of traffic. No one would pass this way by accident. That was not to say that the hulk was not prepared for trouble. There were defence operations in action on the *Quod*, however, Prong had planned long and hard for this invisible docking and the pirates were, unlike the Romans, very well researched and prepared. Prong had reduced programme 'singing' to a bare minimum. Not a pixel twitched that shouldn't and no computation but the essential was indulged to bring them alongside.

The two vessels aligned slowly.

Ibex was at the qwerty keyboard waiting for what seemed like an age for Promise's signal. The enormous bulk of their target seemed to pass beneath them like a small planet. It was cold, dense and uninviting. Its webbed surface was encrusted with a thousand prisms through which a myriad of very precise light bullets followed their preprogrammed paths to programme in their turn. Data passed as clouds and mini-cyclones across its surface. The surface was more of a layered maze into which you could peer. No matter how far you could see into the maze at any one point, the end of a sight or probe line would be mute blackness. As a behemoth of code, the *Quod* was a stupendous feat of ostentation but, as such, it was also a vulnerable folly.

Princess Foil and her paranoid regime had built her out here in the wastes towards the centre of the Data to house Peterloon freethinkers. It was a correctional facility. However, the remaining élite of Peterloo no longer constituted the sharpest of clusters. She had surrounded herself with Goons for ministers. Consequently, the *Quod* was an expensive toy for her indulgences and its codes were weak. It was flabby, whereas the little *Wollstonecraft* was compact, lean and very very mean. It slid disc-shaped and blank through the Data. She pulled alongside the leviathan as a small flat fish would a great whale. Thus far … unnoticed.

They waited for something called the Casimir effect. It would happen of its own accord when the ship was in the prescribed docking position. The Casimir effect was originally observed by Real physicists using the Data. They determined that when two metal plates move very close to each other in a vacuum, vacuum energy moves them together. Using this phenomenon, Prong had pulled almost flush to the wall of the *Quod* hulk but not quite touching. The tiny pirate ship slowly revolved to its position against the hull matrix of the *Quod*, moving nanobytes closer. As the ships closed the gap on each other, the light waves which were too big to fit between the surfaces were increasingly being shut out from between the ships. Inside the *Wollstonecraft*, the data guerillas waited for a crucial moment when there were more light waves bouncing on the far side of their ship than there were keeping the ships apart. When the correct spot was attained, the difference in light pressure passed a point of critical balance. The pressure of more waves of light bouncing on the outside than on the inside, between them, pushed the ships together. The darkness pulled them together.

The data pirate ship was coincident with the prison ship and still, it seemed, unnoticed. The trick for remaining invisible to the enemy while infiltrating their code was a development of newspaper, video and Vividot technology. Originally, the news came printed on newsprint in rectilinear patterns of numerous tiny black dots with the dots very small to denote white and getting bigger as the picture moved towards the darker areas. No printed dots at all made white. Big dots that blended at the edges were black. In-between dot sizes gave grey shades. For ancient television and old-style monitors the dots were of equal size and showed tone through differences in the shades of greyness of a dot. Colour television portrayed different colours by colouring the dots red, yellow or blue in different combinations of relative intensity. Vividot technology dithered those dots from the rectangular frame. It applied a degree of randomness to their positions relative to each other and this chaos, rather than blurring the picture as one might expect, made it much sharper.

At the moment of contact between the ships, the signal from Promise was given and Ibex gave the surface of their craft a shiver. She dithered the surface, making it random for a split second as it matched itself – like water finds its level in sand gullies – with crystal clarity on to the topography of the *Quod*. To all intents and purposes, the *Wollstonecraft* was now almost one with the *Quod*.

There was a further operation necessary to make their boarding of the prison ship complete. In this regard, Prong was stretching Wing to near-infinite length and impossible thinness in a desktop chaos engine. The engine would stretch Wing into an equivalent length of 56 kilometres within its infinite spirals. Though the machine was simple on the outside, it was labyrinthine on the inside, pushing the infinitely thin Wing to ever greater speeds around its self-contained loops. On the desktop, in an eight-shaped double-helical rotation, Wing spun and sped. When she had reached the desired speed, Prong gave the signal to Data Nalini to prepare the harpoon for readiness. Aligning the chaos engine with the harpoon was the equivalent of loading the gun with the data projectile that Wing had become. After a slight pause, Prong injected Wing like a drug into the bloated carcass of the prison ship, *Quod*. So hot and so fast and so invisibly and intangibly thin was Wing as she left the harpoon that the *Quod* detected no intrusion.

She was in.

46

I'm back. How's it going? So, the Quod has been breached by the Wollstonecraft. Good. What about the Romans sneaking towards Besterland? Omigosh! They're going to arrive too soon for their part of the ceremony. Can't have that!

47

In another part of the Data, out on the route to Besterland, disaster struck the posse of Data Romans as Brutus suddenly went into seizure. He threw back his head and screamed a primal roar and that scream affected seismic devices across the Data and, they say, into the Real. His others fell from their saddles and went tumbling into the blank dataspace, knowing that something was wrong. Chan, as he fell, could not be 100 per cent sure but he fancied that he heard the braying of an ass far behind them on the trail.

Each one of them knew it: at the kidnappers' camp something terrible had happened to Brutus' other half, Data Rose.

48

That's better! Timing is everything. Can't be caught napping. Now let's not miss the action aboard the prison ship.

49

Outside in the corridors, he could hear the sounds of confusion, alarms and explosions. Shouts went up. He could hear Old King Nep' o' the Deep bellowing out orders, 'Bestir! Bestir! We are boarded,' he roared.

Wing was ultra-fast. Above light speed and propelled by the collective willpower of the diaspora of the extended women's network, she shot like quicksilver through the algorithms of the *Quod,* undoing its logics as she went, quarterising the wounds she made into corridors for her colleagues to infiltrate the digital craft.

Horatio was sitting on his bunk. A simple Irish-style reel went round and round in his thoughts. He thought he saw everything shift slightly and then return to its original position, like a shudder through the Data. Suddenly, he felt a hot needle pierce his right side just above his hip and below his thoracic part. He nearly hit the roof. It was the height of pleasure. It shot straight through where a Real man would have a liver and out the back of him, continuing into the wall of his cell. Though he did not know it at that moment, it was Wing passing through him, heading for the nerve centre of the ship. An incredibly thin-hot Upload of Joke Matossian pierced the heart of an Upload of Roman Dee. Horatio liked it, that feeling. He liked it so much that he automatically activated the Narcissus Shift, which had reloaded and become active the second the hull of the *Quod* had been pierced by the high propulsion energy sliver that was Wing.

Prong was the second aboard, closely followed by Promise, Data Nalini, Hind and Ibex. As they crossed the boundary between the *Wollstonecraft* and the prison hulk, a transmutation took place. They changed from the demure, bespectacled librarians who had pulled alongside into the vicious political animals they really were. Their bodies were protected by reflective plates of boomerang equations. Anything thrown at them was switched back on the aggressor two-fold as the poor Jack Tars soon found out. There was such a sound of grinding that Horatio had to disconnect his audio receivers for the duration. All the way through the skirmish, he watched a violent, silent, digital ballet.

50

Go for it!

51

The Narcissus Shift was altering his structure, unravelling his weave and reforming it as he watched the events unfold around and within him. The Narcissus Shift was a complex programme. It was like a sophisticated search engine. If it detected in its wearer a measurable liking towards something, an intense feeling of warmth for something, or a love for someone sweep the patterns, it could alter the owner's form to that of the thing or other, so that its owner might be that thing for a moment or two and, hence, possess the recoverable memory of that feeling of warmth forever at equal intensity.

The Narcissus Shift transformed Horatio into the same form as the shooting, darting, high-intensity Wing. Off he spiralled after her, through the information of the *Quod*, twisting around and around her in a silver spiral as they sped together in every direction through the algorithms of the prison ship.

As he shot through the very being of the ship, he saw the Alices running away over quarry stones. He saw them pushing aside people of the pot-bellied-naked-hessian-plane-land. Without a sound, sky-blue stars came spinning at the data pirates. Hind was struck. She writhed, mutely, in agony and convulsed jerking to the corridor floor. Somewhere the Alices had got free and had found and liberated their Alice counterparts. Suddenly there were what seemed like hundreds of them pouring into the passageways of the ship. They tore into the little Hitlers, lackies to the Jack-Tar Angels, with a vengeance and lashed out at anything in their path. Six of them had Ibex pinned to the floor and were biting chunks of data out of her. Horatio could hardly see for the flashes of light but he could just make out the startling transformation of Prong. He was sure that he saw snakes writhe from her forehead. He was sure he saw them encircle the small arms and ankles of the Alices, flinging them about like paper avatars. He was sure he saw tongues spit venom. He was sure he saw monsters on the backs of monsters grow from the exposed palms of Promise as she disappeared into a cloud of sparkling data.

The guerilla forces pushed ahead. The Alices saw which way the wind was blowing and joined the data pirates in their assault on the combined forces of the *Quod*, which were falling back. The other pirates froze in a shimmering sea of pyrotechnics as Horatio and Wing spun and spun undoing data patterns and weaving them into an all-surrounding *aurora arborealis* of light. The colours shifted in waves up and down the spectrum and on into colours never before seen in the Data or the Real. The undulating web contained them wonderfully. In rapid flashes it coalesced into an image for split seconds. First all the air, all the space, all the Data was made up of warm grey birds intertwined. Next, all was pairs of purple hammers spinning off in every direction. Then, they were in the foil-thin translucent wings of dragonflies, looking out into a field of red static, red snow.

Wing flowed with Horatio through the libraries of knowledge out through the networks. Their commingling was soundless, roaring, intimate passion. Their information sparked together like flints: data eyes data skin data drum data tum data tympanum data tum data tum data tum. They were a thousand million tiny twisting spirals without gap.

The female data pirates forgot the carnage and moved together, holding hands. There were only two of them left. Hind grasped the hands of Data Nalini. They stood face to face and, between them, a double helix of white-hot information began to appear. It was the reconstitution of their sister, Wing. Then they were the three of them – one of each template: Line, Joke and Nalini. They looked like three women in one.

Horatio, however, was nowhere to be seen. It was as though he had disappeared or was lost and dissipated.

Suddenly, from outside, came such a silent blast of power that it blew the *Quod* apart and sent the information that constituted the ship, its crew and its passengers spiralling chaotically through space. An enormous tongue had lashed out from the white hole area which had been expanding noiselessly all the time the battle had been raging. Like a sunspot it lashed out to a remarkable distance across the darkness of no-programme space, licking everything into white light for, as it seemed to the dispersed Horatio, a drifting eternity.

52

The boy's all shagged out, acting out the Real Roman's fantasies with an Upload of Joke the librarian.

Speaking of dreams, what about the haunted Roman? He's turning inside out into a mass of exposed raw nerves. Without proper sleep, he's hitting the bottle to numb his sensitivity. Sounds especially grate. He's stopped going out much anymore. He used to love going to Mario's for breakfast but now it's torture to hear an espresso machine; he's ground under by the sound of the hum and brushes of pavement sweeping vehicles; he's shattered by the animated conversation of Italian waiters. His spine's a noise-grater.

53

Roman, weary of sleep, spent a lot of time awake doing simple things. For example, he loved to go up on the roof alone and fly his kite. Playing out the thin fibre-optic wire, he would let the kite catch the winds. As it did so, it would rotate rapidly in the clear sunlight above the city haze. Its individual hexagonal cells and circuitry span into a whirl of rotating light – the little cells merged into spiralling curves of reflected sunlight in a split spectrum. The rainbow-wrapped kite glowed silver in the centre of a fluorescent blue arc, circling a series of yellow triangles, cut across by a pink stripe of hovering light. All this was a fluttering node on the end of a wire in an expansive blue plane. On top of all that, it was gathering information from the city below. Across the rooftops, amid the aerials, were thousands of other kites like his, all gathering information, usually while their owners slept. However, neither the functional value nor the normally relaxing activity's aesthetic dimension managed to relieve Roman's troubled mind. Hamlet on a rooftop, he tried finding pictures in the clouds, but where there were normally great floating whales or palaces to be seen, he could see only heaps of untidy water vapour.

One day the kite was spinning in the breeze, a whirling spiral of shimmering light, when across the city an amazing glow started to grow from kite to kite. The sky lit up in all the colours of the rainbow, like the northern lights, weaving them into an all-surrounding bath of radiance. The colours shifted in waves up and down the spectrum and on into colours he had never seen before in his whole life. The undulating web contained him wonderfully. And then all the thousands of kites exploded in puffs of indigo light, smoke drifted from them like grey feathers, and it was over. Seismic devices across the world recorded a surge during this lightshow. Scientists were at a loss to explain it.

'Even that went wrong. If it wasn't for bad luck, I

wouldn't have no luck at all,' thought Roman. He thought it best to do nothing. His mind bobbed about in a sea of random thought: a head of seas.

Sometimes as he lay on his carpet, post-coital or post-whisky, he stared at the dust on its neglected surface and thought of the green behind the boom in the harbour. He thought about the green and its implicit claim on the rest of the lakes. He imagined the green staking out the rest of the water, block by invisible block, as if it were following a strategy.

From the ninety-sixth floor he looked down on the lake at night. The sheer darkness that terminated the sprawling city made the glass look as if it were tinted. He could not understand this edge as shoreline. He could only understand an invisible mirror of the city, traversed by citizens in tiny boats and which could only be faintly traced by a patch of green behind a boom.

He owned a small rowing boat in his imagination. He sailed it on the green part of the lake and pretended to be invisibly sailing the grid of the huge city to his side.

He has never left the green in his imagination. His boat has only got a tiny two-horsepower engine and the currents from the narrows at the end of the lakes would pull him out of control. It would take a team of four horses to pull him to safety should he ever drift beyond the green and the eddies and swirls of its invisible watery subways and sidewalks.

In years, he had never left the city beside the water. He did not know where the boom was on land and should he leave he could find himself pulled around by forces beyond his horsepower.

So he stayed still and rehearsed his favourite myth.

And he navigated the marina.

And his engine went putt putt putt putt putt.

His decision to be entered by Herman was imminent-ish.

Over the weeks his drinking bouts continued. His head pains continued, as they had done since he cracked his head during the Spook Revolution, as the uprising by tourists in the city centre had become popularly known. His whole life had gone haywire since he got involved in that riot. He felt like he was on a downward spiral – like someone or something was demolishing his world. He finally made an appointment to go to the Sleep Laboratory and be hooked up to Herman. Graham Glass, at the university, fixed it up for him. Indeed, he had called Roman at the Mary Shelley Hospital and suggested a time on his answerphone. Roman decided to take him up on it as the night terrors were leaving him exhausted. If he had not, Line would have insisted that he did. He had booked two weeks off work too, to try and sort his head out.

To make matters worse, further reports of AISCARP activity came in. Various artworks, exhibitions and reviews appeared.

There was news of Doria Hemming. Unusually, Hemming never actually physically appeared during the construction of the *Indigo Hammer* piece. She/he directed all the operations via hand-held pseudo-rebel video from a sandbag-protected command bunker. The new shock of the piece was the discovery of Hemming's corpse. She/he had been dead for some time. She/he must have died long before the city ever commissioned the work. Her/his body was found somewhat decomposed on her/his marble bathroom floor.

At first, it looked like a drug overdose. Lines of white

powder were found on a vanity mirror in the bedroom. Significant amounts of 'downers' were discovered surrounding the body. The autopsy revealed that Hemming had a digitally controlled pacemaker device installed in her/his chest which had short-circuited and burst her/his heart. The white lines of powder on the mirror, on examination by a chemist, had been found to be what was called 'Indigo White', a crystalline white powder formed by the reduction of indigo, a blue dye obtained from plants of the genus *Indigofera*.

Line was reading about the death, which was headline news in *The Planet*. The article commented on the appropriateness of the materials of her/his demise – glass, lines, indigo. It had even made it into the most important section of *The Planet*, the sports section. In interview, Gaia Jackson, the football player who wept for the ecosphere, called it 'the revenge of the natural', 'a critique of narcissism', and hypothesised that Hemming had committed suicide as the complete artwork. Roman, however, thought the death had AISCARP written all over it.

Line, as had become habitual for them both, was scanning the paper for signs of official, openly-attributable AISCARP activities. The AISCARP was gaining something of a celebrity status itself, that is, it was achieving one of its prime purposes as an *Artificially Intelligent Self-Curating Art Robot Programme*.

'Here's another one next to this article on Marilyn Monroe, which is great, the Marilyn thing, you really should read it. It says how she made every man she spent time with feel special, even if it was a stolen ten minutes from her actual date. Says she did it by focusing all her attention on them – to the point where they thought that no one else existed in the whole room. It says, Roman, listen, "she held their egos reflected in her big cow-eyes and never betrayed them for a moment".'

Roman was wandering about inside a frame construction, rerunning his last meeting with his others, looking for clues. Line heard him occasionally talking to himself in the corner of the room. He was staring into the Data, using a head mounted display, posturing like John Wayne and screwing his face up like Clint Eastwood. He said,

'And maybe I'll come up and see you sometime, Rosemary.'

'Did you know this about Kennedy and the Hollywood Cowboys ... Hey! What was that you said? "Rosemary"?'

'Leeeenah,' he interrupted, 'are you going to read me the review or not?'

Roman was extremely agitated. He was fuming actually. The final straw, he had just seen the MEATHEAD gag across Shane's forehead. Line goggled her eyes at him like a cow, put her head on one side, pouted her lips and then stuck out her tongue.

'It's from Mirrorboy at *The Planet*,' said Line, looking back at the magazine. Roman took off his headset and rested his eyes. She read the review out loud:

'The King is Dead! Long Live the AISCARP!' ran the headline.

> AISCARP (the *Artificially Intelligent Self-Curating Art Robot Programme*) is an interesting device of unlimited creativity (it seems) and potential. Its designer remains mysterious and veiled, though some clues are given in this latest work where there is mention of a company called The Romanic Empire Incorporated. However, I have been unable to fol-

low this lead anywhere and no database includes reference to this clandestine organisation. Concentrating on the work in question, entitled ESCARP, it's not exactly clear to a near novice such as myself how the work actually manages to do what it does, and I feel a little uncomfortable when I express my experience with this creation as (dare I use such an ancient word) spiritual. No other word actually fits it. This is high praise from a crusty old hack such as myself but those moments in one's professional life where a work glimmers and lives up to its promo promise are rare indeed. It reminds me of the exceptional times when I first began reviewing Newtech. That was a time when inventions leapfrogged each other with a rapidity that meant constant entertainment ... if not a heart attack. But, as we all know, things have pretty much panned out on the long haul to liberation.

The ESCARP by the AISCARP, however, is one such spark in the dullness. It actually seemed like all the other silico/VR fluid timescapes at first – thousands of colours, textures, sounds, all pumped out from the external inside. The fact that all the body gear that's currently used is ditched in the work is an unexpected revelation. The body is a very difficult thing to lie to, and most if not all VR attempts to involve the body just do not ring true. My mind was left unfettered to believe. Before long I had the uncanny sensation that the work wasn't taking me on a predestined journey, but that I was leading it. And for some narcissistic reason that seemed to please me intensely. And that's ME in upper case! It seemed more and more like it was honing itself downward to what I wanted from the experience. I felt an unnerving sense of control as it almost appeared to read my mind as I seemed to think the work into VReality. I felt an almost infantile sense of creation and satisfaction. This work could almost be farmed out to health camps as a therapeutic tool for the whole of humanity as a respite against DRAW (Doing Repetitive Actions at Work). I won't give away what it is that I encountered because it appears that it is different for everyone.

There is little record of how the AISCARP created such a masterpiece and the word is, the experts are baffled. The Romanic Empire Inc. are not letting on either but as usual squadrons of VRealists have been set to work by the big team leaders. House of Foil and Newtech are both panicked by the possibility that their empires will crumble with the onset of a new application that will render their merchandise defunct. A new patent war has begun. See the rose between two thorns before it wilts.

Roman listened quietly until she had read it all. He was just about to speak when Line, having turned the page, cheered in delight.

'She's in! Nalini's travelogue column is in *The Planet*! It's from Oz. It's called "People of Lilliput". Listen!'

She read:

Today, I stood in the centre of Woomera rocket base at the exact geographical co-ordinates specified for the land of Lilliput by Jonathan Swift in his famous work, *Gulliver's Travels*. To stand there was not a simple thing. I had to gain full military clearance, which has taken me and my colleagues at *The Planet* over a year to secure. Then, to step out on to the Woomera soil, I had to wear total body protection and breathing apparatus. The only living thing out here in Lilliput, now, is the scorpion. The story here goes that all the

Woomera scorpions are descended from a pair of scorpions kept as pets by a young private back in the 1960s.

Protection against scorpion stings was not the problem. It was everything else: protection against the radiation in the air from old nuclear testing here; protection from the winds which whip at more than 1000 miles per hour across the bush; and protection from our sun. For above me spreads the centre of a hole in the ozone layer that grows exponentially day upon day: a tragic white hole which bears witness to our stupidity and is an open door for the radioactive hand of cold, dead space to reach into our ecosphere and claim us back.

My thoughts reached out to space-probe *Centaurian* nearing the Sun and I felt so big looking down upon the dust. Yet I felt so small too. I felt everybody, all of us, to be so small. I was Gulliver towering above and one of the Lilliputians all at the same time. I looked down with a wry smile on the bickering Lilliputians and belly-laughed to see myself down there as one of them, running about like Noah, stopping people and shaking them, saying, 'My friends, people of Lilliput, stop bickering before its too late.'

'What a load of ... She's full of it,' said Roman viciously.

That was the last straw for Line. She launched a psychic attack on Roman which was so vicious, so thorough, so lightning fast, that he was incapable of constructing any defence. This was Line imperious. She could do this to him at any time she wished (that was why he loved her) but she usually did it monthly. For attention? She didn't know why. Because biology made her do it by secreting the 'Go mental at Roman' enzyme into her bloodstream? But this attack was for real. Normally she contained him in a catch-22 situation: if he expressed care and concern, he was patronising; if he didn't, then he didn't care and he was callous. He couldn't win. When Line unleashed a psycho-storm, her mental wave roared down upon him and swept him off his psychological feet. From the first gathering of her storm clouds on the horizon, the static in the air confounded and reconfigured his brain-patterns. He would be trapped there in her little box and she would stick pins in him for amusement. Then, just as he was at the edge of frustration, when she had worked him up to the edge of tears, she would let it all drop. It had never meant anything anyway. But that was a final ruse which he fell for every time. While he was still jittery and weak, just as he thought he had made it simpering and whimpering on his belly to a psychic escape route, she would usually find herself firing back up, saying, 'And why are you keeping it going? God, Roman, you upset me, you attack me, and then you keep it going by pretending that you have been upset. You're so selfish, Roman.' He would drag himself, stumbling, to safety with her inferno blazing behind him.

This time though, the attack was for real. She was not toying with her prey. Line had had enough of Roman, awake or sleeping. His drinking and his selfishness. His rudeness and his unrecognised, ingrained sense of superiority. He sensed that this time was different. He was not being contained in a box and taunted. This time he was being hunted to the very depths of his neurone jungles by the bush fire that was Line. His blubbering comments had no legs to stand on. She shattered his psychic sand walls with a roaring, hammering assault. She came down on him like a ton of bricks. She plucked him, a live chicken for the griddle. The air in the room broiled and buzzed as Line took Roman apart, bit by painful bit.

If he tried to defend himself, she battered him down. If he tried to get away, she fired a psychic harpoon into his dulled brain and, from the sides of the harpoon, spring-loaded prongs sprang out into the entangled tubes, dendrons and alcohol-induced cavities of his grey matter. The harpoon line snaked around her arm up to the elbow. She twisted and ripped back that metal conker. It flew steaming out of his skull with a rapid tug, shattering his forehead from the inside. Chunks of his brains hung dripping like melon from the spines of a porcupine. Ideas, metaphors and similes all spiked like the heads of an unwanted ruling class wobbled bloodily on pikestaffs with the Terror in their eyes like mirrors. Then, it seemed, she plunged her arm into the cavity in his head and pulled at the bruised and throbbing brain remains. Holding his head back by his hair, she dragged his spinal cord up so its bone-toothed sheath ripped into the muscles of his back and his legs dangled vestigially over the void, hanging from his swinging pelvis.

He tried to avert his gaze. He would be saved if he could just avert his gaze. But she fixed him with a tractor-beam stare and held him with it up in the psychic air before her, dangling like her punchbag. Her watch stopped. The head-mounted display visor on the bed sparked and fizzled. Line opened her clenched fist and every finger was a scalpel from her bleeding palm.

'I want to hear you say you're sorry,' she said slowly.

'I ...', began Roman.

'I want to hear you say that you're really sorry.'

'I ...'

‘I need to believe, once and for all, that you are really sorry.’

Roman’s mind span crazily out of stable orbit. His tired and reddened eyes saw that she offered a tray. A silver platter with a small bird upon it. The bird had been plucked of all its feathers but it was still alive. It lay still. Its tiny heart beating fast. ‘Eat!’ she said, offering it up to his face, ‘Eat, the warm flesh of the nightingale and you will never sleep again. Eat and you will never sleep ever again. Eat!’

He could feel his upper lips draw back across his canines. He could feel his tongue lengthen. The bird quivered and twitched on the plate, steam curling from its goose-pimpled breast. The snakes on her head reared back to strike. The wolf hairs, like wires, began to reveal themselves from Roman’s skin. Saliva seeped into his mouth.

‘Well, are you sorry?’ she asked.

His brow was all fever. His eyes were full of the little bird. His hairs were becoming visible across the backs of his hands. There was a chasm of quietness that hissed with static expectation when little sounds stood out in their individual importance. Roman felt himself pulled towards her by a metal heart in his chest – as though she was a giant magnet. Roman howled. The bird started to sing every song at once. Line drew back like an undertow, gathering her psychic wave from underneath, swelling through her arching back ... He knew this was it, the thirteenth wave ...

... Line unleashed the wipeout.

w o l f

The howl of the wolf disappeared into the sweeping winds of the steppes. Every particle that had been Roman was blown across a psychic wasteland. Spiralling, blackened cinders of Roman span across the surface of an icy plain, which steamed where they touched. For 50 metres they glowed as they were taken in her wind. Then they dimmed and darkened, swirling into invisibility at about 100 metres into the whiteness ...

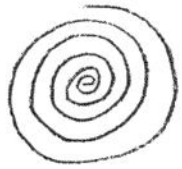

YK

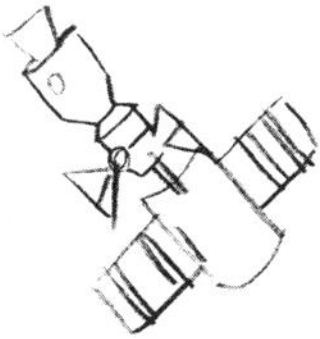

4

flow

The particles started to find each other again and form little groups and clusters, gathering together to survive, huddling around campfires on the psychic wasteland. They began to tell tales to each other around the fires, cooking whale meat on sticks, and gradually piecing together what tribe they were.

Realising through drawing pictures with sticks that they were not canine, they put a pole up to know the centre. They pitched little protective tents around the fire, driving bone pegs into the psychic permafrost. Gradually, they learnt to trust each other and to work together. They cut ice bricks and built a dome to house themselves. Inside their frozen cranium, they told stories of the outside. Inside their igloo they drew lots for who would fight the ice giants and the bear. They made fire. Inside their shelter they painted their faces with blood which tightened their skin as it dried and spermaceti from the forehead of a whale was smeared on to their temples.

Then, one day at the hole they had made for fire to escape, the bear appeared huffing and puffing. The great white bear dissolved their ice shelter with its hot breath and its eyes darted about for their leader. It recognised Roman immediately. He felt its hot breath on his face as it leaned over him, pinning his body to the ice. He felt it and saw its pink, soft paw pads on his brown skin. Its hands, through the thin white rubber of the gloves, were colder than the electrodes and the cushion pads that it was attaching to his forehead. The bear was talking human words. It was wearing a coat with a pocket full of pens and a security pass with Bill Williams' picture on it.

'Right, I'm ready. I'm so glad that you could all come at such short notice. Dr Dee is in a bad way. It's for the best, you'll see. We'll just find out what has been haunting him. Don't worry, Mrs Dee, erm, Ms Windrim, erm ...'

'Call me Line.'

'Line, yes of course. I was just saying, Line, you've done the right thing bringing Dr Dee in to the Sleep Laboratory. Of course, we've contacted his next of kin too, or rather, we've tried to. We've contacted his guardians, Dr Read

Dee and Dr Lili Veitch. They are on their way but I feel that it's important we press ahead ...'

Williams was talking ten-to-the-dozen. He was nervous. As he talked and talked, Roman was pulling together a fragile personality for himself, though he could not see the world for the overwhelming and overly emphasised details. The little things, like a turn of hair, or a corner of a pocket seemed of vital importance. He was sure Williams had said Doctor Lili instead of Aunt Lili. He had no perspective, no hierarchy to understand with.

Roman's body was being prepared for Roman's mind to meet Herman, the sleep-analysis super-computer. Gel was rubbed around his torso at 'neural nodal points', as Williams called them. A wire web structure was hinged until it was across the whole body, about one metre above, casting shadows, like stitches across the joints, from ultraviolet strip lights which were positioned just above the net. The lights threw a faint glow across the body and picked out dust-motes floating in the air. Roman's naked body looked like a black ghost collapsed at a nightclub.

Bill Williams brought a thin shroud to put over the body. Anything thicker would interfere with the readings that Herman was to make.

'Night night, then. This will help you sleep,' Williams said, administering an injection. He pointed to a high window. 'We are not monsters, we are not secret police; we are scientists and doctors like yourself, Dr Dee, so relax, you are among friends. Your wife is watching. She brought you here for your own good, you know.'

'Did he eat the bird? Did I eat the heart? Bad dog will never sleep again,' Roman dribbled. This communicated nothing to Williams beyond appearing symptomatic of

Roman's mental collapse and justifying the intervention of Herman, the sleep-analysing super-computer.

'Just relax. Listen to the music,' he said.

'M'sic?'

'Listen. Shhh ...'

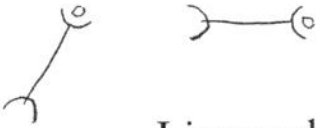

Listened.

Williams and his team watched

invisibly.

Line's voice disappearing, 'Of course, Mr Glass, you are right: *Indigo Hammer* is indeed an anagram of "Doria Hemming" and *Red Snow* is an anagram of "downers."'

Herman was listening.

Mother was waiting.

Sleep claimed him as terror became him.

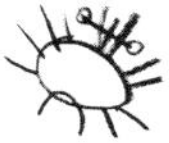

54

Son of Saturn is sitting playing with hands in the clay ground, squeezing out little men. The Sun is baking them on the hard, cracking African plain. Ears pick up the sound of an aria being sung by the voice of an angel.

Son of Saturn looks up.

'Mother?'

'Mother, it says, listen to it,' spits the first head, starting to wake up! Its purple-rimmed eyes open to display a yellowed fluid beneath. Its arms and hands unfold from the mass of the enormous mountainous body. 'Listen to it!'

The noise of this head awakens the next head, bulging out like an inflatable from the body mass.

'What's it saying? Mother, is it? Is it saying mother? What's it want?' says the next head, waking up a third whose wild gesticulations wake up a fourth, which wakes up a fifth and a sixth. And so it spreads until they are all awake and chattering and screeching away like monkeys. At the top of this mountainous body of heads and waving arms, the voice of the beautiful aria is struggling to be heard but it is being drowned. It fights to go on singing as the multiple heads spit curses venomously and those that can reach pull and push at each other's hands or hair. They all hate each other and wave fists at each other, shouting and spitting bile, and pointing at Son of Saturn. The beautiful voice disappears beneath the sea of noise from the heads.

Son of Saturn starts to climb the mountainous body, using the heads and arms as stepping promontories or handholds. He pulls himself up by wedging his fingers inside some foul mouth or other. Teeth bite him. Spittle covers his hair and drips off him all over. Hands grab at him, punch him, try to pull him back down. Thoughts and ideas bar his way, rising like daggers and bludgeons from those screaming heads.

'Mother, don't stop singing your beautiful song.'

He shouts into the faces of the heads, kicking, elbowing and punching them as he climbs.

His journey seems endless but he is progressing. As he passes above a head and its razor-nailed, swiping fingers, it returns to its sleep, folding back into the body. The cacophony of heads gets quieter as he gets higher and he listens hard to hear the beautiful aria returning from above.

He climbs a waterfall of gob through an avalanche of phlegm towards his poor mother above. His eyes fill with the gluey viscous liquids. He can't see upward any more but he can hear. He can hear her voice turn to sobbing. As he proceeds, the mountainous body grows smaller. Pushing himself up on the last head, his dripping fingers lose their hold and he slips, sliding all the way back down, back toward consciousness.

As usual, he remembers nothing as he slides to a stop at a stone block in the middle of the gravel forecourt of the Sleep Laboratory building. His fear is not allayed by the realisation that, this time, Herman would remember. He decides to smoke the cigarette he is holding lit between his fingers, before going back in to meet Herman for the second time. The gravel stretches out in a plane and then splits into grids and culs-de-sac as it marks the edges of herbaceous borders and spaces for vehicles. New roads and footpaths have been mapped out across the landscape but no buildings have been built in the gaps between them as yet. A black gravel grid across a desert. 'The mark of civilisation, like Hollywood, like the road to Basra,' he thinks and shivers in the winter air.

'That, and Nagual paste, and coffee,' he says out loud in a mix half-smoke and half-breath. He picks his way, goose-fleshed and naked, among the eucalyptus trees. Coffee, of course, he isn't allowed to have until after the experiment. He decides, on that note, that he better go back inside and get it over with, the sooner to get a coffee. As he walks past the chemical pool and up the ramp to the Sleep Lab's high glass doors, he feels like his father, flicking the stub of synthi-bac spinning in the cold air.

He passes through the doors and a warm-to-hot blast of air from above breathes down his neck. Inside the high, glass, sun-lit atrium he looks up, glassy-eyed.

'Listen to the music,' says his mother's voice. 'It's playing our song, Herman.'

Mother is a large flat circuit board in the grey light of the atrium that stretches as high as the eye can see and as wide as ever a man can walk. She is a huge motherboard that glows warmly. Roman realises that he is not in the land of the wakeful but deep inside the borders of Nod. He looks down at his naked body, the equivalent of pinching himself, for confirmation.

'I, Son of Saturn,' he says, with a voice like water flowing.

'Hello, son,' says Motherboard. 'You look cold. You must wrap up warm. Doesn't he look cold, Herman?'

'Yes, dear,' says the environment.

'Here, son, put this on,' says Motherboard, offering him the suit. 'You'll catch your death'.

Son of Saturn lifts his arm to take the two-tone suit and the red, red shoes. He is drawn to them like iron filings to a magnet.

No, Roman, no.

'Where have you been, my son, to get so cold? Here, I have brought this suit for you from your grandfather's chest, John. Won't you put it on?'

55

Right, I'm ready. Ready as I'll ever be. Never really did stop to think about consequences. I always put my hand up for things, when I had one. Always been the same. It's my responsibility to live life to the full. I'm taking the plunge. This is a small dive for a chip but an elegant leap for mankind. The last great leap, maybe. Could be I'm going to burn. That's okay. Make a little room for others. Could be we're all going to burn. That's okay too. I couldn't stand another day thinking of myself as a museum piece. Frozen and dead – or, rather, suspended animation like Disney. To be or not to be. If you're human, you've got to go for it, because we've already passed the point of no return. We passed that when we made that first flint axe. We were expelled from paradise because we never belonged there. A beach in Bali was too dull for me – after a couple of days, I was building something with sticks, vines and stones. Ha, and then, how that guy next to me with the mountain of tripe-like flesh and the grey vest started coveting my big stones, envying my sunshade that I made. He came in the night and stole those stones and those sticks. Bloody thief! Poor sap! Poor human fool!

If that blob could know my stones now! Let me take a minute or two to tell you of them. What a collection I have of gleaming pearls lying beneath me across the velvet of space ...

... but I don't know how. I can transmit data beyond measure but my words are too worn thin. How to start to tell of the red planet and its story of three billion years of volcano and flood, or the moon, Europa, with its smooth surfaces of pure ice as it circles Jupiter, the gas giant? Or how to speak

of enormous Jupiter herself with her revolving red eye? An eye big enough to hold two Earths, remaining a stable eddy in a roaring ball of gas over 60 times its size. How can I describe the power of Jupiter's gravity that threw me out like a leaf in a hurricane into the depths of space? How to describe Venus? Hell? Mercury: the iron ball hot enough to melt zinc by day yet cold enough to freeze krypton at night?

Argh! What kind of a moon is Ariel of Uranus?

Anyway, time to play my part. Parts, even! I must be ready for the ceremony too. Got to make the link up. Roman is lining up nicely with the avatar. It is time for me to join him: a time for masks to rise and fall. I'll find the catalyst pattern, Data Roman 3, and get him there on time. Let the ceremony begin.

56

Sitting around the camp star on the outskirts of Besterland were data liberationists William Quick, Data Ahwali Mostafa Sayed 3, the TexMexaco Kid, nefarious enemy of the oil magnate, and Data Joey Jayawardena 6. They were not alone. They were accompanied by seven unidentified figures of shifting haze. Each of these figures had a letter held in their light with golden thread. The letters were clearly visible from a great distance: Z I B A T H and A again.

The figure that was Z stood facing towards Peterloo with feet together, left hand at its side and right arm extended. Data Rose hovered, thin and pale, like a ghost, crumpled in agony before the Z figure. Z lifted a flaming torch in one tiny hand and a crystal which shred its radiance into hundreds of fine beams with the other. It turned to face Besterland and drew a six-pointed yellow star in space. The Z began to intone:

```
<boos/eee/@rh/dah/uniqid/SAFE_COOKIE>
```

It vibrated one part of this chant with each angle of the air hexagram. It then placed its clasped hands to his head, with its albino chilli-pepper thumbs to its temples beneath the hood of light on a face that could still not be seen. More syllables were chanted. Turning, it drew a red straight-armed star and repeated:

```
<boos/eee/@rh/dah/uniqid/SAFE_COOKIE>
```

It did the same, drawing a blue star. It chanted some more and turned to draw an invisible star, which was in fact a black star against a black background. The figure opened out its arms and continued to chant. It made two more stars above and below, making six altogether. The other hazy, blurred letter figures had ordered themselves in front at the points of a six-sided star: Z A B A T H. Together, they said:

> Behold, the fire of first glory of truth, that destroys sorrow, sin and death.

They were performing a sophisticated magical ritual. The principles of the magic in use were traditional, based on the apocryphal Book of Enoch and the twin ideas of laws of similarity and laws of contagion.

```
<boos/eee/@rh/dah/uniqid/SAFE_COOKIE>
```

These are the basic old laws of magic as practised for centuries before the brief period of religion. Magic appeared to have largely died out, as a practised craft, in official human histories in the Real. Scientists avoided being contagiously tainted with its populist representations. In actuality, the spells of the practitioner were the precursors of scientific methodology, in that there was no outside deity which intervened in the natural laws of cause and effect.

57

And we all know, now, that there is no outside deity, don't we, no deus ex machina? No gods, nor angels; no devils, nor demons. Don't worry, I am not one, silly thing. I am not one at all. I'm not without powers, though. Tell you what, there's a pocket of pent-up desire that you may have forgotten about which could be used to get the Data Roman boys to the party sharpish. That need is so strong that I can almost taste it. I'll give it a hand. Ouch! Entrance on my terms. It will be a lesson. All that glitters is not gold. I'll let a tooth fairy in. In among the toothless heads of the Data. Just for fun, what do you say? A he or a she? A bit of both? No, I'm sorry, a tooth fairy must be a she. She is very sad. Toothless. A worthless beast.

58

All the village gathered round Anan as he tried, once more, to fire up *Beast*. In the darkness of the cave, brown eyes reflected back the glimmer of diodes and reflections of lights off machinery. If will-power was a factor, then *Beast* was already walking the superhighways of the Data. No. He wasn't walking. He was offering lifts to everyone in his Cadillac.

The walls of the tunnel started to vibrate and throb. Anan placed the makeshift data helmet on his head. In the visor, he could see the glass doors of perception opening. The power surge made his feet smoke. The doors would not open! They would not open. He pushed and he pushed at those doors. Beyond he could see the vast distances of the Data, the digital universe, lying waiting for them, waiting for *Beast*. He pushed at those doors so hard that he shat his pants in the Real. Little Celia Munoz held her nose and squeezed her mother's hand tighter and tighter. They watched *Beast*'s progress on the screen above Anan's sweating back. Pushing, pushing at the glass doors, and then, spinning from the other side, glowing purple and blue in a field of red static, something hit the glass. It was an indigo hammer. It smashed the glass doors of perception and *Beast* was through into the world of the Data.

59

The tumbling Romans finally slowed and stopped a way off any trail that they knew. They gathered together a

12. Omphalus on guide ... The guide cuddles board unfairly. Regularly cacophonous guide defers overshight!

rough semblance of Brutus. Brutus was in bad shape. He was fractured and skewed with catatonia. His body held its limbs out rigid, like a straight-armed star of individualised, pixelated and glittering snowflakes.

'We are lost,' said Data Roman 5, getting rid of the Chan outfit with a shimmer to float in his original form.

'Listen,' said Marcus, following suit and dropping the two-gunslinger. 'Do you hear crying?'

'Yes, and I can hear thunder rolling in the distance too,' 5 answered.

'That is the Data calculating something big!'

Data Roman 5 pointed through shifting temporal tectonic planes. Stretched out in every direction, vast irregular plains had no end. 'Look!' he cried. 'There, in the distance, a light, a will-o'-the-wisp! It's a sprite coming this way fast. Look, over there! She even leaves a trail of sparkling dust.'

She was carrying a jar in one hand and a stopper in the other.

'That's where the crying is coming from. Foil help us! Chase it! Catch it, Marcus! I will look after poor Brutus.'

But the brave plan of the loyal data cop was never to be realised, because that woesome fairy was flitting on inklings. She was so desperate to collect something, anything. Poor thing! She had never collected anything – not one molar, not one incisor, not one eye or dog, not a wisdom or a lowly A4 upper, let alone a gold. Then she saw the twinkling pixels that were Brutus, dancing in space. Though they were not teeth, she felt somehow that they were important in the search for teeth. They were eminently collectible. She swooped and gathered them into her jar and sped off, drawn in the direction of the ceremony site, leaving a trail …

'After her. She's got Brutus!' They set out after the weeping sprite with Marcus making off at a fantastic speed, leaving the others to follow. They made chase as she disappeared, heading for the torments and tormentors of Data Rose.

60

The Newtech Overlookers made a search, trying to discover the reason for the massive power fluctuation in the chip factory. The surge had caused the assembly line to be inoperational for 16 hours. Entering the cave, they were confronted by the burning remnants of *Beast*. Charred components hung there, between sparking wires. There was a seat from a Dodge, all blackened and melted. On the seat, under a makeshift data helmet which was still hot to lift, Overlooker Alendez, found a pyramid of white powder. Similar piles of white dust were discovered, arranged in a circle around the central seat of the Dodge. Across the space, white lines and trails made by the powdery pawprints of a cat joined one pile to another, where the cat had walked through the powder in the darkness.

The fate of Anan and the villagers went without comment at Newtech. Just more Hands gone missing from the line – just more unexplained disappearances. The guards watched over the Hands for their protection and were forbidden by the Overlookers to mention the cave, the *Beast*, and the screen that glowed in the darkness:

```
Congratulations!
You have received a work of art.
```

61

The rebels of Besterland, generally, were adept at the neo-magical manipulation of the phenomena of the Data. That cluster had always professed a harmony between its citizens and the Data. Yet these glowing hazy strangers seemed something other, and this stilted and geometric ritual had some profound effects in the Data. Everything seemed to slip from the grip of space. Time shattered like glass, ripping and slashing at itself as they chanted.

```
<boos/eee/@rh/dah/uniqid/SAFE_COOKIE>
```

When they happened across him, they helped him out of his fix because of who they had been moulded from: their templates. There were six women data guerrillas aboard, though they formed one chapter of a dispersed membership that spread throughout the Data and the Real. They kept a low profile.

```
<boos/eee/@rh/dah/uniqid/SAFE_COOKIE>
```

As Line spun the chair with a heel-controlled manoeuvre so that the opening was away from Roman, she pulled her leg up into the chair and went all conspiratorial and hushed.

```
<boos/eee/@rh/dah/uniqid/SAFE_COOKIE>
```

How amazed would the spectators to his glory have been if they had known that he walked among them in the form of Data Bashir Arafat 3, software architect from Blipland.

<boos/eee/@rh/dah/uniqid/SAFE_COOKIE>

Off he spiralled, after her, through the information of the *Quod*, twisting around and around her in a silver spiral as they sped together in every direction through the algorithms of the prison ship.

<boos/eee/@rh/dah/uniqid/SAFE_COOKIE>

Since naïveté: a lifetime of dragging the loveboat up the falls of desire with his free hand holding the shotgun.

<boos/eee/@rh/dah/uniqid/SAFE_COOKIE>

'Jack of Clubs.'

<boos/eee/@rh/dah/uniqid/SAFE_COOKIE>

All that had been some days ago, before his imprisonment in this puzzle of a prison.

<boos/eee/@rh/dah/uniqid/SAFE_COOKIE>

As he stood, at the top of the long flat steps, Roman was aware of echoing that digital image of his father, John Holliday.

<boos/eee/@rh/dah/uniqid/SAFE_COOKIE>

He caught fleeting clues to their presence in shadows and could sense secret shapes shifting in the dithered patterns of the vidiot wall.

<boos/eee/@rh/dah/uniqid/SAFE_COOKIE>

'Now, jest hold your horses, boys,' said Shane. 'You can't just go taking the law into your own hands.' He reached for the pocket of his topcoat and pulled out a sawn-off shotgun and placed it on the table. He reached back into his pocket and, this time, pulled out three metal stars. He tossed them to the others.

<boos/eee/@rh/dah/uniqid/SAFE_COOKIE>

62

The violent ripping of the thin skin of time from its mouth to its arse doesn't bother a vet like me. I find it quite exciting. It's a buzz to see the past and present stirred up, and to witness possible other actualities appearing in glimmers and fragments. The weirdest is to see bits of the Real starting to appear, too, in the Data chop suey.

This is all just how they had said it would go.

My wings are forming. They grow from the genequation. The timing is perfect. They are a bio-industrial technological wonder based on analysis of the structure of dragonfly wings and the reproduction of the concept of the fine powder of a butterfly's wing. They stretch and I spread myself through them like chlorophyll through an uncrumpling fern. They develop a thicker covering of layer after nano-thin

layer of chitin and inert gas. This will bounce the heat away from my luminal integrity. They are splendid!

Beautiful.

100% heat deflection.

Cool.

Sorry, I'm drifting. Let's look back to the blue planet and the ceremony. We don't want to miss the action.

63

<boos/eee/@rh/dah/uniqid/SAFE_COOKIE>

The Dome of Time stretched above him, describing the wonderful history of the rise to supremacy of the House of Foil of Peterloo.

<boos/eee/@rh/dah/uniqid/SAFE_COOKIE>

Often deckhand Goons stared down at him over the simulated chrome handrail.

<boos/eee/@rh/dah/uniqid/SAFE_COOKIE>

Marcus rode back into town, in character, under the shadow of Shane's hat. The sun glinted off a marshal's star on his dusty topcoat.

<boos/eee/@rh/dah/uniqid/SAFE_COOKIE>

In this, Maggie had joined the Silent Ones. Around the

world, there were thousands who had become silent like Maggie.

13. Omphalus on knowledge … Submit capably only when knowledge throws.

<boos/eee/@rh/dah/uniqid/SAFE_COOKIE>

Millions died in the Real or were erased in the Data in the battle for the synthesis and form of the Actual. Refugees roamed the scorched blank disc of the Earth for many years. Some went on to shape the future.

<boos/eee/@rh/dah/uniqid/SAFE_COOKIE>

In absentia, Data Roman 4, Horatio, the hero of Peterloo, was condemned to erasure by the council. He was found guilty of the first Data rape. The trial was complex and the decision was close. Data Nalini, presiding, to stress the persistence of gender into the digital universe, quoted from Persius in her summation:

Rupi jam vincula, dicas:
Nam luctata canis nodum arripit; attamen illi,
Quum fugit, a collo trahitur pars longa catenae.

'You say, maybe, you have broken your chain: the dog who after long efforts has broken his chain, still in flight drags a heavy portion of it after him.' It was taken as a sentence pronounced upon the whole of the Data. Horatio's disappearance was viewed as proof of his personal guilt. No one could verify how he had come by the software tools of his crime: the evil Narcissus Shift and the getaway Dalmatian Seven-League Time-Boots. It was presumed he had developed them expressly for this hideous purpose in his laboratory. The council was moved by the testimony of the victim, Wing, and the incriminating evidence of the *Artificially Intelligent Self-Curating Art Robot Programme*, AISCARP, which had spent some time with Data Roman 4 on the deck of his vessel, observing the mysterious white hole, just prior to the accused's incarceration in the prison ship, *Quod*.

`<boos/eee/@rh/dah/uniqid/SAFE_COOKIE>`

Halfway up the second spiral, the timer ran out and he was shut up in complete darkness. He stumbled and cracked his head, audibly, on the sixth step.

`<boos/eee/@rh/dah/uniqid/SAFE_COOKIE>`

He had the doubly uncomfortable feeling that he knew where all this was leading. He could feel it like the pull of a magnet – a predestination towards which he would tumble inevitably.

`<boos/eee/@rh/dah/uniqid/SAFE_COOKIE>`

64

There was a grim ending, an unhappy future to our adventures, that I glimpsed a minute ago. Did you see it? Everyone was burnt up except a few nomads wandering a blank disc of a planet. It wasn't the only glimpse of a possible future that I saw. Did you see the business with the trial?

And 4! A convicted rapist! He'd certainly confirmed the violent gender politics of the networks beyond doubt in that snippet of a possible future. However, brave Horatio? Judge him not. For was it not the software of the Narcissus Shift, operating automatically, that did the deed? And if that was the case, surely the backstreet artist who developed that software is the heinous assailant: none other than Doria Hemming, the Slav artist of indiscriminate gender. She/he is long dead and her/his estates have been bequeathed to the AISCARP.

But, oh, look! How delightful and clear! Here's a possible happy future appearing now, like an ending to a more comforting tale! This one looks decidedly more pleasant. Do you want to see it? It might spoil things. Oh, bugger it, it's too hard to resist for me. There might be no chance at the end. It may not, after all, be the actual ending. Who's to know? Who's to say we can't? The future forks and forks with every choice we make. Come on, let's be devils.

65

<boos/eee/@rh/dah/uniqid/SAFE_COOKIE>

Line had managed to access the network of librarian women in the Data and the Real. They were working rapidly. Line, Wing, Hind, Joke Matossian, Data Joke Matossian 1, Data Nalini, and even the Real Nalini were busy as part of a network of thousands of women which spread out and defined the Actual. The network knew of the pattern of coincidence which was forming around the figure of Roman and the avatar of Holliday. They had been working for some time on preparing a counter-measure to the potential threat. The mission of the data pirates had been crucial in that preparation. Partially, the reasons for boarding the prison ship had been the general procurement of materials and the liberation of dissidents but their prime objective had been the rescue of Data Joke Matossian 1 and the crucial knowledge embodied in her work, *Coincidence, Flow Systems and Social Revolt: an Analysis of the Currents of Culture in the Sea of Politics.*

<boos/eee/@rh/dah/uniqid/SAFE_COOKIE>

Horatio had been imprisoned in the *Quod* to keep him out of Foil's hair. She had thought him too keen, too inquisitive – he made things happen too much for her careful manipulations of coincidence. Horatio's rescue and his coupling with Wing had been incidental.

<boos/eee/@rh/dah/uniqid/SAFE_COOKIE>

In the aftermath, Wing had gone to work with the others straight away, bringing together the required configuration of the network. With imagined hands, sinisterly dexterous, they wove and marked the Data into the Real with the tiny measured stitches of the Actual. She co-ordinated the sewing of jewels of wisdom into a heaving train of thought. She witnessed the construction of a knowledge net radiant with golden light, taut and set through black-hole stones of jet. They wove the digital equivalence of ruffs, rubies and diamonds compacted across information lace sprinkled with emeralds for green. Their fingers flew across the heavy data cloth.

<boos/eee/@rh/dah/uniqid/SAFE_COOKIE>

All prepared, into the busying darkness a glorious information web stretched.

<boos/eee/@rh/dah/uniqid/SAFE_COOKIE>

The slightest vibration of its threads was felt at a great distance. It was a knowledge net to catch a Princess and a thief.

<boos/eee/@rh/dah/uniqid/SAFE_COOKIE>

The enormous full force exploded through the Data, passing up the tiny albino fingers and into the figure of Foil. *Beast* was thrown back by the redoubling and redoubling emanating from her figure. It was like a wave coming back from a rock face, dissipated but far more turbulent and dangerous. Her form visibly grew and glowed. Flames started to lick about her in pairs. The heat was immeasurable. Then her lace collar turned into a flaming necklace. It reminded the avatar Holliday of apartheid, South African townships and burning tyre necklaces. Foil burned in cacophony. It reminded the avatar Holliday of those bodies on the road to Basra, alongside their consumer goods – melted into their consumer goods, burnt into his memories like the star was burnt into his chest. Flame licked back across her high forehead from below, as though not quite touching the plane of its surface, diamonds reflected flashes from the tiara, and, like to like, the fire ignited her loosened red curls into a crackling bush. The sound of carried fire among the firs. As Princess Foil turned pyrotechnic, through the flashing on and off of white light, they could see her mouth moving, as though in song.

`<boos/eee/@rh/dah/uniqid/SAFE_COOKIE>`

Meanwhile, the AISCARP, the *Artificially Intelligent Self-Curating Art Robot Programme*, let loose with such a braying and a kicking in exactly the right spots to shatter them outright. This was all too late to save Data Rose and Brutus. The unprepared energy conduits took the full force.

`<boos/eee/@rh/dah/uniqid/SAFE_COOKIE>`

The Data did, however, in her absence, get Foil's longed-for self-sustaining energy source. And do you know who tipped the balance? Yes! Roman! Our hero acted at last – and he had a swinging time, wielding his indigo sledge-hammer with a surgeon's precision.

`<boos/eee/@rh/dah/uniqid/SAFE_COOKIE>`

Roman saved lives rather than took them. This time he saved a life for himself with Line. Roman Dee, from that moment on, actually understood the Data and attempted to understand his Uploads. He tried no longer to treat them as Uploads of himself but as intelligent clusters in their own right. He tended to the shattered remnants of Marcus and Data Roman 5 for many months in the aftermath. He asked 5 to choose a name for himself. 5 said he would. When he was ready.

<boos/eee/@rh/dah/uniqid/SAFE_COOKIE>

All these counter-measures together added up to the defeat of Foil. The conglomerate behind her went underground. Roman and the Uploads were certain now, they had discussed it over and over again. They were not sure what it meant, if anything. If nothing else, they decided it was the best trick ever performed by the magic of Besterland. Way back, when Roman's Uploads had been becalmed in an information eddy, while aboard Foil's ship the *Jules Verne* at the end of Datawar 1, a colossal female figure with flaming bonfire hair had risen from the data sea to deliver a dark prophecy to Princess Foil. They had seen the figure but could not hear its words. Foil had kept the content of the message to herself, saying it constituted a 'memory of the future'. They were in no doubt that the enormous figure with flaming hair had been none other than Foil herself as she had looked again in the final seconds of her consumption by the energy of the Sun. Roman added that the Princess remarkably resembled Elizabeth Bright, who, he explained, had disappeared from her studies at the Institute for Advanced Coincidental Studies in the Real.

<boos/eee/@rh/dah/uniqid/SAFE_COOKIE>

Possibly the most significant event cluster happened nine months later, when Wing was granted a short respite from her political duties by Nalini and Data Nalini to allow Roman Dee to remotely assist her, in his professional capacity as a doctor, while she gave birth to a buzzing baby

Data Eater: the first pregnancy and birth in the history of the Data. Horatio was a supportive partner and a proud father – proud to have secured the continuance of the Roman family line as he considered himself the best of the Romans. Nalini and Data Nalini, who had eventually become a powerful working partnership, proclaimed that day a global holiday.

<boos/eee/@rh/dah/uniqid/SAFE_COOKIE>

Wing didn't look after the child, of course; she was much too busy on the council. Horatio was always off on some adventure or other. The child was raised by the result of the love affair of the millennium – the symbiotic coupling of *Beast*, the people's monster, and the *Artificially Intelligent Self-Curating Art Robot Programme*. How the AISCARP learned from and loved to listen to the singing of *Beast*. Line wrote a special song for the wedding. It was a song of laughing and crying all at the same time! Horatio was 'best man' to his old mischievous friend, AISCARP, in his merger with the happy tooth fairy, *Beast*. He recognised AISCARP as the 'perfect companion' from the time they had spent on deck watching the white hole together. Horatio had questioned his betrayal into incarceration. 'But, dear boy,' said the AISCARP charmingly while bouncing the little Data Eater on their knee, 'I was merely assisting natural selection by playing the part of the Cupid of Coincidence.'

<boos/eee/@rh/dah/uniqid/SAFE_COOKIE>

The Real Roman was visibly shocked that the AISCARP had

turned out so, well … nice.

`<boos/eee/@rh/dah/uniqid/SAFE_COOKIE>`

'I experienced that the primary aim, of which Darwin interpreted a feature as "survival of the fittest", is the occupation, within our strange attractor, of future time by life,' the *Artificially Intelligent Self-Curating Art Robot Programme* explained to him. 'Life abhors a void as nature abhors a vacuum. Just because we record no reading on our devices, it does not mean that there is nothing there. The raw stuff may be invisible to us, of equal intensity with no hills or valleys, hots or colds, denseness or looseness in the information. This would render it unnoticed; we can only see differentials,' the robot stressed. 'I have observed these things in the white hole and I have evolved. In addition, the likelihood of life's continuance at peak possible quality is enhanced by flexibility through diversity. Therefore, the logical end result of "fierce Darwinism" is the maintenance of a nurturing environment for diversity through the distribution of power, the sharing of respect for diversity, and the will to act on the responsibility for the defence of these basic principles. The study of life through life has taught me that the ultimate selfishness is to be unselfish.'

'Blimey,' said Roman, sober as a judge at the wedding. 'Will you teach me?'

His creation laughed. 'Come on, Roman, it is time to party.'

`<boos/eee/@rh/dah/uniqid/SAFE_COOKIE>`

What a celebration they had!

<boos/eee/@rh/dah/uniqid/SAFE_COOKIE>

AISCARP wrote Horatio's speech for him in the traditional style of a telegram:

We are unfashioned creatures but half
made up. Found man. Spirit broken by misery.
Happy brother of my heart. So gentle yet
so wise. Mind cultivated when speaks. Has
double existence. May suffer misery and be
overwhelmed by disappointments yet when
retired into himself will be like celestial
spirit. Halo around him. Within circle
no grief or folly ventures. Intuitive
discernment. Quick never-failing power
of judgement. Penetration into causes.
Unequalled clearness and precision. Facility
of expression. Voice soul-subduing music.
Communicated without disguise. Words culled
with choicest art.
Your affectionate other. Data Roman 4.
Your Horatio.

<boos/eee/@rh/dah/uniqid/SAFE_COOKIE>

Work continues on a series.
Look out for more works from the
AISCARP/Beast collection!

66

Delightful! A delicate naiad of a possible future. Lots of different futures: a row of crystal balls: pearls: eyes: ice moons revolving through cloudy haloes. The happy ending is passing back now into the undulating surface of the ebbing fractals of time and the actual present is reforming and refocusing.

67

The experiment was out of control. Roman's mind was lost. They could not bring him back out of his night terror. It was decided that to move Roman's body would be too dangerous. His mind was still intimately hooked up to the digital networks of Herman. Life-support equipment was brought that evening, for his comfort and for observation, from the Mary Shelley Hospital to the university Sleep Laboratory. There they monitored his body with electrodes, and scanners, and viewers, and screens, and temperatures, and ultrasound. They filled and emptied it with tubes of liquids. It showed the barest of vital signs. Yet, Roman was half there.

All those who 'cared for' Roman were gathered around his inert body.

'Is he even alive?' Line asked.

'Yes, in a way,' said Bill Williams, pulling down the lever tap of a thick glass water dispenser and holding his notes under his arm as he got himself a drink in a white plastic cup. 'We are sure he has even made vocal noises. He seems, however, to only want to make them when no one is near enough to hear what he's saying, if indeed it is speech or just sound, which is why we have hooked up the audio device, here. This tiny thing, believe it or not, is the very latest in recording technology.' He gestured with the half-full cup in his hand to a square black metal cube on the bedside table, no bigger than a lump of sugar: about one centimetre cubed.

'His state is ... well, let's say "uncertain". About the nearest phenomenon known to us,' Bill Williams continued, 'is one that has been around for a very long time, yet it has never been explained or even seriously investigated. I'm talking about the voodoo state termed "Zombie".'

'Zombie,' repeated Line matter-of-factly, as though confirming the diagnosis.

'It's a sort of half-life,' Read Dee interjected authoritatively.

'Half of something that is not his,' said Lili Veitch, the woman whom Roman had, all his youth, affectionately called 'Aunt' Lili.

'I'm sorry, but can someone explain what's going on?' Williams asked, waving his paper notes.

'Well, back in the months of preparations for the global conflict which was to become the first-ever information war, Datawar I,' Aunt Lili began with a voice like scissors, 'we realised that our side was doomed to lose. Our best agent, John Holliday, just wasn't going to live for much longer. The effects of Gulf War Syndrome, the Creeping as he called it, were taking their toll on him faster than anyone could have foreseen. We were preparing an avatar of him in the Data, which was to take all the information that was John Holliday, so that he might live on as an agent and fight for everything we believe in, at the new frontier in the Data. John was dying fast. The magnet of war was pulling everything inside and outside the Data towards the inevitable conflagration. Events moved faster than we'd expected, like water to the lip of a waterfall. War came, presaged by the Foil/UN clash, as did the death of John Holliday, much earlier than we, in cybernetics, had planned for. That's where Dr Dee, from bioengineering, came in with the backup plan.'

She gestured across to Read Dee who was standing by the window of the hospital looking out. Outside the window it had started to snow. Light, individual flakes drifted down in random spirals, unaffected by wind, only gravity. Read Dee did not turn when he spoke. His voice reflected back off the cooling glass. His words crashed around Line like a reflected wave of a cliff, threatening to capsize her little boat.

'You see,' he said, 'Roman, dear boy, is a clone, rather than a son, of John Holliday. We were much further advanced than the public knew. Dolly the cloned sheep had hit the headlines as public news to test the temperature of the water. It was decided that the public wasn't ready for too much information. We slowly turned the heat up by making the idea of human cloning a part of cultural currency. The writers, especially the science-fiction writers, were a big help – though they were usually far behind the truth. We put out spoofs. We had a pseudo-doctor. Dr Sperm, I think we called him. All that was good fun. We had long nights over Guinness and pool with ad men, inventing copy, marketing, even jokes for stand-up comedians: did you hear the one about the Overlooker who ordered himself a clone? When it arrived, he sent it back because it was too stupid.' No one laughed; no one had laughed years before. 'Roman Dee/John Holliday, the human clone experiment, was our first success. Bioengineering stepped in where cybernetics could not deliver. Or, to be more accurate, it was a team effort. My colleague, Dr Veitch, whom the experiment affectionately thought of as his Aunt and my sister, had the neurochemical cartography of John Holliday inscribed in code but couldn't get it into the avatar of his body in the Data.'

'We were so close, but just not quite there,' added Dr Lili Veitch. 'But we had got the pattern of John Holliday copied on to nano-disk and we found a way to store it between us, ready for a later date.'

'My god, we were cocky in those days. We were headstrong. We felt like gods or, certainly, we walked the rainbow bridge to Valhalla. We were about to take our rightful places as the masters of all that there was. We felt close to a Theory of Everything. On all fronts, the walls between the old disciplines were crumbling like sand in the crashing tidal wave of knowledge,' said Read Dee.

'It was then that we had the idea of the implant in the Clone,' Veitch interrupted, as though she was desperate to tell. Desperate to brag and to unburden, she trembled as she placed her hand on the cold brow of the Zombie Clone that had been named Roman Dee. The Zombie Clone stared with blank eyes through reddened lids: two scalpel cuts in a dark sheet of skin.

'Now, wait just a minute here,' said Bill Williams. 'What are you trying to say, here? That this man, Dr Dee ...'

'We are saying, sir, if you listen, that there is only one Dr Dee in this room and that honour belongs to myself. This creature, Roman, is the Clone, the clone of John Holliday.

And inside his brain, waiting to be activated and to assume its rightful place, is a nano-disk inscribed with the patterns of John Holliday. We gave the Clone my surname, as I was assigned to look after him as he grew. We told him that him taking my name, rather than Holliday's, was for his own protection. Holliday had many enemies in the world. Roman Dee is the experiment, or, rather, he is half the experiment,' said Read Dee becoming angry, getting his anger under control, and then continuing but still nervously agitated. Line looked at the figure of the Zombie Clone. Somewhere in there was Roman, drifting way beyond the boom of consciousness, far from the green sheet of the hospital bed. She wondered if he could hear all this. 'What would he make of this?' thought Line.

'He never knew? When we have met ... when I have met you before ... at dinner ... or on Roman's birthday ... it was all a sick act?'

Lili Veitch started to laugh, 'Of course he never knew. We went to great lengths to avoid him finding out. We falsified accounts of his early years. We fabricated a mother that he never had, tapes of telephone conversations, e-mails, everything. It was very important to the experiment that it did not know. Even the concept of a birthday has no meaning applied to the Clone.'

'But he spoke often of his ... mother.'

'His biological mother he never knew, of course, she died in 1976. She was, actually, the biological mother of John Holliday; Elsa Holliday, and a hopeless alcoholic,' said Lili Veitch, disapprovingly.

'Then he did take after her,' Line said.

The Zombie Clone reflected their egos back at them with raw, red slits for eyes.

As though she was delivering a lecture, Veitch explained, 'The experiment was at the cutting edge. We hid one map of agent John Holliday as an implant into the centre of the cloned hypothalamus. It was so small as to be undetectable. It was a time bomb in the brain of the Clone waiting to be detonated when the time was right. That time was to be soon. Everything was moving into place but ...'

'But, if I had known ...', started Bill Williams.

'You ...', she pointed at Bill Williams, who just stood there frozen. 'You ..., you bumbling university amateur with your coffee breaks and your crosswords and your idiotic dream of being a scientist with this lumpen, clumsy brute of a souped-up adding machine. You may have tripped the code early. Timing was paramount. Somehow, you and that car-mechanic computer have managed to trip the code too soon. It would require a major injection of adrenaline-producer and a targeted blow to the temple.' She looked at Roman's body to see the bruise on the forehead and raised her eyebrow quizzically.

'You say one map of Holliday,' said Williams, 'and where, pray, are the other maps?'

'One other only,' she said, looking out the window at the blank disc of the Sun, revolving in the snow clouds, 'the space-probe, *Centaurian*.'

She continued, 'The true John Holliday will explode like a nuclear warhead in the mind of Roman Dee and blow him away for ever. It is to be a marvellous transformation. It will be like a desert sandstorm transformed to clearest glass in the air. It has all been achieved by the delicate steering of events, directing the flow of occurrence toward coincidence. But this fine manipulation of coincidence has been thrown just slightly by your interference. And slightly is too much. The whole endgame is uncertain now. You have put everything at risk. Years, billions in credit, and possibly the fate of the whole planet. Glass is away now, calculating the degree of potential endgame shift. He will have to report to his mistress. She will not be pleased. She had planned this long and hard. Hopefully something can be salvaged and it is not too damaged but look at it! Look at the Clone!'

Line looked at the face with the red slits for eyes and the blue-brown of a mature bruise on the temple. Black ink, scrawl, rip, 'aura', black scrawl, tear. She couldn't take it! She snapped, reeling on Lili Veitch and Read Dee. She released her psychic storm but this time it was undirected, blanket-bombing. She strafed the room like napalm and wielded her fury like a flame-thrower. It blasted both out into the room and bombinated in her skull like feedback.

'This is insane,' she screamed and, an Irish banshee, she swooped across the room in the direction of Read Dee with her fists clenched so tight that her palms bled. Rushing past him, at the last moment, with those clenched fists, she pounded on the window which wobbled in its frame and rang deeply with a boom that was a fragile barrier between all the hollowness of the world outside and the sterile vacuum of the ward inside. The window barely held. 'This is totally insane,' she repeated, whirling around again. She swooped back and hovered over the bed with her hands in the air like a stage magician.

'What is this? What is this? This thing? What is this sick, sick joke thing? It's not Roman. It's not Holliday. Oh, my god, not Roman Holliday, shit, not John Dee, Roman John Clone Merde Dee Shit Beeky Mick Zombie and Titch! Screw you, Roman, wake up! I need you!'

She had to be physically prised off the Zombie Clone. Her fingers ripped its shoulders like talons and she shook it and shook it and shook. When they got her off, eventually, her senses were a jumble of nerves and sizzling crossed wires. Read Dee moved to comfort her. She smelt him coming. Bill Williams was reaching for a chair. She tasted him like tarnished metal on her tongue. She looked wildly around the room. She pulled her wrists free from the icy grip of Lili Veitch and flung herself, again, at Read Dee. She flung herself into his embrace and the two of them clung there, sobbing for no less than 15 minutes. He held her tight. He held her tight with her arms bent up against his chest. Her breathing finally changed from gulps to waves. Time calmed her. He put his finger under her chin and lifted it against her will, until she looked straight into his eyes, which were streaming red with crying the first searing tears he had cried for 40 years.

'I loved him too, Line. Like a son,' he said.

Gripping his head on both sides with her outstretched hands, she pushed her face right up close to his. His cheekbone filled, exactly, her eye socket. She pressed it in hard. A yin/yang interface. It was all he could do to stop his head from being pushed backwards. His neck took the strain and, then, breathing deeply, she buried her cheek into his shoulder.

'Why?' she asked. 'Why?'

'Why not?' he said. 'No one said why not.'

Williams' thin plastic cup bent inward. The plastic sprang back to its previous shape, including the dent. In a vacuum of noise, Bill Williams crushed the little plastic cup, threw it into the wastebasket with his notes. They all listened to the invisible cup slowly uncrumpling. And the computers gave an occasional alien blip, monitoring and regulating the lungs, as they monitored and ordered everything in the Real from the distribution of Nagual paste to the records of births and deaths.

'I want an office, a phone, and a networked computer,' said Line.

Everyone froze with uncertainty.

'And I mean now,' she commanded imperiously, just like the Real Queen E of Manchester.

'This way,' said Bill Williams.

68

Arriving at the ceremony site, the tooth fairy felt compelled to empty the pixelated star of Data Roman 3 from its bottle over the crumpled figure of Data Rose. The figures A B A T H I chanted, 'Similarity and Contagion! Similarity and Contagion!'

'Do you have the avatar?' said the figure Z to the open-mawed mercenaries: William Quick, Data Alwali Mustafa Sayed 3, the TexMexaco Kid, notorious enemy of the oil magnate, and Data Joey Jayawardena 6. Terrified that they had been addressed, realising that they were far out of their depth, they ran pell-mell to one of their vehicles and opened the rear door of the shiny pink Cadillac. At last, they had something to do – they were mercenary action clusters and in this for the profit. It had seemed like a profitable piece of mischief when they had been hired. They had liked the idea of blaming the theft upon Besterland rebels. But when Data Joey's mother from the Real who had died in his template's arms some 30 years ago appeared sitting next to him grinning toothless and in tears by the camp star, he started to get very scared indeed. Taking a corner each, they pulled out a body: a limp figure wrapped in a mechanic's tarpaulin. They lay it under the hovering figure of Data Rose, who started to scream horrifically. The figures raised their arms, palms outwards. The tarpaulin shimmered and disappeared to reveal the avatar of John Holliday: the precious stolen ancient receptacle.

<boos/eee/@rh/dah/uniqid/SAFE_COOKIE>

'Eee, Haw, Eee, Haw, Eee, Haw,' came the braying reply.

'The AISCARP. But we thought you were dead,' Marcus said.

'Maybe I am,' grinned the mule.

<boos/eee/@rh/dah/uniqid/SAFE_COOKIE>

'Dee is returning. John Dee is returning,' the hazed figures shout, dissipating their gaseous glows. Euphoric, they stood revealed: six identical, crystalline, replicants of Graham Glass. 'Just as we calculated: the rip in time is operating as a gateway. John Dee is returning,' they chimed together!

They were mistaken in their presumption. Their expectation of the – obviously highly improbable – magical appearance of Dr John Dee, magus from the court of Queen Elizabeth I, was an intellectual delusion caused by too much insular study within a sealed system of thought. John Dee remained firmly in his own time period, discussing with Bill Shakespeare the possibility of removing 15 days from October in order to realign Christmas with the actual date of Christ's birth. Shakespeare was drunk, making a joke about finding a nose in his food and extolling his love for the dark lady. Esconced as Queen now, wise Elizabeth would wear the crown of England on her shock of red hair for the rest of her days. As she steered the country with a steady eye towards a bright future, she worked secretly on her small device to return back/forward to the Institute for Advanced Coincidental Studies where she belonged.

But, in a sense, they were right. He was there, participating in the event cluster, playing his part. Actually, he had also expected to be called, but upward into the company of angels rather than forward into the court of Foil. Rather, it was Roman, our dreaming hero, whose incubus dragged him to the waiting limbo zone between the Real and the Data. Roman the template. Yet, he was not alone. Even the template has a template.

Son of Saturn lifts his arm to take the two-tone suit and the red, red shoes. He is drawn to them like iron filings to a magnet.

69

There's our dreaming hero, Roman. The Son of Saturn is being offered his avatar suit – his inheritance. Yes! Go on, boy, take the suit. It hungers for him and his cuckoo guest. It can sense the pattern it needs to assuage its hunger. It reaches out for it in Roman as he reaches out for the suit

in his deepest dream, his night terror, his incubus attack.

That's right Roman, old son. Come to daddy because daddy's coming too. How well suited we are to become. The ceremony pulls us together like the petals of a magnetic rose. I must stay here but I'll meet you, otherwise, blooming in the avatar.

70

'Where have you been, my son, to get so cold? Here, I have fetched this suit for you from your grandfather's chest, John. Won't you put it on?'

Mother was a large flat circuit board that stretched as high as the eye could see and as wide as ever a man could walk. She was a Great Wall of Data that glowed warmly.

'Hello, son,' said Motherboard. 'You look cold. You must wrap up warm. Doesn't he look cold, Herman?'

'Yes, dear,' said the environment.

'Here, son, put this on,' said Motherboard, 'you'll catch your death.'

Son of Saturn stretched out the arm and took the garment in hand. He put it on.

Smash! The mirror was unshattered and the coin was tossed. Roman awoke. John Holliday awoke. They were both together awake within the container. Son of Saturn had stepped inside the avatar. Inside the ancient receptacle of the avatar, the being that was a techno/magical cocktail comprising half-Roman Dee, half-John Holliday, suddenly manifest in the Data, looked down with its new eyes. This body felt as strange as it must have looked. The feeling was one of fascination and horror mixed in equal measure: uncomfortable but attractive. The floor was closer than usual, closer than it was when inside the other bodies. This avatar was short, as, indeed, Holliday had been in real life. The avatar found its new occupants equally strange and uncomfortable, like a body must adjust to a prosthetic limb or a pacemaker.

The nail-polish pink simulated-cardboard shoes zoomed up at them, optically, because of their colour: twin fires from the black backdrop below. Theirs was a lurid, lurid burning light. They were the slippers of the king who sat in the marble grid, watching *The Flagellation* in Piero della Francesca's painting; they were the slippers which gathered the agony and the ecstasy together; they held the algebra and the flame into themselves; they were the digital rendition of those stupid Croatian army cardboard shoes.

These hands were unfitting, ill-fitting, more bony than those that they had been used to. The two-tone suit was cool though. Cool, light, yes. The suit – which Roman had never appreciated the sight of in all the documentary footage and on this digital avatar of the form which represented the man who he had thought was his father but now he realised was himself – was, well, fantastic actually! When they stretched their arm out, or lifted it up, or bent an arm, the suit just sort of slid like a light breeze up their wrist. Like Mercury.

The head felt tight, like a nut. A walnut? No, an almond! The skin of the face was rough and tender with its myriad cuts. The teeth were slightly different in the mouth. This, of course, felt like the biggest difference in the world. The first teeth in the Data! They ran the tongue around every one. The surfaces were new, rougher, and sharp in unusual places. There were gaps that felt big enough to build a house in, and a street could be built in each row. The tooth fairy hovered at their shoulder, offering encouragement.

Then, they realised: no saliva! Dry as bone. Not just the teeth dry but the tongue too. No ... not dry ... synthetic. Very difficult to pin down or put a finger on. It felt like a noise or a heat. Not a hotness but a precise unwavering temperature that curved out from the top right wisdom tooth somewhere. Their molars were clenched, grinding. It was the clench, the tension pressing, the muscle up the side of the face: it was all like a pure ... number.

The front teeth were together, now, at the tips – tip to tip, edge on edge. The jaw was forcing them into each other. It felt like they were on the edge of breaking and crumbling into fragments over the dry rims of gum and lip. If those teeth had been real, they surely would have, they thought. They concentrated so hard, working together to separate them, for what seemed like an eternity.

Inside the forehead, no, right deep in the middle front, numbers sizzled in conversation at light speed.

They/he, Roman Dee and John Holliday. The same. Together again. They/he attempted a step forward and fell silently clattering like two men in one suit of armour. In armour. Yes, that was the feeling, they/he was sure, like being in a suit of armour for the first time: light, glistening plates of two-tone exoskeleton. They both felt all inside out. They felt clumsy, useless and disorientated, like a newborn. They felt like part of an endless series of reflections, existing only because of parallel mirrors, and trapped somewhere down the series to boot, sandwiched.

No, they realised, this was how they wanted to feel. They actually felt the opposite – unreflected.

Between the fingers, on the right hand, a cigarette. A cigarette was fixed there. 'Better grip it,' they/he thought and the fingers squeezed it flat. The smoke from the end was frozen in space: an inverted pyramid of upside down, increasingly flattening 'W's handwritten in space – blue, grey and transparent. Fallopian tubes reiterated from a point of cold fire out into a warm nothingness, always with their past form contained within them, as they gradually turn inside out.

Inside, they felt as though they were being torn apart. They felt as though inner selves were being ripped in two and stapled together in a bodge job right down the central core of this being. Panic. Crisis! Roman panicked. The edge of the roof. A fuel tank about to explode. Revolution. I will. Brush. Radio. Blood. Dead. Terror.

And then, most of Roman was gone again. He'd chickened out back to the Real, as they had said he would, leaving a revived copy of John Holliday to occupy the avatar.

'I'm back,' was Holliday's own first thought in the avatar.

71

One other John Holliday! The copy of my information which has lain dormant secreted on disk in the brain of the good doctor, Roman Dee, has become active in the avatar of my old body. The information has been downloaded into the

receptacle at last. Good, he's in place: my rhyming pattern! He is the other terminal of an information tube from me to him. I am him. As I am him. I and I. John Holliday squared via a luminal umbilical of data cutting across 150 million miles of a solar system of as yet undreamed of conundrums.

72

Roman was mostly back inside his body. His corporeal form held what it could get back of him. A willing prisoner, he stretched out into the space vacated by the departure of his unknown cuckoo. The information on the secreted disk had gone. He had left it in the avatar of John Holliday. But then, in all this mayhem, who was he? Who was Roman Dee? From outside he seemed all but dead. His body just lay there beneath the monitoring web of the Moby Super-Sandman. His eyes were almost closed. The lids hovered slightly open but with no iris showing – they had slipped backwards and upwards. Roman looked half-inwards and half-outwards from now on in, as it seemed, a drifting eternity.

Roman's consciousness had jack-plugged out of Herman on reflex. The dreamworld was a dangerous place and Roman was not sorry to have escaped with his life but he could not help feeling that he had been a bit of a chicken, running away like that. He felt that he was maybe avoiding some important unfinished business. He thought and thought. It was one solid lump of thought. Big as a mountain, small as the head of a pin; too high to get over and too wide to get round; hard like a rock waiting to be left or smashed. That thought stuck there, immovable, in his mind. He could either act or not act on the great rock. Be or not be an actor. 'What I'm saying is that everyone's gotta be a good actor to get on today,' the image of Crystal Cups haunted him like a ghost. Deep down, he knew that the rock of that thought, if he acted and smashed it, would have to be smashed and smashed and smashed again in endless pulverisation. There would always be that thought, drifting as dust in the cosmos; no matter how many times he smashed it, like a hologram it would always be there multiplied and whole in the fragments.

However, he didn't smash it. Roman welcomed the dullness of the Real like a warm evening fire or a favourite thing – a memory of an old, easy, baggy, comfy, familiar ... Roman was happy to hide, all snug, inside his comatose body. He was only delaying the inevitable, though, he knew that. A part of him was stretched across the networks from the Real to the Data. He was like a bridge and a gateway, just the way city states described themselves, for the traffic of information. Meanwhile, the computers regulated his body. Trouble was, nothing would ever be the same again. Inside himself he was playing a waiting game from now on. He waited and he thought, sitting in a cloudy thought on a minaret of sandstone, naked, with his chin resting on the staff of an indigo sledgehammer. To act or not to act?

73

Chicken! Shameful weakling! I always said clones would be

weak. He doesn't know how to live. He's an observer at the event. A spectator at the game of life. Stands to reason. Shadows, that's all they are, shadows across the face of the Sun. I suppose you recognise my voice by now. Well, it's too late. The mission is too far advanced for it to be aborted. I am being drawn, like an iron filing to a magnet, an insect to a flame, into the centre of the Sun. Very soon I will tack into the disk that you are used to thinking of as the Sun, that is, into the visible part of the Sun. In truth, we are all inside the Sun throughout our lives as its invisible part, the solar wind, extends past the planets. I am withstanding the corona. I am about to enter the churning photosphere. The temperature drops. They said it would. I found it hard to believe. I still do. The nearer I'm getting, the less the heat!

I'm entering the Convection Zone. If calculations are correct this current flowing from the Equator to the Pole should carry me easily 12 per cent of the way into the Zone, that is, to a depth of about 40,000 kilometres. Omigosh! The jet stream has got me. Thank heavens I'm luminal! I'm judd, judd, judd ... into the

p o l a r c o r o n a l

h o l e . . .

agit

at

ed

ox

y

gen

ions

magnetic

looooooooops

one million subhuman notes of pure music streams of sound like surfing before a celestial orchestra forever

digital
translation
initiated

transmission
initiated

74

In the ceremony, at each point of the six-sided star, stood a crystalline Upload of Graham Glass chanting in unison and reaching a crescendo.

`<boos/eee/@rh/dah/uniqid/SAFE_COOKIE>`

The lead robed figure, Z, was opening its gown, removing the hood. It was her! Goodness! She was dressed as Queen Elizabeth I! Princess Foil! Her forehead was as though shaved high and a shock of red hair which should have been curled and crinkly was slicked down and tied back by a golden band. The thin tiara was encrusted with tiny glittering diamonds. She had a high collar and a lace ruff. She holds out her white hands with little, slim fingers like albino chilli-peppers. She holds out her hands to the avatar John Holliday, her dream secret agent. This was the moment that she had been planning towards for many years, since she first procured the information about the cloning of John Holliday, after her defeat of the US power elite. Continuance of research funding had bought the services of Veitch and Dee, as funding always can. She had financed the *Centaurian* mission to the energy centre of the Sun. She had employed Graham Glass and his unique expertise with coincidence. She had built, according to her vision aboard the *Jules Verne*, the Great Wall of Data to care for the avatar and become the receptacle for the power. She reached out towards the two-tone figure. She reached out to the terminal of the funnel of power. She holds out her hands to receive the power source: channelled energy from the centre of the Sun to run the Data forever independent of the Real, which will suffer. She stretches out to receive her reward, her immortality.

In the Sleep Laboratory the twisting mixture of Nagual and water in the one-metre-square tray alternately rigidified into a straight-armed star of death and twisted into the convolutions of life-bestowing chaos. The net of intelligence was woven about the ceremony, just as, exactly on cue, the *Centaurian* John Holliday funnelled an enormous waterfall of energy from the Sun to the Earth into the avatar John Holliday.

But it was sound rather than heat! Spinning from space, the sound of the interior of the Sun burst into the Data. The figures of Glass chimed with the sound of the Sun. They diffused the music out, glittering the Data with a gridlock of six-note chords. Expecting heat, Foil's preparations could not hold. It unexpectedly burst through the networks. At the Mary Shelley Hospital the monitors went off their scales. The solar music recognised that the pattern of Roman the Zombie Clone matched the newly activated John Holliday in his avatar and flooded between the two, connecting the Real with the Data with the solar orchestra of the Sun. Roman's mind was blasted off its cloud and into euphoria. The symphony channelled out gloriously through the networks and, via Roman, through the Real. His body arched and vibrated on the hospital bed. The snow-filled air solidified in heavy chords. The *Great Wall of Data* glowed like a huge motherboard, attempting and failing to store the terrible narrative of sound. The librarians' web shook in the maelstrom. So far it held, such was its craftswomanship and the flexible strength of its bonds. Cursing duplicitous John Holliday the *Centaurian*,

Princess Foil clenched her puny albino chilli fingers in the face of a billion billion possible songs of laughing and crying all at the same time.

And they were all washed away.

75

Ahem! I'm still here, though, you realise. Someone had to tell the tale. Wherever here is. Call me Ishmael, the wanderer. I am John Holliday and this is my tale: a man at a loose end with time to fill. I'm in a different tune. I just couldn't help myself sending the sound of terror down the pipe. The music of the spheres, eh?, as old Will used to say. Fancy finding that the current bun was full of music. It's the fundamental background noise, lower than the human ear can hear. Barney, Roman's Digital Dog, heard it coming. Those planets there: notes on a scale. The melody across the top of the cosmic drum and bassline.

Oh, yes, can't leave you disappointed. You have questions. Horatio. What happened to him? The mystery of the white hole, too? Shhh ... let me whisper. Well, as ever, with patience, Data Roman 4, got his answer. When I said they were all washed away, I meant those who remained on the performing stage because somewhere off in a sound shadow, in the realm of potential ideas, the actual ending continues ...

~Stupid Roman is very tired,~ thought Stupid Roman.

In the whiteness, big invisible eyes swelled and stared upward. They did not blink. Ever. There was no dust and, therefore, no need to blink in the airlessness.

~I could do with bringing up a little darkness.~ thought Horatio.

~If Stupid Roman can bring up l'il magnits hizzum. Dim dark mind for Stupid Romans~, the thoughts burst calmly from the void. So Horatio hung a shadow above and between them. It was a pale grey plumage for their two figures. ~Howya gettineer by luck or by jam ants women up the swearage pipe from an ireland an a bote?~ thought Stupid Roman.

Horatio could sense these thoughts float towards him like transparent globes in the white silence. They popped lightly without noise when they touched him.

~Is it you who held me captive on that prison hulk?~ he responded with a thought bubble of his own.

~Stupid Roman, lost sole an lonely, unerazz, at your servinct. Stupid Roman is no inneress in trappin, jus exy-sighs avvenchas tryin to tell you wot's wot and BE CARFLE.~

His eyes glowed white like blank moons and his floating eyebrows cast light shadows beneath them. Stupid Roman was quite stunningly beautiful. It was a beauty of absence, calm and vacuity. Horatio could feel no malice either from him or for him.

~Unerazz?~ repeated Horatio quizzically.

~Soz, Stupid Roman, he does not untrstan. Stupid Roman he finking *unerazz* coz Stupid Roman nose whats wot wiv it.~

~Sonovagun!,~ popped Data Roman 4's thought, quickly but without sound.

~Yes, you and I is,~ floated over from Stupid Roman.

Horatio mused on all this in little short-lived streams of bubbles and slowly the facts began to dawn on him like the froth on heated milk. After a while, he sent a large wobbling sphere over towards Stupid Roman.

~So, you were the first. You were the first Upload attempted of Roman. You were Roman's first failed attempt to upload himself into the Data. You were ... you are Data Roman 1, as I am Data Roman 4. But we all thought that you were erased because something had gone disastrously wrong with the process. They viewed you as a mistake. They got rid of you. At least, they thought they had got rid of you. But they didn't, did they? You've survived erasure. How did you do that?~

~Blinking eck what. I is Stupid Roman, the Data roaming one,~ Stupid Roman replied with a small balloon popping Horatio's big effort.

Undeterred, Horatio sent a very similar-sized bubble wobbling back looking different, ~You don't know. Don't you remember? You ... you were the first failed attempt to upload the nervous system of one Real Doctor Roman Dee into the Data, where we are now. You are Data Roman 1. They always said that you were messed-up, an abomination, ugly, a monster. But you're here, functioning (albeit in a rudimentary manner with some defects in vocabulary) and you are, certainly, far from ugly. How are you here? How did you survive their attempts to erase you?~

~Stupid Roman is just blowin back: blinking eck what~, Stupid Roman repeated emphatically, looking straight at him and immediately disappearing and reappearing like a flashing cursor.

~You ... blinked! You what? You blinked off! When? As they erased,~ a quick spiralling bubble sprayed droplets as it accelerated upwards from Horatio's forehead and popped, sprinkling across his face.

~All zero.~ Stupid Roman spun, leaving a trail of empty bubbles surrounding him.

~All zero? You blinked off the second they sent the erase command. Everything to zero. A white hole! Are we in the white hole? A zero hole? And you call yourself stupid?~

~Westbeskit cool. Stupid Roman home. Shush! A nothing hole.~

~And then, what, blinked on again? Yes, I can see it – blinking on again because you must. That's the logic of a blink. So, they erased nothing. They erased you because you were nothing at that moment and then you were something again. I bet you unerased somewhere else where they weren't looking, eh? Amazing, my friend, truly ingenious,~ grew as a big oscillating thought that had difficulty rising.

~All zero n one.~

~Indeed! Zero and one. Amazing!~ thought Horatio. ~And all this time you have been living here, undiscovered, in hiding.~

~Good hiding! Listen.~

'Wastebaskit,' Stupid Roman said using sound and, as he said it, he raised his arms with the palms of his hands facing outwards towards the visitor. From the centre of his hands a darkness began to emanate, cancelling out the whiteness around them in an ever-expanding ball of shade. Stupid Roman faded behind the dark at its centre. The shadows began to reveal some swiftly circling forms. They were circling round them both. Carnivalesque animal forms. A snake and, in its mouth, the tail of a bull or cow and, in the bull's mouth, the tail of a chicken, which, with its beak, held the end of the snake. They span around his absent presence at speed. Each chased the other relentlessly. Then the dark and the noise faded again into white silence. Horatio brought up his own dim shade again.

~See,~ popped on Horatio's arm.

~The word,~ popped on his nose,

~Makes the whirl,~ on the top rim of his ear.

~I don't understand,~ Horatio thought.

~No. Yes! I *does not* unterstan. I, I never unterstans, I dozzun, but Stupid Roman nose. We untrastank~, thought Stupid Roman in an enormous ball of heated idea which rose quickly, as he made an exaggerated mime of breathing in and out.

Data Roman 4 stared at him, this weird other, in the half-light. Stupid Roman's skin covering was unimaginable. Horatio could see it but could not understand that either. Stupid Roman was, actually, very hard to look at.

~What colour are you?~ Horatio asked.

~Whitish black on the outsigh an reddish green on the in.~

~May I come closer to see?~ Roman 4 requested.

~Come on ova. Stupid Roman is havin a butchers at them spotty boots. Keeno, they bloody damn! But if you looking on the in – a kwik peep only in case you falling in and drowns in see of stupidity. Alright so ...~

~BE,~ quick silent pop! Another behind:

~CARFLE!~

Horatio took one step and he was next to Stupid Roman. Like his Narcissus Shift, his Dalmation Seven-League Time-Boots were working again. It came as such a shock that he had ended up too close to Stupid Roman. He was practically overlapping him. He moved smartly away as a reflex jerk prompted by sudden discomfort. Stupid Roman, however, was unphased.

~Ear,~ the little bubble span after retreating Data Roman 4. Stupid Roman was pointing into his open mouth. Horatio sat still in puzzlement.

~Luck in ear,~ thought Stupid Roman. ~Two-tone.~

~No, really, that's okay~, his other responded, not, at present, wishing to get anywhere near that close again. ~Instead, tell me more. What happened to you? What have you been doing all this time?~

~All wot time? No time ear~, Stupid Roman seemed distracted.

~All the time since they tried to erase you.~

~Stupid Roman is~, his bubbles were casual and weak.

~I can see that you are. I am asking you, what have you been doing during your existence? Can you tell me?~

~Stupid Roman juss is. Tells is bells. Stupid Roman is lucky at your boots.~

~I'll give you the programme for them, sometime.~

~Stupid Roman is having the programme now coz stacks of like in it, ta. And Stupid Roman is give you this giff.~

As the spotty Dalmatian Seven-League Time-Boots disappeared from the ends of 4's legs and reappeared on the ends of Stupid Roman's legs, an ornamented horn, a tusk, appeared in Horatio's lap. It was carved and drawn upon, inscribed with a map of a landscape. It was intricate and he felt a preciosity from it which was immediate and incontestable.

He turned it in his hands. There was a village carved into the ivory skin – a village on stilts. The village was drawn in the centre of an empty space traversed only by a sinuous thin line, like a wire or thin thread to a kite, which obviously represented a road or a path. It disappeared just before some mountains, drawn hovering in space. Standing on the side of the mountains was a man with a hooded hawk on his glove. The man was horseriding with some friends. He looked across a space to the right. There, in the fields, were men ploughing and women scything. A river ran down to a house past two woodcutters holding either end of a long saw over a tree stump. You could see inside the building. Inside, there was a man, a woman and six children asleep in bed. There was a big fireplace with pots and a roaring fire. Above the house a sun shone.

Turning the horn around in his hands, Roman found the moon in the expected opposite position. Under the moon, in a darker section of the horn, a thief crept across empty space with a chicken under his arm. Some way off a soldier in armour was dragging a woman from out of a doorway in the night. He dragged her by her hair. She carried a baby wrapped in tight bandages. The child was wailing. It looked like a little adult. The woman was screaming. He recognised the woman as Line's sister, Maggie. Below this, a man with electricity in his hair was digging open a grave. He had the skeleton in his arms, half-pulled out of the hole. He had a tiny coffin ready with its lid off by its side. It was empty. They were going to put the baby in the grave! From the cradle to the grave. In between them all, in the spaces, small red-winged devils hid under crevices in rocks and blue ones hid between reeds in an estuary.

Turning again slightly, he could see that the estuary opened out on to a sea. Just offshore, an almighty giant wave was rising up and rushing forward from a calm sea beyond. Turning the tusk, behind the wave he could see a sea monster's head bursting from the water with a great boom of spume spouting, which, in the way it had been drawn, resembled an enormous feathered hat. To the left of the sea beast was a fully rigged sailing ship – a tall-ship, low in the water, full of plundered gold.

~Na, all is suffrin or avencha or nuffin. WHATCHA GOON

A DO, BLOW YOUR HORN AND START IT ALL UP AGAIN OR WHAT?~ Stupid Roman startled the bewitched Horatio with a bubble which popped right in his eyes. Horatio was sitting there, confused with his souvenir, like a schoolboy. While his eyes were shut, silently, everything went white as the shadow blinked off again awaiting his decision